D1010278

Also by Catherine Arnold

DUE PROCESS
IMPERFECT JUSTICE

WRONGFUL DEATH

Catherine Arnold

A SIGNET BOOK

SIGNET
Published by the Penguin Group
Penguin Putnam Inc., 375 Hudson Street,
New York, New York 10014, U.S.A.
Penguin Books Ltd, 27 Wrights Lane,
London W8 5TZ, England
Penguin Books Australia Ltd,
Ringwood, Victoria, Australia
Penguin Books Canada Ltd, 10 Alcorn Avenue,
Toronto, Ontario, Canada M4V 3B2
Penguin Books (N.Z.) Ltd, 182–190 Wairau Road,
Auckland 10, New Zealand

Penguin Books Ltd, Registered Offices:
Harmondsworth, Middlesex, England

First published by Signet, an imprint of Dutton NAL,
a member of Penguin Putnam Inc.

First Printing, March, 1999
10 9 8 7 6 5 4 3 2 1

For Linda

ACKNOWLEDGMENTS

Special thanks to the Hon. Brandt C. Downey III, for guiding me through Florida criminal law and procedure, and attorney R. Jerome Sanford for sharing his expert knowledge in federal court procedure. Thanks also to Dr. Joseph Sicignano for more information than I ever needed to know about mental depression and expert psychiatric testimony.

Prologue

The small, two-room cabin located in the vast Canadian northern wilderness, hundreds of miles from civilization, was an odd setting for this man. Built from rough-hewn lumber and cheaply furnished, the cabin creaked and groaned as the north wind increased in velocity, its noise drowning the sound of crackling logs in the brick fireplace. A light dusting of snow bounced off dirty, single-paned windows and settled on top of the six-inch accumulation of the previous day.

Dressed in jeans and an old plaid shirt, he sat in a plain wooden chair in a room lit by the fire and a lone gas lamp, a room now chilled, despite the fire, by the frigid air outside the old cabin walls. He looked at his watch, put down the book he was reading, struggled into his parka and boots, and went outside.

Twenty minutes later, he returned, moved to a corner of the front room, opened a cabinet, dropped a desk panel, and switched on a battery-operated transceiver.

There was nothing but the sound of dead air for four minutes. Then, the man heard a voice.

"This is Tony, over."

He leaned forward, his lips inches from a microphone, pressed a switch on the transceiver, and said, "Go ahead, over."

"There's a problem here, a big one."

"Explain."

"He killed himself."

The man hesitated a moment, then smiled. "When?"

"This afternoon. Blew his brains out. We gotta forget this."

Instantly, the man's face reddened with anger. "You listen to me," he yelled. "Nothing changes. Hear me?"

"I can't do it. I just can't. I feel sick all over."

"You do what you're supposed to do or you'll regret it. You feel sick now? I promise you'll feel a lot sicker if you screw this up."

"I can't."

The man banged his fist on the small desk and fought to control his temper. His mind raced. Something had to be done to calm this idiot down.

"All right," he said. "We'll make a small change in plans. You do the job, then come up here."

"Come up there?"

"Yes. Have your people deliver the other package and then the three of you come here. We'll talk and work it out. I'll make it worth your while. But if you screw up, I'll do what I said I'd do. You'll spend the rest of your life locked up. Don't for a minute think you can defy me. You understand?"

"But he's dead. What's the point?"

"That's not your concern. You follow orders, period. Then you come up here."

"How?"

Again the man's mind raced. "Hold on."

A minute later, he was back on the radio. "Drive to Cornwall, Ontario. You know where that it?"

"Yes."

"Leave your car there. Take a bus to Toronto. From there, you a take a commercial flight to Winnipeg. Got it?"

"Yeah."

"Good. You remember the name of the guy who worked for you last year, the guy with one eye? Don't mention his name on the air."

A pause, then, "Yeah, I remember."

"There's a man in Winnipeg with the same last name. He owns a small plane and knows where to go. He's in the phone book. First name is Jack, but he goes by the nickname of Skid. You may have to make several calls before you find the right man, but you do it. Tell him it's on my authority, and he'll bring you here. Got it?"

"What then?"

"I'll have it all worked out. You'll be a very rich man."

Another pause. Longer. "I don't think I can."

"One last time, Tony. You have a choice. You can be rich or you can spend the rest of your life in jail. Which do you want?"

"That's not a choice."

"Exactly. We have to get off the air now. I'll expect you here by Monday dusk at the latest. If you're not here, I'll start the wheels in motion. You won't like it."

There was a final pause. "I'll be there."

He switched off the radio, stood up, put his parka on, grabbed the lantern again, and headed back outside. As he worked to bring the long string antenna back to earth, he smiled to himself.

The man was dead. Even better than expected.

One

While the prosecuting attorney tossed questions at the witness, Liz Walsh reached across the bar to the defense table, tapped her boss, Karen Perry-Mondori, on the shoulder, and handed her a folded paper.

Karen glanced quickly at the note.

"Check with me before you leave," her secretary had written. "Don't worry, Carl and Andrea are fine, but you have an urgent matter to take care of."

Probably papers to be signed, Karen thought, then slipped the note under her legal pad, and returned her attention to the interrogation.

She was in her usual element, the prosaic confines of the always busy Pinellas County, Florida, Criminal Courthouse, engaged in one of several ongoing trials. This trial was, like most of them, unspectacular, unattended by media or family members, just another in the never-ending grind, the unceasing procession of criminals of whatever persuasion brought before the bar of justice.

For three days, Karen Perry-Mondori, the defendant's attorney, had conducted herself with her usual unruffled composure, exhibiting patience and serenity, even when provoked by Judge Joseph Brown's misogynistic taunts, including his continuing refusal to use her proper last name. Judge Brown lived to torment female attorneys, and Karen made a point not to provide him ammunition for one of his renowned attacks.

She objected at the proper times, most times just raising her hand like someone making a bid at an auction. At other times, when the conduct of the prosecutor was clearly excessive, Karen voiced stronger objections, but even they were offered with a curious lack of her usual feistiness.

To the uninitiated, Karen's objections might have appeared to have been made as a matter of course; required, but not honestly felt. To those familiar with her courtroom manner, however, her behavior looked more like the calm before the storm.

And so it was.

This case was about to come to a shuddering halt.

Karen's calm demeanor had lulled the young, aggressive prosecuting attorney, Spencer Ferguson, into a false sense of security. And now, with this witness, the assistant state attorney, the representative of the people, was throwing caution to the winds. His face contorted in anger as he led the witness shamelessly, piling improper question atop improper question, his outrage over the defendant's alleged crimes obvious to an attentive jury. He wasn't simply prosecuting, he was putting on a show, and the jury was buying all of it.

With her trap firmly set, Karen finally sprung it. After repeated objections, all of them sustained, she rose slowly to her diminutive five-foot-two height, her entire comportment an expression of sadness. "Your Honor, the defense wishes to make a motion."

Judge Brown leaned forward, brows raised over eyes bloodshot from one of his infamous hangovers, as if anticipating what was coming next. Karen had

been before him many times, and while the judge
persisted in his sexist comments, he was also familiar
with the lawyer's expertise and, on occasion, had
granted her grudging respect.

"Very well, Ms. Mondori." Judge Brown beckoned. "Approach."

Karen and Spencer Ferguson approached the bench.

"We're asking for a mistrial, Your Honor," Karen
said in a soft voice. "The jury is hopelessly inflamed."

Before the prosecutor could speak, the judge
waved a hand and snapped, "You may step back."

He then turned to the jury. "Ladies and gentlemen"—resignation edged his voice—"we're going to
have to discuss a matter of law for a few minutes.
The bailiff will take you out of the courtroom at this
time. I remind you not to discuss this case among
yourselves. This shouldn't take long, so don't bother
with the Coke machine."

As the jury was led out, the two lawyers resumed
their positions at their respective tables.

Karen suppressed a smile of satisfaction. She didn't
want Judge Brown to accuse her of employing femi-
nine wiles, one of several charges, including raging
PMS, which he frequently leveled at female attorneys. To that end, she had dressed with great care
each day of the trial, pulling her soft, shoulder-length
brown hair back in a severe bun, forgoing makeup
that emphasized her large green eyes and high cheek-
bones, and dressing in long, boxy jackets that called
no attention to her full breasts, tiny waist, and slender hips. Her only concession to vanity had been
three-inch heels, worn more to increase her elevation
than complement her trim ankles.

Now, her yellow legal pad clenched in her left
hand, in a voice devoid of passion, she stated her

case. "Your Honor, I have noted nine incidents of profound impropriety on the part of the state attorney, either in the form of direct comments to the jury, or a series of intentional and improper questions directed to witnesses, all of which were designed to inflame the jurors' minds. The state attorney's actions are extremely prejudicial to my client.

"In each instance, I have asked that the comment, or question, and the witness's answer, be stricken from the record and the jury directed to disregard. While you have seen fit to do so in each instance, too much damage has been done. At this point in the proceedings, the combined weight of the state attorney's inappropriate remarks cannot but be felt by the jury.

"Jurors are human, and this jury must be irrevocably biased in the matter now before this court. You have admonished the state attorney on six separate and distinct occasions, yet he persists. In the interests of justice, I must move for a mistrial declaration."

Karen, pleased to have completed her motion without a single ill-mannered interruption from the irascible Judge Brown, noted that her opponent, Spencer Ferguson, was staring at her slack jawed.

"This is nuts," Ferguson bellowed. "Just a cheap trick by a cheap hotshot."

Karen smiled at him. "I'm a lot of things, Mr. Ferguson, but I assure you, I'm anything but cheap."

"Cut the chatter," the judge snapped.

Seething, Ferguson faced the judge. "If I was out of line, I apologize, but the fact is, the defendant is as guilty as they get, and that's what's important here, not that I stepped over the line a couple of times. I promise it won't happen again, but to let this guy off the hook this way would be a total miscarriage of justice. The evidence is irrefutable, and Ms. Perry-Mondori knows that. This is a stunt, that's all. You declare a mistrial on this and we'll have to do it all over again, a waste of time and money we can ill afford."

The judge shook his head. "That's it? That's all you have to say?"

"Why don't we poll the jury?" Ferguson said. "Ask them flat out if they've made up their minds."

"The law is quite clear on this point, Your Honor," Karen countered.

Judge Brown glared at her. "I'm aware of the law, missy."

Karen turned silent as His Honor continued to glare. "You set Ferguson up, right?"

"No, sir."

"I think you did. I saw this coming two days ago. You gave him enough rope to hang himself, right?"

"No, sir."

"He's right about one thing, Ms. Mondori. It's a cheap stunt and I don't like it one little bit."

Karen leaned forward. "With all due respect, Your Honor, I'm not the one at fault here. This is not a cheap stunt and I deeply resent your comment. Throughout this trial, I have objected to each breach of procedure on the part of the prosecutor. I have asked for admonitions six times. You granted those requests, and well you should have. Justice would have been better served had you taken Mr. Ferguson aside and made him understand that his behavior had to stop. I would—"

"That's enough!" The judge, fire in his red-rimmed eyes, waved her quiet.

There was a time to push and a time to be quiet. Karen knew the limits.

The judge turned his wrath toward the prosecutor. "You should know better than this. You thought you were being cute, but all you did was mess things up. You're a disgrace. If I declare a mistrial, it makes us all look bad, but if I don't, I'll be overturned on appeal. I like that even less. I have no choice."

Ferguson looked ready to explode. "Your Honor! You can't! We've spent years bringing this bastard to trial. The evidence is—"

"Don't yell at me, mister." The judge waved a finger at Ferguson. "You brought this on yourself. Sure, you've got the evidence, the witnesses, the whole nine yards, and you've thrown it all in a cocked hat by being a smart ass. Instead of playing by the book, you let your zeal cloud your judgment."

Quickly Judge Brown turned to the court reporter and ordered, "Strike that. Strike all of it after the motion."

"We also ask that bail be continued," Karen said.

The court reporter looked to the judge, who nodded, then leaned forward, his hands formed into fists. "Bring back the jury."

Both attorneys remained quiet as the jury was brought back.

"Ladies and gentlemen," the judge intoned, "it is with deep regret that I inform you this trial will come to an end immediately. The prosecutor in this case has acted improperly, and, as a result, I have no choice but to declare a mistrial. I thank you for your time and attention, and I apologize for the fact it's been wasted."

The judge declared the mistrial, granted bail continuance, adjourned court, slammed his gavel, and stormed out of the room. His black robes trailed behind him, giving the appearance of an enraged mutant bat from some low-budget horror film.

Ferguson glared at Karen across the aisle between the tables.

"This is unconscionable," he snarled. "This guy walks and you're responsible. Another five thousand kids get hooked on crack, another ten thousand lives are destroyed, another million tax dollars go up in smoke, all because of you. Whatever happens from this day on, you're responsible."

The soft smile left Karen's lips. "You're quite wrong, Mr. Ferguson. It's you who is responsible. You let your ego get the better of you when you chose to grandstand. That stuff looks good in the movies, but there's no place for it in a real courtroom. Maybe you've learned something. Frankly, I doubt it."

Her client was at her side, tugging on her elbow. "What's all this mean?"

She whispered in his ear. "It means you're still out on bail while the state decides whether to try you again. I expect they will, so don't leave town, understand?"

"You mean we'll have to do this all over again?"

"Probably. We'll talk about it later. This is not the place."

John Farrow, a twice-convicted drug dealer facing a long sentence, groaned. "Jesus. I don't think I can go through this again."

Karen gripped the man's arm and squeezed hard. "Be quiet," she whispered. "Go home. Say nothing to anyone. I'll do the talking. Just sit tight until I call you. Understand?"

"Okay," Farrow said, then turned and almost ran from the courtroom.

Watching him go, Ferguson spat on the floor. A burly bailiff started moving toward him. As Karen gathered up her court papers and shoved them into her attaché case, Ferguson was on his knees, wiping up his spit.

Outside the courtroom, Karen's secretary hurried toward her. Judging by Liz's distraught appearance, Karen assumed something was terribly wrong. The usually placid Liz hadn't looked so catastrophic since a year ago, when Walter Sinclair, partner in the prestigious law firm of Hewitt, Sinclair, Smith & Perry-Mondori and suffering the terminal stages of cancer, had committed suicide.

Karen was thankful Liz had assured her in the note that her husband and daughter were fine. Even so, a sudden chill sliced down Karen's spine as she greeted her secretary. "What's happened? You look upset."

Liz chewed on her lower lip for a moment. "Your sister-in-law called."

"Claire? Is something wrong?"

Liz nodded. "We need to talk privately. My car's in the lot, parked beside yours."

They pressed into the elevator with eight other people, saying nothing until they were outside the building, walking in the bright Florida October sunshine and toward their cars. Karen's agitation over Claire's call grew and she grabbed Liz's wrist. "So, what's going on?"

Liz, always the cool professional, but now near tears, looked into her questioning eyes.

"Karen, there's no easy way to tell you this," she said gently. "Your brother killed himself about an hour ago."

Two

Karen felt as if someone had punched her in the stomach. Her mouth was open, but she couldn't catch her breath. She wanted to move, but her feet seemed rooted to the asphalt. The benevolent sunshine had become oppressive heat, flushing her face and making her weak. Memories of U.S. Senator Robert Jameson, her half-brother, flooded her mind, and she leaned against her car, absolutely breathless, staring at the pavement, ashen faced, her lungs fighting for air. She tried to speak, but her voice sounded more like a moan.

Liz clutched her arm and spoke soothingly. "I'm so sorry, Karen. So very sorry."

Finally Karen found her breath and her voice. "Claire told you Robert . . . killed himself?"

Liz nodded. "She was almost hysterical."

Karen ran a hand through her hair, dislodging the hairpins in her bun, as she struggled to regain her lost composure. "My God, this is unbelievable. I must call her."

She walked around her car, unlocked it, and grabbed her cellular phone. With shaking fingers, she punched in the numbers for Robert's Virginia home.

The telephone was picked up almost immediately. "Karen, thank God! Did Liz tell you?" Claire sounded very near hysteria, her words punctuated by quick gasps.

"Yes. She said Robert has . . . committed suicide."

"It's true," Claire said. "He shot himself in the head. Oh, God. He's dead, Karen. Can you come up right away? I need you here." She started to weep.

Although close to tears herself, Karen had a score of questions. She repressed the desire to ask most of them, but she had to ask two. "Have you called the police?"

"Yes, they . . . they're here now. In the garage . . . with Robert." Claire was barely coherent.

"What on earth would cause Robert to do such a thing?"

Claire struggled to answer, but all she could say was, "Oh, Karen, I can't. Not now."

"It's all right," Karen murmured. "I'll be there as soon as possible. Within hours."

"Thank you."

Like a combination-lock tumbler clicking into place, Karen's mind addressed the immediate problem. "The police are there now."

"Yes."

"Are you certain it was suicide?"

"Certain? Oh, yes. There's no question."

"Have the police talked to you yet?"

"No. They've just arrived, really."

"Let me speak to them."

In a moment, Karen heard a man's voice. "Ms. Perry-Mondori?"

"Yes. I'm the senator's sister and Mrs. Jameson's attorney."

"Lieutenant Jack Brace, Fauquier County Sheriff's Office."

"I understand"—she struggled to keep the anguish

from her voice—"my brother has committed suicide."

"It would appear so, ma'am."

"Appear so? You're not sure?"

"Just a figure of speech. It sure looks that way. My condolences, ma'am."

"Thank you." She grasped the cell phone tighter to steady her shaking hand. "Was there a note?"

"Yes, but it really doesn't tell us much. I'll be asking Mrs. Jameson some standard questions so we can sort this out a little. Nothing serious."

"I'd appreciate it if you'd wait until I get there before you ask more."

There was a pause. "Are you a criminal lawyer, Ms. Perry-Mondori?"

"Yes."

"Well, there's no reason for concern. There's no evidence of foul play. It's not like Mrs. Jameson's a suspect or anything."

"I understand. Nevertheless, until the cause of my brother's death has been officially declared, I'm instructing Mrs. Jameson not to answer questions unless they're asked in my presence."

Brace paused again. "We're allowed to ask certain questions, and we'll be doing that. Surely you're aware of the law. You're in Florida?"

"Yes."

"Well, as I said, Mrs. Jameson is not a suspect, so there's no cause for you to be concerned. We'll stay well within our province, I assure you. If you like, we'll remain at the house until you arrive, if you're on your way."

"With any luck, I'll be there in three to four hours."

The detective sighed. "Are you licensed to practice law in the State of Virginia?"

"I am." She had passed the Virginia bar several years ago, when her firm picked up an important client with homes in both Richmond and Florida.

"Very well. We don't wish to cause additional problems for Mrs. Jameson. She's pretty dazed right now. Understandable, given the circumstances. I'll ask only those questions that have to be asked. Anything else can wait until you get here. We have plenty to do."

Claire came back on the line.

"The police will be asking you some questions," Karen said. "Answer only those relating to what you heard and what you saw. Nothing else. Don't get into any speculation as to why Robert might have done this. Understand?"

"Yes . . . but I have nothing to hide."

"I know, Claire, but whether you realize it or not, you're in shock. Lord knows, so am I. It's always best to speak to the police only in the presence of an attorney in situations like this. Please do as I ask."

Claire hesitated. "Very well."

"Will you be all right until I get there?"

"I don't know," Claire said in a faltering voice. "You're right about the shock. I feel numb. I've called my mother—and Martha. And Dr. Richards. They're all on their way."

"That's good," Karen said, her mind reeling. "Hang in there as best you can." In spite of her own need for answers, she saw little point in questioning Claire further.

"I'll try. I'm sorry, Karen. I know how close you two had become."

"Yes." To keep her tears in check, Karen focused

on details. "I must make plane reservations. I'll be there as quickly as possible."

Claire was weeping when Karen broke the connection.

She replaced the phone in her attaché case, then turned to Liz, who waited beside the car, her face a picture of pain and confusion.

"I'm so sorry," Liz said again.

"I still can't believe it," Karen said. "Suicide. It seems so impossible."

Liz patted her arm.

"Look," Karen said, "I'll go home to pack and call Carl. In the meantime, book us three seats on the next flight to Washington. Call me as soon as you have reservations. I'll need about an hour and a half, no more."

"Of course. Would you like me to drive you to the airport?"

"No, you have enough to do. We'll leave the car at the terminal. Ask Brander to cover for me until I get back." She rubbed her forehead. "I don't know when that will be. You'll have to juggle things."

"I will. Don't worry about it. You go and take care of your family. I'll take care of things at this end."

Karen gave her a hug. "Thanks, Liz."

As she fought the traffic on U.S. 19, Karen's mind was a thousand miles away, in Virginia, in an old house an hour's drive from Washington, where her brother lay dead.

She found Robert's suicide utterly incomprehensible. Robert was a strong man, a fighter, a maverick, shrugging off the worst life had to offer, embracing the best, moving forward, always forward, with optimism and enthusiasm.

She and her half-brother hadn't always been close. Up until a year ago when Karen agreed to represent Mafioso Angelo Uccello, they'd gone their separate ways.

When a leader of the Miami arm of the Cali drug cartel had come gunning for Uccello, and Karen and her family as well, Robert offered his home as a refuge. By focusing the spotlight of his Senate investigative committee on the drug runners, he had saved the lives of Karen, her husband, Carl, and daughter, Andrea, and arranged for Uccello to disappear into the Federal Witness Protection Program.

Since then, Karen's affection and respect for her brother had grown. Their families had exchanged frequent visits, and Andrea had come to adore her Uncle Robert.

And now Robert was gone.

Suddenly Karen felt an emptiness so strong it forced her to turn off the road into the parking lot of a shopping mall. She stopped the car, closed her eyes, then leaned back in the seat, and let the tears flow with gut-wrenching sobs. She was gripped by pain, oblivious to the stares of passersby. It took five minutes to pull herself together.

When she finally parked her Beemer in the driveway and entered her house in Autumn Woods, an exclusive area of Palm Harbor, her tears had stopped.

She set down her attaché case in the front hall and struggled again for control. Robert's death had brought back a flood of memories, including the vicious murder of her former au pair by the cartel's assassins in this very hall. Andrea had been traumatized by the event, and for a while, Karen and Carl had considered moving. After consulting their daughter's teachers and Leo Zimmer, her therapist, they'd concluded that leaving the only home the child had ever known would be more stressful than the memories.

They'd redecorated instead. No one would ever guess that at one time bullets had riddled these walls.

A few months after the conclusion of the Uccello case, one of Karen's colleagues in the Clearwater Bar Association moved to California. Her au pair, Rahni Shah, decided to remain in Florida, so Karen had hired her. Each day, Rahni prepared meals, drove Andrea to and from school, and cleaned house. Rahni's quiet disposition had proved especially helpful toward Andrea's recovery, and, after a stressful day at the office, Karen appreciated coming home to the order and tranquility Rahni created.

Almost thirty, a few inches taller than Karen, slender with fine features and jet-black hair pulled back in a braid, Rahni greeted Karen. In a musical voice, accented by the rhythms and inflections of her native India, she told Karen the plane's departure time, called in a few minutes earlier by the super-efficient Liz.

Karen placed a call to Carl's beeper, then rushed upstairs, dragged her suitcase from the hall closet, and carried it into the master bedroom. She had begun removing lingerie from her bureau when the bedside phone rang.

"You called?" Carl asked.

"It's Robert," she said, fighting not to cry again. "He's dead."

Stunned silence resonated for several seconds on the other end of the line. "His heart?"

"Suicide."

"Are you sure?"

"Yes, I spoke with the detective."

"I'm sorry, Karen. What will you do?"

"Liz made reservations for the three of us to fly out of Tampa an hour and a half from now."

"I can't. I have a patient prepped and ready. The surgery will take at least that long."

"Claire was hysterical on the phone. I should leave as soon as possible."

"Of course. You go ahead on the three o'clock plane. I'll break the news to Andrea when I get home, and the two of us will take a later flight."

"You're sure?"

"Don't worry about Andrea and me. We'll be in Virginia before bedtime."

"It will be cool there this time of—"

"I'll pack warm clothes for both of us," he assured her, and she could hear the concern in his voice. "Karen?"

"Yes?"

"Check out that detective."

"Why?"

"Robert was the most optimistic guy I know. If he killed himself, I'll turn in my license to practice medicine."

As Karen approached Robert's house, she spotted a panel truck parked about a hundred feet from the gate, its large, white parabolic dish pointed skyward. Television people. Vultures. Parasites. The first of an expected, vast gathering of bloodsuckers.

Several cars were parked within the confines of the wrought-iron fence surrounding the Virginia house, two of them Fauquier County police cars. Two uniformed policemen stood by the gate.

She brought her rented car to a stop, groped for

an unfamiliar handle, and rolled down the window.
"I'm Karen Perry-Mondori, the senator's sister."

"You got some ID?" a laconic cop asked.

While Karen showed her identification, the other
cop got on the phone. In a moment, the gate swung
open, and Karen drove the Ford up the short drive
to the front of the house and parked it beside one of
the police cars.

"Aunt Karen!" a young man called. He bounded
down the steps and lifted her off the ground in a
bear hug. "Thank God, you're here."

"Richard."

Karen had finally learned to tell her twin nephews
apart, recognizing Richard by his contact lenses and
his outgoing manner. Michael wore glasses, and was
the shyer of the two. Both were tall and big-boned
with well-muscled bodies like their father, and even
better looking, with chiseled features, dark hair, thick
eyebrows over long-lashed eyes, and full, strangely
sensual lips. Through some magical circumstances,
they'd benefited from both parents' genes, retaining
the best, discarding the worst, as if able to participate
in the choosing.

Richard had played football in high school and
then college, but Michael preferred the solitude of
golf, though sports had always been a secondary interest for both. Since middle school, fervently encouraged by their parents, they had concentrated on
getting good grades. It had paid off. Richard, the
extrovert, was in his second year of law school and
in the top five percent of his class. Michael, a quieter
version of his minutes-older brother, was in medical
school, garnering equally good marks. Both, at
twenty-three, knew exactly what they wanted.

"Where's your mother?" Karen asked.

"She's upstairs, asleep. The doctor was here and gave her something."

"How is she?"

"Awful. I've never seen her so messed up."

"When did you get here?"

"An hour ago. The local police are inside, and the FBI showed up just after I arrived. They've all been waiting for you."

"Good. You okay?"

"I don't know. I never would have imagined anything like this could happen. Not to Dad. Jesus. The ambulance arrived just after I did. They've taken Dad away."

"Where?"

"Walter Reed, I think. It was the FBI guy's idea."

"Did your mother tell you what happened?"

Richard gripped his aunt's arm. "She told me he killed himself. Shot himself in the head. She won't tell me anything more until she's talked to you."

Karen blinked with surprise. "She didn't say why he did it?"

"Not a word. God, I just can't imagine Dad doing such a thing. He's so positive about everything all the time."

"Where's Michael?" Karen asked.

"He left Stanford two hours ago. I'll be picking him up at the airport when he gets in just after seven."

"Carl said he and Andrea will be arriving at 7:30 p.m. Maybe you can give them a lift, too. What about your grandmothers?"

"Grandma Taylor will be here later this afternoon. Dad's mom comes in tomorrow."

"Did you talk to my mother?"

Richard nodded, a wary look in his eyes. "Mom

called her first. Grandmother Perry's pretty upset. She wants you to call her right away."

"I'll do it later," Karen said, looking skyward for a moment at the prospect of confronting her cantankerous mother. Then she tucked her arm through Richard's, and they walked inside.

Three policemen stood in the living room of the old house, one uniformed, the others in plainclothes. Richard departed and Karen introduced herself.

"I'm Lieutenant Jack Brace, Fauquier County Sheriff's Office. I talked to you on the phone," the shortest of the three policemen answered.

"I appreciate your patience, Lieutenant."

"No problem." Brace pointed to the other men. "Sergeant Fisk is the one in uniform. He's with me. In the blue suit is FBI Special Agent Donald Tucker."

Karen turned to the FBI man. "What's your interest?"

"Just routine. Whenever a member of the United States Senate dies of unnatural causes, we're required to submit a report. I'll simply be assisting Lieutenant Brace. We don't wish to add to your grief in any way."

Odd talk from the FBI, Karen thought. Someone must have given them sensitivity training. Usually they took over an inquiry, throwing their weight around like nine-hundred-pound gorillas, heedless of the feelings of victims, other law-enforcement agencies, or anyone else.

Karen's practiced eye fixed on the three men. Tucker was young, maybe thirty-two, well dressed, with eager eyes that accentuated the FBI look about him. Brace, on the other hand, was older than she was. He looked like an accountant, possessed of a studious face, large black-framed glasses covering soft brown eyes, and straw-blond hair parted in the middle of his round head. He was dressed in a rumpled brown suit, and his brown shoes were dull and scuffed. Fisk was about forty and looked every inch a cop. His shoes gleamed.

"Have you talked to Mrs. Jameson?" Karen asked Brace.

"We talked to her some. Just routine."

Karen detected a note of disapproval. "And what did she say?"

"Not much. She was in the bedroom when she heard the shot." Brace seemed reluctant to furnish more.

"Tell me all you know, please, Lieutenant." Accustomed to graphic crime scenes, but not when members of her family were involved, she steadied herself for the details.

"He did it in the garage. Sat down in the far corner and put a .38 in his mouth. Mrs. Jameson called us right after she found his body. Two of my uniformed officers showed up, secured the area, and I arrived about ten minutes later."

Karen winced. "May I see the note?"

Sergeant Fisk picked up a clear plastic envelope from the coffee table and handed it to Karen. A handwritten note inside the envelope read:

My dear Claire, I know how much this will hurt you and the others I love so much, but I have no choice. Absolutely no choice. I know you'll realize that in time. I hope you'll also realize that what I said was the truth. It simply never happened.
                    With all my love, Robert.

Lieutenant Brace took the envelope from her. "Do

you have any idea what he meant by 'it simply never happened'?"

She shook her head. Nothing about Robert's death made sense, least of all his final note.

"What about his having 'no choice'?"

"I can't imagine." Karen thrust her hands into the pockets of her suit jacket. "On the flight up here, I thought about nothing else, trying to determine what could possibly have driven my brother to do such a thing. I have no answers, and the note, aside from being cryptic, tells me nothing. What else did Mrs. Jameson say?"

Brace shrugged. "Just that he'd been depressed for a couple weeks. She didn't think it was serious and had no idea what caused it. Was your brother in some kind of trouble?"

"Not that I was aware."

"When's the last time you talked to him?"

Karen thought for a moment. "Wednesday night. We talked on the telephone, planning a visit. My husband, daughter, and I were coming here next weekend to enjoy the fall colors."

"Did he discuss his depression with you?"

"No," Karen said. "I had no idea he was depressed. He sounded normal, basically upbeat. Oh, sure, there were the usual frustrations, like everyone has. He did express some dissatisfactions, though he never pinpointed the exact problems."

"So he was evasive?" Brace said.

"No, that was his routine. He'd discuss generalities, but never specifics. He felt constrained by the rules of his office, which he took most seriously."

"So his depression could have been work related?" Brace asked.

"Maybe," Karen said, "but even when Robert became unduly perturbed about his job, the condition was always temporary. He understood the nature of politics better than anyone I've known. He certainly never let the vagaries get to him. I've seen him upset, annoyed, disgruntled, and disappointed, but I've never seen him in what I'd describe as a depressed state."

"What about . . ." Brace hesitated, embarrassed. "I have to ask this, you understand. . . ."

"Go ahead."

"A lady friend?"

Karen frowned, thinking of Claire having to answer these questions and remembering her own pain during the Palmer case when false allegations had been made about Carl's fidelity. "It's possible, but I sincerely doubt it."

"Why?"

Karen took a moment to select her words. "During our growing up, Robert and I suffered the traumas of a highly dysfunctional family. As a result, he and I both as adults have made a priority of providing our spouses and children with a secure, stable, and happy home. As for Robert and Claire's relationship, I can assure you that this was a marriage in which both worked very hard to keep it fully alive."

"Sounds heartwarming." Lieutenant Brace sighed. "But if this note is legit, something was bugging him."

"What do you mean," Karen asked, "*if* it's legit?"

"No need to worry," Brace said. "Mrs. Jameson says it's his handwriting."

"I agree," Karen said. "It's Robert's handwriting all right. Even so, are you *sure* this is a suicide?"

Tucker, who had taken a chair in the corner, decided to stick his oar in. "About ninety percent. I've examined the evidence Brace has gathered up to this point, and murder appears out of the question. The position of the body and gun, the entry and exit wounds, the powder burns, the lack of appearance of any struggle—"

"So there's nothing to suggest it *wasn't* suicide?" Karen said.

"There's more to check before we make a final determination," Tucker answered quickly. "First we have to talk to Mrs. Jameson at length, which we really need to do as soon as possible. I understand you're a criminal attorney."

"Yes."

"May I speak candidly?"

"Please do."

"You didn't help by telling Mrs. Jameson not to speak to us. There's no reason to consider her a suspect. You've just wasted everyone's time."

Karen glared at him. "I'm sure you'll not mind if I speak just as candidly?"

"Go ahead."

"I've lost a brother, Agent Tucker. Wasting your time is the least of my concerns."

"I see."

"Experience has taught me," Karen added, "that no one should talk to law-enforcement officers without an attorney being present. I'm sure it comes as no surprise to you that innocent people have been charged with crimes they did not commit."

"That's a rarity, Ms. Perry-Mondori."

"Nevertheless, it happens. I've seen it. I've defended people who've been victims of it. My first instinct was to advise my sister-in-law not to say anything until I arrived, but I allowed her to talk with Lieutenant Brace, so you have no call to speak to me like this."

Tucker's face reddened, but he said nothing.

Karen turned to Brace. "I hesitate to repeat myself, but are you *convinced* this was a suicide?"

Brace's eyebrows rose. "Do you have some reason to think your brother's death was murder?"

"I just find it hard to believe that Robert would do this. Hours after the fact, I still find it incomprehensible."

Brace nodded. "I'm sure. We'll have to do an autopsy, but I'm not expecting any surprises. One of our best forensic experts has already examined the scene, and his preliminary report confirms suicide. No signs of struggle, no illegal entry into the garage. And while we waited for you, we took statements from the gardener and the maid. Neither saw anyone on the property who shouldn't have been here."

"Where are they now?"

"The maid's up in her room. We let the gardener go home. He was pretty shook up."

Karen turned to Tucker. "Richard tells me you've taken Robert's body to Walter Reed."

Tucker nodded. "We want the autopsy done there for a number of reasons. No reflection on Brace's people, but your brother *was* a United States senator."

"I understand." Karen glanced out the front window. "The press have set up shop in the street. Have any of you talked to them yet?"

"Nope," Brace said, "but it can't be avoided."

Karen frowned. "What do you plan to tell them?"

"Simply that your brother died of a gunshot wound, we're pretty sure it was a suicide and have no reason to suspect it wasn't. We won't release the note, but we'll confirm there was one. We'll refer all questions to the family spokesman, who, I take it, is you."

"Yes, and I appreciate your deference, Lieutenant."

"No problem. When do you think we can talk to Mrs. Jameson at length?"

"I want to speak with her first, then you can take her statement. I understand she's asleep at the moment. . . ."

Richard entered the room. "Mother's awake, Aunt Karen. She wants to talk to you."

Without another word, Karen turned, left the room, and hurried up the stairs.

Three

"I killed him," Claire said.

Karen, stunned, not quite sure she'd heard correctly, quietly closed the bedroom door behind her, then stood beside the bed, leaning over an anguished Claire, who firmly gripped a white linen sheet drawn tightly under her chin.

"What did you say?" Karen asked softly.

The last time she'd seen Claire had been less than a month ago at a dinner honoring Robert for one of his many achievements outside government, an award bestowed for his successful chairing of a committee responsible for establishing a privately owned hospital in one of Miami's poorer Cuban communities. He had convinced a large and diverse group of local business interests that investing in a hospital catering to the poor was good public relations. To almost everyone's astonishment, the businessmen had agreed and quickly built the hospital.

The hospital welcomed the indigent, and while it would always lose money, its very existence significantly enhanced the public image of those companies that had contributed the money to build it and committed to keep it going. Only a few knew that Robert was testing a concept he hoped would eventually be used nationally. To him, full corporate involvement

in crucial community concerns was the key to break-
ing unproductive dependency on government as a
problem solver.

At the dinner, Claire had looked ravishing in a
full-length designer gown, her skin glowing, her blue
eyes shining with pride as she stood beside Robert.
That she was still madly in love with her husband,
and he with her, was obvious to everyone in the
room.

This day, this terribly shocking day, Claire's patrician features were appallingly twisted by pain, and
she seemed to have aged ten years in a few short
weeks.

Karen hugged her and felt Claire's hot, quick
breath on her neck and the wetness of tears.

"What are you saying?" Karen repeated in an urgent whisper.

"I killed him," Claire sobbed. "I might as well
have taken the gun and shot him myself."

Karen expelled a long breath, gently extricated herself from Claire's grasp, and eased her sister-in-law
back onto the pillows. "We'll talk about this later.
Has the doctor given you something?"

"Yes."

"How long ago?"

Claire tossed her head back and forth. "About four
hours ago."

"Did the doctor leave you something?"

"In the night table."

Karen found the sedatives, read the handwritten
label instructions, and tapped one tablet from the
vial. She gave it to Claire with a glass of water, then
replaced the vial in the night table. As she closed the
drawer, she noticed a small oil stain. To her horror,

she realized this was where the family gun was usually kept.

"We'll talk later," Karen repeated. "You get some rest."

"I must tell you now," Claire insisted. "I can't hold this in. God, I killed him, Karen!"

Karen brushed Claire's hair, damp from tears and sweat, back from her eyes. "You've had a tremendous shock. You should rest."

"Just listen. Please!"

Karen plumped Claire's pillows and sat on the edge of the bed. "All right. Tell me what happened."

Claire stared at the ceiling. "I still can't believe it. He was frantic, so anxious for me to believe him, and I denied him."

"Believe what? How did all this happen?"

"Did you read the suicide note?"

"Lieutenant Brace showed it to me."

Claire turned her face away. "He killed himself because I didn't believe him. I should have pretended I did, given him an out, but I couldn't, not this time. He was hiding it all this time, and when I finally realized it, I was sick."

"Realized what? What made you sick?"

Claire's beseeching eyes held Karen fast. "I could live with it now, given the chance, but I don't have that chance. He's gone. It's too late."

Claire was barely coherent, but Karen's inflamed curiosity pushed her. "Concentrate on exactly what happened. You told the police Robert was depressed. Depressed about what?"

"Until a few weeks ago, I thought he was fine. But lately, he's been so morose. Then today . . ."

"What happened today?"

Claire took a deep breath. "He got a tape in the

mail. A videotape." She covered her eyes with her hands. "It was hideous."

"A videotape?"

"Before he showed it to me, he told me it was either some kind of fakery or . . . he was afraid he was going crazy. He thought he was hallucinating. He said I had to see the tape so he'd know if he was going crazy." Reluctantly, she pulled her hands away from her face and looked at Karen. "Oh, God, if only he'd never shown it to me."

"What was so hideous about the tape?"

Claire seemed bewildered. "It was Robert . . . and a young girl. They were in bed. Together."

Karen's stomach began to tighten. "In bed?"

"Yes, Robert and . . . a child, really. They were having sex. When I saw it, I almost vomited. He swore it never happened. And then . . . I told him I didn't believe him, that he was sick and depraved. I ran here, to the bedroom, closed the door and locked it. He stood at the door, insisting it was all a lie, that the tape was some awful fabrication. He said he didn't know how he got on the tape, that it simply never happened."

Claire clutched Karen's arm. "You have to understand something, something I've never told anyone."

"What?" Karen could hardly breathe.

"Robert had been a senator for less than a year when it happened. I was looking for something in his desk and I found a . . . magazine. One of those awful things, men with little girls . . . having sex. I confronted Robert. He was furious. He told me he was on a committee studying pornography and the magazine was one of the exhibits. He hadn't wanted to leave it at the office, he said. He was so upset with me, angry that I'd even think he'd be interested in such trash, and I felt so ashamed for having questioned him about it.

"But today, when I saw that tape, I knew he'd lied to me back then. It was so . . . horrible. There was no mistake this time."

Claire was sobbing now, eyes closed, shaking her head from side to side, her tears forming tiny rivers as they ran toward her ears. "I can still hear him, pleading with me. I didn't know what to say. I was just so shocked I blurted out my feelings without thinking."

Karen, mesmerized by the horror of the story, pushed Claire further, feeling guilty for doing so. But she had to know. "And then?"

"He went away. A few minutes later I heard the gunshot."

Karen looked into Claire's eyes and saw pure hell.

"I rushed downstairs," Claire continued, "and saw Toshi, the gardener, running into the garage. I went to the garage through the kitchen, and Toshi was standing, just staring at Robert there in the corner, on the floor, a gun in his hand with . . . blood . . ." Claire covered her face with her hands again.

Karen's stomach clenched with a pain that almost bent her double, but she had to know the truth, for her own sake and to advise Claire when the police questioned her.

"Back up a little," Karen said, trying to get events fixed in her mind. "You saw a videotape in which Robert was having sex with a young girl?"

Claire shuddered. "Yes."

"And you think he killed himself because you didn't believe him when he told you the tape was a fake?"

Claire nodded.

"And you believe this is something he's been doing all along? Is that what you're saying?"

"What else could it be?" Claire gasped. "I'd forgotten all about that magazine, but when I saw that tape . . . that tape was *real*, Karen. There's no mistake. It was Robert."

Karen felt very cold. "Where's the tape now?"

"In the safe, along with the package it came in."

"Did you tell the police about the tape?"

Claire shook her head violently. "I showed them the note, that's all. I had to. But I couldn't bring myself to give them the tape, or to tell them about it."

Claire grabbed Karen's arm. "No one must see that tape. It's bad enough that Robert killed himself, that he had this . . . problem. If that tape ever fell into the wrong hands . . ."

"Has anyone else in the household seen it?"

"No." Claire sat up suddenly and gripped Karen's shoulders. "They wanted money."

"Who?"

"There was a message on the tape, blackmail. Will they still want the money, now that Robert's dead?"

Karen had a quick mind, but the facts were coming too fast. This information was difficult to assimilate, especially when her intellect was numbed by shock. She could see the sedative beginning to take effect. Claire's mouth was open and, despite her near-panic, her eyes were beginning to close. Karen pressed her sister-in-law back on the pillows.

"Who is Robert's personal representative, Claire? There are details that must be taken care of."

Claire's eyes widened with dismay. "I am, but I can't do it, not now, not after all this. You're good at details. Will you handle the arrangements, and the will, please?"

"If you're appointing me to take over as personal representative . . ."

"I am."

Karen nodded. "I'll take care of things."

Claire closed her eyes and clutched Karen's hand. "I'm so glad you're here. Robert trusted you so. Now, you'll have to protect us, Karen. Not just us, but Robert's image. He was such a good man. We can't have his life belittled because of just one . . . awful . . . perversion."

"You get some rest."

Claire peered at her through half-closed, leaden lids. "This is like some dreadful nightmare. Can you make it just a nightmare, Karen, so when I wake up, things will be as they were?"

Because she couldn't give Claire the answer she wanted, Karen said nothing.

Claire closed her eyes, finally giving in to the effects of the drug. In a minute she was fast asleep. The doctor, probably recognizing the magnitude of Claire's shock and the need for time to successfully counteract it, had prescribed a very strong sedative.

Karen stayed with her sister-in-law five minutes longer, then gently pried her hands loose. With a heavy heart, she went downstairs where the policemen waited.

Four

"She say anything?" Brace asked.

"She's still in shock," Karen told him. "Most of what she's saying makes no sense. It would be best if you waited until tomorrow to question her. Let her regain her senses."

Brace gave her a wary look. "She said nothing to help us?"

"No."

"You're sure?"

"I'm not trying to stall you, Lieutenant. Robert and Claire were very close. Their relationship has been strong since the first. Losing him, especially this way, is extraordinarily traumatic. Naturally, she doesn't know what to make of it." She shook her head. "Frankly, neither do I. If you'll give us until tomorrow to pull ourselves together, I'd appreciate it."

"Fair enough." The policeman handed her a card. "Call me when she's ready to make an official statement."

"I'll do that."

"Oh, your nephew went to the airport. He asked me to tell you."

In addition to Michael, Richard would bring Carl and Andrea when he returned. An overwhelming need to see them surged through her. "Thanks. And thanks for stationing your people at the front gate. I appreciate that very much. We all do."

Brace shrugged. "It's the least I can do. Your brother may have represented Florida, but we liked him a lot around here. He was a rare bird, a politician with clean hands. We'll miss him."

"Thank you again."

Brace turned to leave, then stopped. "Ms. Perry-Mondori, I must have a reason why he did this so I can close the case. There's no need for the media to know whatever details you can give me, but I can't just let it go. You understand?"

"I assure you, as soon as I know anything, you'll know."

Tucker extended his hand. "I'll leave with the lieutenant. I'll get whatever I need from the local officials.

"Thanks." Karen showed all three policemen to the door, then went into the kitchen.

The cheery atmosphere of the spacious room, furnished in late nineteenth and early twentieth-century American pieces, contrasted starkly with the tragedy that had just occurred.

The kitchen is the heart of a home, Karen thought and recalled an occasion last winter when her family and Robert's had gathered around the hundred-year-old trestle table, laughing, talking, and eating. The gigantic wood-burning stove had pumped warmth into the room while they watched snow fall and icicles form outside the French doors. With its Early American wallcoverings and all modern appliances cleverly concealed behind wooden panels that looked like pantry doors, the room seemed like a time capsule from another era.

Robert and Claire loved the house they had owned

for eleven years like a fifth member of their family. The redbrick, triple-gabled, two-story former farmhouse that once stood alone among open fields was now surrounded by urban sprawl. Claire had personally refinished the gleaming hardwood floors, and her special touches, including fresh-cut flowers from her garden, were everywhere.

Karen stared out the window above the sink into the gathering darkness. This house, the Jamesons' home away from their Miami home, had necessitated a sometimes brutal commute for Robert, but he had liked it that way. His distant residence had given him an excuse to avoid all but the most essential of the interminable parties and receptions that begged his attendance. And the house provided Claire a retreat from the hurly-burly, not-quite-real world inside the Beltway.

A lump formed in Karen's throat. Robert would never have to worry about a snowy commute or his social calendar again.

She turned from the window and scanned the room, looking for any hint of what had happened there earlier. With much trepidation, she opened the door leading to the garage. The place was dark. Both cars had been removed and sat in the driveway. She turned on the light and peered in, gritting her teeth when she spotted what she was looking for: the scene of the tragedy, the far corner, the wall stained by blood, the floor marked in chalk. Resisting the urge to turn and flee, she stepped into the open space.

Her foot hit a basket on the floor by the door, and she flinched as a trowel rattled among other hand tools. The domesticity of Claire's gardening basket presented an ironic contrast to the grisly scene at the opposite side of the space.

Karen walked slowly to the marks drawn in chalk and stared down at the telltale signs of sudden death. She began to shake as a mordant odor invaded her nostrils.

A thin white string was affixed to the floor, running to a point about three feet up the wall, indicating the angle of the bullet. A splash of dried blood surrounded a small hole in the wall, ringed in black by a felt-tip marker. She could see where the police had dug the slug from the wall.

She stood there, taking it all in, drawing her own conclusions from the evidence. She could almost see it, Robert sitting on the floor, his legs drawn up under his chin, a gun in his hand, the barrel shoved in his mouth, its hammer cocked. And then . . .

Her eyes filled with tears. She turned and walked quickly back to the kitchen, closing the door behind her.

"Will you be wanting dinner, Ms. Karen?" Ursula, a family fixture for fifteen years, asked.

A quiet, attractive woman in her late thirties and devoted to the family, Ursula stood in the middle of the kitchen, still in uniform, blond hair askew, eyes wet with tears, stunned, yet wanting to carry on as though nothing had happened.

"I don't think anyone is very hungry," Karen said softly. "Why don't you take the night off? If anyone gets the urge to eat later, we'll just help ourselves."

"I'm so sorry. For Mrs. Jameson and you, but especially the boys. How awful they must feel." Ursula sniffed and dug into her apron pocket for a handkerchief.

"Have you talked to the police?" Karen asked.

Ursula nodded, blew her nose, and wiped her eyes.

"What did you tell them?"

Ursula hesitated for a moment. "Just that I didn't hear the shot. I had no idea what was happening."

Karen guided the maid to a chair and motioned for her to sit. "You didn't hear the shot?"

"I was vacuuming my room. I didn't know anything had happened until I turned off the vacuum and heard Mrs. Jameson screaming. I found her standing at the door to the garage, just screaming."

"No one else was in the house?"

"No, Toshi was in the garage, just standing there staring at the senator's body."

"Did you hear anything before the shot?" Karen asked.

Ursula looked into her eyes, then dropped her gaze to the floor. "That's why I decided to vacuum my room. They don't fight much, you know, and when they do, I try not to listen."

"What were they fighting about?"

"I don't know. They were in the den, and when they started to argue, I went to my room. Then I heard them upstairs, so I started to vacuum. When I finished, I heard Mrs. Jameson screaming."

"Where was she when she screamed?"

"Downstairs. When I came rushing down, she was standing in the doorway to the garage, so I guess it was there."

"What did you tell the police?"

Ursula looked into Karen's searching eyes. "I didn't tell them about the argument. Just the scream and me running to the garage."

Ursula began to weep, and Karen patted her shoulder again. "Did the police talk to Toshi?"

"Yes. All he said was he heard a shot, ran to the garage, and found the body. Then he heard Mrs.

Jameson screaming and saw me come up behind her."

"Who called the police?"

"Mrs. Jameson."

"Were the cars in the garage?"

"No, Toshi cleans the garage when he comes, so the cars were in the driveway."

Karen gave her a brief hug. "You get some rest, okay?"

"By the way, Mrs. Jameson's mother arrived while you were in the garage. She's upstairs with Mrs. Jameson now." With a weary motion, Ursula hoisted herself to her feet and left the kitchen.

FBI agent Donald Tucker sipped the coffee offered him by Lt. Brace and carefully set the heavy mug on the man's desk. "Good," he said, smiling.

Brace sipped his own coffee, then laughed. "You lie like a rug, Tucker. Marsha lets that stuff cook all day." He reached forward and picked up Tucker's mug. "I'll tell her to make some fresh."

Tucker smiled. "I was hoping you'd say that."

Brace let out a bellow. A woman in her sixties entered the room, and he lifted his coffee mug. "Make a fresh pot, will ya, Marsha?"

Marsha busied herself making fresh coffee, then left the men alone while it dripped through.

"So," Tucker said, leaning forward, "what do you think?"

Brace waved a hand. "It's suicide all right. First thing I did when I got there was check Mrs. Jameson's hands. No powder marks. She was in real shock, too. Besides, two other people were in or near the house. I doubt she'd've killed him in their presence. And then there's the gun."

"The gun?"

"Yeah. There's people who will use a gun and others who won't. Claire Jameson isn't the gun type. Too refined, if you know what I mean. If she was goin' to kill her husband, she'd use poison or something less messy than a gun."

Tucker nodded. "You know them well?"

"Very well. Great people, like I said. Besides, when I talked to her and the help, I didn't get the feeling they were trying to hide anything. Then there's the note and all. Finally, Frank's a good forensics man, and he's convinced."

"What did he say?"

"He found powder marks on the senator's right hand. The pattern was a little off, but that's probably because Jameson was holding the gun at an odd angle." He sighed deeply. "Like I say, Claire's just not the kind. And the help . . . no way. The security system was turned off 'cause the gardener was there. No matter. He'd've seen someone coming in the front. We talked to the neighbors in the back, and they didn't see any strangers hanging around, and you know how neighbors are. They've got the eyes of eagles, especially keeping watch on the people next door. One lady heard the shot and kept looking out her back window. She never saw anybody."

Brace tugged at his chin for a moment, then slapped a hand on the desk. "No, it was suicide all right. You think different?"

"Not really," Tucker said.

"But something's buggin' you. What?"

"Must be my natural antipathy for criminal defense attorneys. Karen Perry-Mondori told the senator's wife not to talk to us until she got there. It seems defensive to me."

Brace grinned. "You just don't know them. The Jameson family is real tight. I'm sure there're secrets there, like with any family. Perry-Mondori, being an experienced trial lawyer, didn't want her sister-in-law blabbing things that have nothing to do with this, and I can hardly blame her. Best thing to do is shut the hell up. You called her on that to her face, and she said as much."

"In no uncertain terms," Tucker said, remembering.

"Have to appreciate the circumstances, son. Those people are the salt of the earth. Mrs. Jameson shows her roses at the county fair every year, and the senator is always helping out folks around here. The man represented Florida, so it was no skin off his nose to refer some complaining citizen to his own man, but he never did that. Just quietly went about doing what senators do, getting things straightened out for folks."

Brace put his feet on the desk and leaned back in his chair. "About a year ago, we had this kid dying from some strange Asian disease. Jameson arranged for a trip to Disney World for the kid and his family. Paid for it out of his own pocket. Kid died about a month later. Funny thing was, the senator and his wife insisted nobody know they paid for the trip. I know because I made the arrangements. When's the last time you heard of a politician missing a photo op like that?"

Tucker remained silent.

"He was a fine man," Brace continued. "We're really gonna miss him."

Marsha stuck her head in the door. "I've got another one of those television people on the phone. You still want me to refer them to the sister?"

"You bet."

Marsha sniffed. "The lady lawyer's not talking to anyone, they say. They want to send a crew over here."

"Tomorrow," Brace said. "Not until tomorrow."

"You can't do that!" Marsha said.

"Why not?"

"You stall them much longer," she said, "and they'll make you look bad."

Brace sighed. "Tell 'em I'll make a statement in an hour. You write it up for me." He turned to Tucker. "Anything you want to say to the press?"

Tucker shook his head. "I'd just as soon they didn't know I was there."

"Suits me," Brace said. "Get on it, Marsha."

Marsha retreated to the outer office, and Tucker shrugged. "I wonder what made him kill himself?"

"We'll know soon enough," Brace said. "Once Mrs. Jameson gets her head straight, I'm sure she'll have an explanation. Something real personal, I'd imagine."

"Yeah," Tucker answered. "About as personal as it gets."

"I miss Uncle Robert," Andrea said.

Karen held her daughter close. Andrea and Carl had arrived less than an hour ago and joined her, Richard and Michael, and Mrs. Taylor in the kitchen for sandwiches, although no one had much appetite. When Andrea could barely keep her eyes open, Karen had carried her to the guest room where she and Carl would sleep and placed her in the trundle bed.

"Goodnight, sweetheart." Karen kissed her sleepy daughter and tucked the covers around her. "If you need us, Daddy and I will be in the den."

She left a night light burning and closed the door.

The house was quiet. Mrs. Taylor had returned to Claire in the upstairs bedroom, and Michael and Richard had disappeared into the room they shared when home from school.

Carl was waiting for her in Robert's den, where Robert's collection of old and rare first editions blended with his modern electronic equipment, generating a unique, if quaint, warmth.

A few years from fifty, Carl was still ruggedly handsome, his European good looks a match for any continental film star. Just under six feet, all muscles and taut skin, with smoldering dark eyes, thick dark hair, and full lips, he attracted her as much today as he had the day she'd met him.

"Do you want a drink?" she asked.

He shook his head. "I can tell by the look on your face you know more than you've told me."

Karen locked the door. "I don't want any unexpected interruptions."

"Finally, alone together." Carl grinned and pulled her into his arms. "This could be interesting."

Karen tilted her face toward him, her expression grim. "It is, but it's not what you think. I'm going to show you why Robert killed himself."

Before Carl and Andrea had arrived from the airport, Karen had located Robert's will and burial instructions. Among the papers was the combination to the safe embedded in concrete in a corner of the room.

Carl released her, and Karen peeled back the carpet, spun the dial and opened the safe. The tape was there, as was the package.

"This," she held them up for Carl, "arrived earlier today."

"Who sent it?"

Karen turned the package over. It was devoid of marks except for an address handwritten in block letters. "There's no return address, no canceled postmarks, so it must have been hand delivered, probably placed in the mailbox that stands just outside the gate."

"Why didn't you give it to the police?"

"Sit down," Karen nodded toward an easy chair. "When you see it, you'll understand."

While Carl sat, she removed the tape from its protective plastic sleeve, inserted it in the video player and turned on the television. When she tried to run the tape, she saw nothing but snow and, for a moment, wondered if Claire, in a panic, had erased what was there.

"Try Rewind," Carl said.

Karen rewound the tape and again pressed the Play button. Almost immediately, block letters flashed on the screen:

A MESSAGE APPEARS AT THE END OF THIS TAPE. DON'T MISS IT.

Carl leaned forward. Then the screen filled with an image of two people, a man and a child.

Robert and a girl of ten or so.

Carl snapped back in his chair as if slapped. Karen felt her throat constricting. Wanting to vomit, she took some deep breaths as the scene continued to unfold.

Robert was enjoying himself immensely, smiling, his forehead gleaming with sweat, his deeply hooded eyes at times shut tight, at others wide open as he faced the camera. His naked, milk-white skin reflected the harsh lighting with an almost phosphorescent intensity, and his movements matched the rhythm of the staccato rock music emanating from the background stereo system.

His companion, a blond-haired girl, appeared enthralled with the sexual prowess of her fifty-two-year-old lover and kept repeating his name in varying degrees of passionate timbre, ranging from deep-throated huskiness to shrill screams of ostensible lust. Robert, apparently concentrating on the moment, or possibly forgetful of the child's name, confined his comments to singular adjectives, most of them enunciated in clear, crisp tones.

"It's Robert's voice," Carl said.

"And his face and body."

The king-sized waterbed oscillated turbulently beneath them as the two lovers increased the tempo, their bodies slamming together noisily. And then, the child screamed.

The image suddenly disappeared, replaced by another message.

UNLESS YOU PAY US ONE MILLION DOLLARS IN CASH, WE WILL MAKE THIS VIDEO PUBLIC. YOU WILL BE CONTACTED.

The screen turned to snow.

Carl's dark, Mediterranean face had paled. "I need that drink."

"Claire told me what to expect. Still, it's incomprehensible. Impossible." Karen moved to the bar concealed in a closet and poured two snifters of brandy.

When she returned, Carl was on his knees before the VCR. He rewound the tape partway, ran it forward, then freeze-framed it and examined it carefully before rising. "There's no evidence of fakery."

She handed him his drink and filled him in on all Claire had told her.

Carl was silent for a moment when she finished. "So Claire thinks if she had believed Robert's claim that the events on the tape never happened, he'd still be alive?"

Karen nodded and took a long sip of her brandy. "Claire insists the tape is real. What do you think?"

"Robert was not a stupid man. To perform like that, much less with a child, in front of a camera is the act of an idiot."

"Maybe he was under the influence of some drug?"

Carl shook his head. "He was clear-eyed, coherent. Besides, to put it bluntly, if he were drugged enough to be coerced, he'd have been too sedated to get it up."

"Then the tape's a fake?" Karen asked, feeling haggard from the cumulative effects of grief, stress, and two fingers of brandy.

"What's Andrea's all-time favorite video?" Carl asked.

"*Babe*." Her eyes widened as she grasped the implications of his question. "Computer-manipulated images of animals speaking and acting like humans."

"And so smoothly and seamlessly created, not even the gigantic screens of a movie theater spoil the illusion."

Karen fought back tears. "Poor Robert. And poor Claire. She was so certain this was real."

"I didn't say it wasn't."

She took a deep breath. "Okay. It's *unlikely* it's real. And if it *is* a fake, it's professionally done. Computer manipulation must require expensive equipment. Narrowing down the places in this country where such a film could be produced should be relatively easy."

"You'd better expand that search worldwide. The hotel room in that film was in Europe."

"How could you tell?"

"The electrical outlet behind the bed, definitely European." He set down his glass and opened his arms. "Come here."

Karen settled on his lap and rested her head on his shoulder. "I'll FedEx the tape to Bill Castor in the morning. He can find someone to analyze it and figure out where it might have been produced."

Bill Castor, who worked on several of Karen's cases in the past, was a private investigator with extraordinary contacts and reliable discretion.

Carl nodded. "Sending the tape to Bill will also remove it from the house, so the boys can't see it. They idolized their father. This tape would destroy them."

"That's why I'm not giving it to the police. Not until I have solid proof it's a fake. I have to protect Robert's reputation. That's all of him that's left."

"The sooner the police have the tape," Carl reminded her gently, "the sooner they can catch the blackmailers."

"The district attorney will handle the felony indictment when the time comes." She sat up, her mouth set in a determined line. "I intend to file my own charges."

"What kind of charges?"

"The bastards who made this tape had to have big money. When I find out who they are, I'll sue for wrongful death and strip them of everything they own."

Carl grasped her shoulders and began to massage

the tension from her knotted muscles. "The people who made the tape obviously have no scruples. Perhaps you should let the district attorney deal with them. You have enough to handle, helping Claire and the boys."

She stiffened, in spite of his soothing ministrations. "Have you ever known me to back away from a fight?"

He gave her a rueful smile. "Not where justice is concerned."

"If these wealthy blackmailers do face felony charges, between their expensive defense teams, crowded court dockets and teeming prisons, they could receive laughable sentences." Her green eyes blazed with indignation. "Robert was a good man. I want the people who pushed him over the edge to suffer for the rest of their lives, just as Claire and the boys will."

Carl stood and lifted her in his arms. "You can fight the good fight tomorrow, after a full night's sleep, all right?"

"All right."

Karen placed her head on his shoulder and closed her eyes, but she didn't doze. As Carl carried her to the guest room, she compiled a mental list of tomorrow's tasks.

Deflecting the media was at the top.

Five

Caught in a macabre nightmare, Karen tossed, turned, and flailed her arms. Horrific visions of torn flesh, blood, empty eyes, and a wild-eyed, middle-aged man screwing a naked little girl glutted her mind.

She jolted awake and sat up in bed, panting, her body bathed in perspiration, her eyes staring at the nearest of three bedroom windows, her conscious mind fighting to get its bearings. Carl, undisturbed by her turmoil, dozed beside her, and Andrea slept like an angel in the trundle bed.

Their room faced the front of the house, where light from four pole-mounted streetlamps on either side of the driveway barely seeped through the heavy drapes, giving the room a look of bleak solemnity. As her highly disciplined mind reluctantly released her from the terror generated by the ghastly nightmare, another emotion took terror's place—despondency.

The wave of initial shock provoked by the impossible combination of Robert's sudden death and the hideous videotape had subsided, replaced by grim grief. What had been a flood was now a trickle, a heartache that only time would heal. Intellectually, Karen knew that, but her unconscious mind, not subject to direction, chose to focus on the immediacy of her searing pain.

She brought a pillow to her face and wept like a child.

Until yesterday, crying was something she hadn't done since the tragedy of her au pair's murder. Now, for the second time in less than twenty-four hours, she found herself unable to fight the compulsion.

She'd had so little time to enjoy her relationship with her brother, and now he was gone. Death was bad enough, but the manner of his passing and the circumstances that precipitated it were unbearable and placed a crushing weight on her soul. For a few minutes, she gave herself to self-pity, surrendering to a seemingly inexhaustible store of misery. Then, almost imperceptibly, the fighter in her rose from slumber and forced her to confront the need to find answers, to move forward again.

She glanced at the glowing digital clock. Five-thirty. Exhausted as she was, she knew sleep was unattainable now, so she dragged herself from bed and stumbled to the shower. Pulsing water cleansed some cobwebs from her mind. Head pounding, stomach churning, she dressed quietly, left Carl and Andrea to sleep, and closed the guest room door behind her.

The kitchen light was on. When she entered the room, she was astonished to see Claire, dressed and carefully made up, sitting at the table, a cup of coffee in her hands. Claire proffered a brave smile. "Good morning. Couldn't sleep?"

Despite Claire's stouthearted effort at camouflage, she looked terrible. Her face was puffy, her eyes red-rimmed and swollen, the variegated pouches beneath them almost screaming for attention.

"Good morning," Karen said. "How are you feeling?"

Claire's smile faded. "Like death." She gulped coffee. "No, I take that back. Death would be a blessed relief. I wish Robert had killed me before he killed himself. It would have been more merciful than leaving me with this terrible guilt."

Karen squeezed Claire's shoulder, then sat beside her. "You've got to stop blaming yourself. There's no point to it."

"I know, but—" Tears formed at the corners of Claire's eyes. "Did you see it?"

"The tape?"

Claire nodded.

"Yes," Karen said gently, "but I'm not convinced it's real."

"It's real, all right." Claire became more animated. "You must destroy it. I only kept it for you to see, so you'd know. The children must never see it. They're devastated enough already. *No one* must ever see it."

"I'll take care of it."

Claire sagged back in her chair. "Thank you."

"What did you tell Michael and Richard?"

"That I didn't understand why Robert killed himself. I discussed the note and said I wasn't sure what it meant, but I'd try to figure it out." Her lips quivered. "My poor boys. Richard idolized his father. Since he was a toddler, all he wanted was to grow up to be just like Robert. I remember how proud he was the day he was admitted to Yale Law School. . . . He won't want to be like Robert now."

Karen let her talk, hoping her concern for her children might give her strength.

"And Michael." Claire wiped away a tear. "Dear, sweet Michael. He'll make such a good doctor. He's my sensitive one. The slings and arrows of politics wounded him deeply. Whenever an opponent attacked Robert, Michael took it personally. This will devastate him."

"They're strong young men. It will be hard for them, but they're survivors."

Claire rested her head in her hand. "Thank God, you're here to help. I can't think, can't function. I thought if I got dressed and tried to act normal, it would help. It hasn't. I don't want the boys to see me like this. Maybe I should go back to bed."

"If you want to," Karen said.

"You don't approve?"

"I didn't say that."

Claire smiled wanly. "I sense it in your voice. You're so like Robert. You find it difficult to lie."

"Okay," Karen said, "I think you should try to hang in as long as you can. The sooner we can all get past this, the better. Right now, you're hurting, but you'll get through this because you must. There's no alternative."

Claire flashed another wan smile. "You're so strong. Robert had that same strength. Until yesterday. Now—"

Karen said nothing. With Robert, it had been more than strength. As she'd come to know him better over the past year since the Uccello hearing, she had learned more details about his philosophy of living and the events that had shaped him during the long years of their estrangement.

He had always been a man with a mission. His political aspirations had been spawned by his disenchantment with the war in Southeast Asia. His overall philosophy embraced conservatism, but on the issue of the war, Robert, well dressed and clean shaven, had joined hands with the drugged-out hippies and draft card burners on the steps of the Capitol building long before the rest of the country turned its back on Vietnam.

Robert had felt the way to change things was to get involved, and so he had, first as a campaign worker for a Senate incumbent who also opposed the war, then, after an eight-year career in corporate law, as a candidate for the House of Representatives. With little money, but boundless energy and enthusiasm, he'd won his first campaign.

Once in the House, he'd quickly learned the futility of being a total outsider, so he'd gone along to get along, but always with an eye to the ethical bottom line and a keen sense of why he was there. His ethical principles had been bruised, but not broken, and the respect he'd earned from those he served was heartfelt. After two terms in the House, he ran for the Senate and won by the slimmest of margins. Subsequent campaigns had yielded significantly better results.

Again, Karen doubted it was possible for such a man to involve himself in something as perverted as the videotape had implied.

Claire was staring at nothing. Karen, her curious mind demanding answers, decided to act like a lawyer for a few minutes. "Do you mind if I ask you some questions before Richard and Michael wake up?"

Claire's eyes refocused. "Questions?"

"Yes. Some pretty personal stuff."

"Oh."

"Forgive me," Karen said. "But I'm not as strong as you think. If I'm to get through this myself, I need to understand Robert's death, and that means having as much information as I can get my hands on."

"What kind of information?"

"Aside from that one instance with the magazine, was there ever a time . . . that you even suspected Robert was a pedophile?"

A slight rush of anger flushed Claire's cheeks. Good, Karen thought. Anger was sometimes the best medicine.

"I told you about that?" Claire asked.

"Yes, last night."

"I hadn't realized."

"Well?"

Claire straightened in her chair. "You can't be serious."

"Claire . . . I'm simply asking."

"The answer is no," Claire said firmly. "That time with the magazine . . . his explanation was entirely credible. I thought I'd made a mistake and felt terrible. I was sure Robert was telling the truth, and he never gave me a reason to doubt him. Until I saw that hideous tape." Claire's anger ebbed. "He fooled me completely."

"This next one," Karen said, "is a bit rough."

Claire set her jaw. "Go on."

"Did Robert, when he was with you, ever exhibit any offbeat—"

"Kinkiness?"

"That's as good a word as any."

Claire frowned. "Of course not," she said firmly. "Must we really discuss this?"

Karen nodded. "I'm trying to determine the probability that the tape is real. People don't become deviates overnight. Usually there are indications, some subtle, others more overt."

Claire sighed. "Go on with your questions."

"So you're saying his sexual behavior was normal?"

Claire nodded. "No whips or chains or dressing up, if that's what you mean. Robert's the only man I've ever known, so I have no means of comparing, but from everything I've read, he was normal, whatever that means."

Claire stared off into space for a moment. "He was a tender and considerate lover, undemanding, yet quite passionate at times. He made me feel desirable, even after all these years. I'd say that makes him quite a man." She sighed. "I'm not sure what that makes me."

Karen smiled. "It makes you someone very special."

Claire wrapped her arms around her body. "Not that special, obviously."

"Anything else?"

"What am I supposed to say? What signs was I to look for?"

Karen reached over and touched her hand. "I'm sorry. Forget it."

"No. Now that you've brought it up, I want to answer. What should I have been looking for?"

"I don't know."

"You're not making much sense."

Karen sighed. "I realize that."

Claire looked away for a moment, then turned to Karen, her gaze level. "I don't know what's expected or common these days, but he was . . . almost prudish, in the best sense of the word. In the early years of our marriage he had his little dalliances, but I never took them to heart. Beautiful, intelligent young women throwing themselves with total abandon at a married man for reasons even they probably didn't understand. I certainly didn't. I'd get angry, but in the end, I just accepted it."

Karen hid her surprise. As happy as Robert and Claire had always appeared, rough patches in their marriage seemed unbelievable.

Claire smiled wanly. "I didn't accept his peccadilloes at first, until I realized how meaningless they were. Robert always loved me and put me and the boys before anyone or anything."

Karen got up, grabbed the coffeepot, refilled Claire's cup, and poured one for herself.

"That's why I was so incredibly shaken when he showed me the tape," Claire said. "It was like a bomb had gone off in my head. I couldn't *imagine* him doing such a thing, but there it was, clear as day. And he kept insisting that it wasn't true." She paused. "You know what troubles me most?"

"What?"

"I was angriest that he thought I was stupid. He'd never been condescending before. He could never keep his affairs secret, always coming to me with tears in his eyes and confessing like a child. I threw things and slapped him, screamed and yelled and threatened to leave him, but except for that one time, I never really meant it."

"You left Robert?"

"Years ago. But being away from him made me realize what a good man he really was. And my leaving, even for such a short time, scared him enough to straighten him out. Until this."

Claire took the coffee cup in both hands, sipped, and placed it back in the saucer. "When Robert insisted the tape was a fabrication, I was furious, more for him thinking I was an idiot than for his actual behavior. Isn't that odd?"

"Not really," Karen said. "We all react irrationally to the incomprehensible. Part of your mind was denying what it had seen, while another part accepted it. The dichotomy caused you to focus your anger on something else, on what you saw as excuses."

"Perhaps."

"You said Robert had been depressed the past few weeks. Did you two discuss it?"

"Some, but Robert doesn't like to talk about his work. He likes to leave it in Washington."

"Then his depression was work related?"

"That's what he said. He kept insisting he was fine, but I knew he wasn't. Usually, I'd let it go for a few days before I'd press him. This time, I let it go longer. Perhaps—"

She started to weep again, then wiped her nose with her napkin and continued.

"He did mention some bill. Not the details, but that he was having trouble getting support for it. But he's used to that. I can't imagine him so upset over his failure to persuade others to join him in some cause."

"Could his depression have anything to do with the tape?"

"I simply can't imagine it," Claire said softly. "Last night, I thought about asking the boys if . . . well, I wondered if Robert had ever—"

"Claire, stop it." Images of Andrea, laughing with her Uncle Robert, flashed unbidden through Karen's mind. If Robert had molested his niece, would Andrea have told her? Could Karen somehow have guessed it? She refused to consider the unthinkable. Not unless the tape proved authentic. She stood up, looked out the window for a moment, then turned back to Claire. "When did you move the gun?"

"What?"

"You used to keep the gun in the bedroom. When did you move it?"

Claire looked puzzled. "About a month ago. I read something about burglars going straight to bedside tables for guns, so I asked Robert to put it somewhere else. He moved it to the den, in the drawer beside the television. How did you know we moved it?"

"You said you locked yourself in the bedroom. Unless the gun had been moved, Robert wouldn't have had access to it."

Claire lifted her hand to her mouth. "Oh . . ."

Karen changed the subject. "The media vultures are still out there. We're going to have to tell them something. The sheriff's office has already issued a statement."

"What did they say?"

Karen poured herself more coffee and returned to the table. "They came by last night and gave me a copy. They were obliged to report that Robert committed suicide, and they mentioned the note, but not its contents. They've assured me they won't divulge what he wrote, but I suspect some enterprising reporters will ferret it out soon enough. We need to make a statement as soon as possible."

"What kind of statement?" Claire asked.

"One that explains credibly why Robert killed himself. The note doesn't mention the tape, but does make reference to something Robert says never happened. We must address that."

Claire was wide-eyed. "How can we?"

"We certainly can't reveal the truth. We'll have to fashion a statement that can't be thrown back in our faces should the facts eventually come out."

Claire looked terrified. "What are you suggesting?"

Karen gripped Claire's hand and held it tightly. "You need to prepare yourself for another shock."

"My God, I can't take much more. What shock?"

Karen chose her words carefully, wanting desperately to dull their impact, while knowing the exercise was futile. "I could be wrong, but the possibility exists that a copy of the tape will be made public at some point, probably soon."

Claire looked as if Karen had hit her. "Why? Robert's dead."

"Two reasons. Whoever was blackmailing him didn't expect him to take his own life. They asked for a million dollars, and now they know they won't be getting a penny from him. But you're alive. They may demand money from you to prevent the destruction of Robert's reputation."

"They'd come to me?"

"It's possible. If they don't, they may release the tape as a warning to others."

"Others?"

"Robert may not have been the only one on their list."

Claire shook her head in wonderment. "I don't understand."

"I looked over the tape carefully." Karen spared her sister-in-law the embarrassment of knowing Carl had studied it, too. "*If* it's real, Robert was aware he was being photographed. For him to allow that meant his rational thought processes were somehow suppressed, possibly by some kind of sophisticated mind control. If they can do that to a man like Robert, they can do it to anyone. Releasing Robert's tape would make sure others they've managed to—"

Claire was weeping. Karen put her arms around

the sobbing woman. "I know this is difficult, but you have to hold on."

Claire gripped her hand. "I'm sorry, but I can't hear any more right now. I just can't."

"It's okay." Karen released her. "Let's concentrate on the statement."

Claire sat up and wiped her eyes. "Can't we say Robert was depressed for reasons not understood and leave it at that?"

"That would simply stoke the fires of speculation. I need to give a credible reason for the depression, something unrelated to his personal life."

Claire sighed. "I can't think right now. I leave it to you, Karen. Think of something that will satisfy the jackals of the press."

Claire rose unsteadily and left Karen alone in the kitchen.

Six

Two hours later, Karen stood inches away from a cluster of microphones just outside the gates of the Virginia house and confronted the all-seeing eyes of a dozen Minicams. She held a sheaf of papers, copies of a one-page statement she'd typed earlier.

"My name is Karen Perry-Mondori. I'm an attorney and Senator Jameson's sister, and I represent the family in this very sad matter. I have a statement to make, copies of which will be distributed to all of you."

The blinding floodlights distorted her vision, but she didn't have to read the page she couldn't see. She knew by heart what was written there. "Robert Jameson took his life on Friday, October twenty-fifth, while suffering from severe depression. He left a note, the contents of which will not be made public. To the best of the family's knowledge, Senator Jameson's depression began about three weeks ago and may have originated with his belief that he had inoperable cancer.

"Senator Jameson had been suffering from migraine headaches for over a month and refused to see a doctor. We believe he feared his headaches were caused by a brain tumor. Whether he, in fact, *had* a brain tumor, we don't know. We can't comment

further, except to say that we will release the results
of an autopsy as soon as they become available.

"Senator Jameson's career has been a distinguished
one. We hope the American people will remember
him for his many accomplishments and not for the
sudden impulse that caused him to take his own life.

"He will be buried near his home in Miami on
Wednesday. A memorial service will be held in
Washington the following Monday. The family asks
that in lieu of flowers, contributions be made to the
National Institute for Mental Health."

She handed the copies to one of the reporters, and
the feeding frenzy began as men and women, fearful
of missing out, jostled one another in their haste to
procure the statement. She stepped back in front of
the microphones. "I hope that you, in deference to
the suffering of the senator's family, will let this matter rest. I won't be answering questions, so please
don't ask them. If you want to stay out here, there's
not much we can do about it. I assure you, your wait
will be in vain, for this is the only statement we'll be
making until after the autopsy results are released."

She turned to leave and the reporters hurled a
score of questions at her. She ignored them all.

By two o'clock, Karen was at Dulles Airport,
watching her mother bull her way through the crowd
disembarking from a Miami flight. For over thirty
years, Martha Perry had refused to set foot on an
airplane. The mention of flying had always brought
a gleam of panic to the indomitable woman's eyes.
It had taken the unexpected death of her only son to
force Martha onto a plane. From the tight, white line
of her unsmiling lips, the experience hadn't sweet-
ened her already sour humor.

As her mother's blazing eyes found Karen, the older woman waved a copy of a newspaper and bellowed, "Have you seen this?"

Karen cringed. Her mother's voice seemed to echo throughout the terminal.

"I watched the *Today* show this morning," Martha continued at full volume. "The way they carried on, you'd think nothing else had happened in the entire world."

Karen moved forward and took her mother's arm. "Mother, please keep your voice down."

Martha paid her no heed. "And before I left Miami, I saw you on television making some ridiculous statement about depression, for God's sake. Why didn't you say something sensible?"

"Mother—"

"You had to tell all the world he was depressed, some mentally sick person?" She gestured with her free hand and continued her harangue. "What the hell's the matter with you?"

With her jaw set, Karen gripped her mother's arm tighter and guided her toward baggage claim. "Not here, Mother," she hissed.

"What's the big secret?" Martha exclaimed. "The whole damn world knows, thanks to you. Now Robert is disgraced. You could have prevented that."

"Stop it," Karen snapped.

"I won't stop it." Martha jerked away from Karen's grasp. "I'm surprised you're even here. I expected Ursula."

"He was my brother, Mother, and your son."

"Not *my* son. Turns out he was his father's son. *My* son wouldn't kill himself. He'd fight whatever the hell it was to the bitter end. I didn't raise quitters.

His father's genes caught up with him in the end. Weakness was his father's forte, not mine."

Karen suppressed the strong desire to slap her mother in the face.

In her seventies, Martha Perry looked ten years younger. Her dyed-brown hair was carefully coiffed and styled to frame her stern face. Tall and slim, she radiated a bulldozer kind of confidence, a self-assurance born of necessity. Long before Karen was born, Robert's father, the ill-fated Jameson, beset by financial problems, had run away, leaving a faltering department store and a young son. Martha had wallowed in self-pity for about five seconds, then swung into action.

First, she took back her maiden name. Then, with little money and an iron will, she worked twenty hours a day until her store expanded. By 1948, Martha had six stores and a hefty fortune. When her husband died that year in a Los Angeles flophouse, she ordered the body buried in a pauper's grave.

Karen had known nothing of her father, except that he wasn't Jameson, until a year ago. Her birth had resulted from a brief liaison during a moment of weakness in Martha's march to money and power. Her mother had instilled in Karen and Robert certain values, but had given them little love or affection. For most of their young lives, the children were cared for by a nanny. When it was time for college, they both picked Yale, more to be away from their mother than any other reason.

Martha hated lawyers with a passion, and when first Robert, then Karen announced their intentions to pursue a career in law, Martha refused to speak to either of them for years. Upon graduation, Robert returned to Miami and Karen settled in Central Florida. With consummate effort, they gradually rebuilt a tenuous bridge between themselves and their mother. For years, that precarious relationship with Martha was all Karen and Robert had in common while they both searched for the same thing—grudging approval from a domineering and obdurate mother.

They never received it. Now Robert never would.

Karen grabbed her mother's suitcase from the carousel. "This it?"

"Yup. I travel light."

"How's business?"

"What do you care? You two never had an interest."

"The stores were your domain, Mother, not ours."

"They could have been. As it is, I'm leaving the chain to employees. No one else gives a damn. They'll probably convert it to cash before my body's cold, but—"

"Let's not start, okay?"

Martha sighed. "Why did Robert kill himself? On the phone last night all you said was he was sick, and you couldn't say more because the line might be tapped. On TV I heard you say he was depressed, but not under a doctor's care. Why'd you say that?"

"Because it's true."

"How do you know?"

"Does it really matter?"

"Damn right. Suicide is the coward's way out, unforgivable, even if he was in terrible pain from some dread disease. But he looked pretty good to me the last time I saw him."

"Not now, Mother."

"Not now? On television you made it appear there was something weird about—"

"Mother." Karen's patience was at an end and she glared at the older woman. "Shut the hell up. We'll discuss this in the car."

Karen's forcefulness subdued Martha until they reached the car. Then, as they drove toward the Virginia home, she started again. This time, Karen didn't hesitate. She told her mother everything—about the magazine, the tape, and the blackmail attempt. When she finished, Martha was uncommonly speechless.

"I want you to understand something," Karen said.

Martha stared out the window. "What?"

"Claire has been shattered by this. She believes she was married to a man she didn't know, a man who's left her with a terrible legacy."

Martha said nothing.

"The boys don't know about the tape," Karen continued, "and I don't intend to tell them unless it becomes necessary. In the meantime, I want you to be as pleasant as you possibly can. None of your usual crap."

"I don't know what you mean."

"Yes, you do. One wrong word from you, and you'll be on your way back to Miami, if I have to hire a team of security guards to haul you off. You'll tuck away your aggressive hostility as long as you're here. Understand?"

Martha took a deep breath. "You make me sound like a bitch-on-wheels. I busted my rear end raising both of you, and what did I get in return? You both broke my heart."

"Because of our career choices?" Karen asked. "You hate lawyers. And politicians. Doctors, too. There isn't a profession you don't hate. You wanted us in the store, pure and simple. That store's all you ever cared about."

"That's not true."

"It *is* true. You have that marvelous gift of selective memory. I can well imagine why your husband ran off. He was afraid of you, terrified he wouldn't measure up. As if anyone could measure up to your lofty standards."

"You're being cruel." Martha sounded hurt.

"The fact is, Mother, you are a domineering, selfish, callow woman. So be it. You have a right to live your life as you see fit. But not to inflict pain on others.

"In the past, to avoid confrontation, Robert and I have taken our lumps. We looked at your motivations and determined that you just like to inflate your own ego. But now, with Robert gone, I'm not going to tolerate your usual bullshit."

Martha opened her mouth as if to speak, then snapped her jaws shut.

"Claire is deeply wounded," Karen said, "and very vulnerable. Richard and Michael are crushed by the loss of a father they loved and idolized. With their whole world upside down, I will not allow you to dump on that family. You'll be sympathetic, tolerant, and kind, or I'll cart you off so fast you'll never know what hit you."

Martha stared at her with awe. "When did you get to be so tough?"

"I'm not being tough. My brother is dead and I'm grieving. I have a mother who is insensitive, opinionated, and cold. I've lived with that fact all my life, but I won't allow you to hurt Robert's family."

"Really?"

"Really."

Martha's face twisted with anger. "Let me tell you something, Ms. Know-it-all Smart-ass Lawyer. You're as bad as me if you think your brother was screwing little girls. Robert was right about that tape. It had to be a fake."

"I didn't say I believe the tape is real. I'm working to find evidence it isn't."

"I don't need evidence," Martha insisted. "I know Robert like I know you. I'm your *mother*, damn it. Robert's not the kind of man who screws children."

Karen slammed her hand on the steering wheel. "A moment ago you said he was his father's son because he killed himself. You had no trouble accepting that he committed suicide."

"Not anymore, I don't. Now that I know about that tape, it's all crap. Robert didn't screw little girls, and he didn't kill himself. He was murdered, if you want my opinion."

"I don't," Karen said harshly.

"I expected an experienced lawyer like you to be more skeptical."

"For God's sake," Karen exclaimed, "it's because I *am* an experienced criminal lawyer that I accept nothing unless the evidence is irrefutable, and the evidence for Robert's suicide is as irrefutable as I've ever seen. The jury's still out on the tape's validity."

For a moment, Martha was quiet. "I don't care about the evidence. There's no way on this earth Robert would either kill himself or do such a perverted thing. No way. You'd better start believing that."

Karen didn't answer. There was no point. Although the evidence presented an almost iron-clad case for suicide, she had her doubts. Like her mother, Karen never believed Robert capable of taking his own life. Maybe neither of them had known him as well as they thought. For the rest of the journey, they traveled in silence, each lost in her separate world.

When they arrived at the house, Lt. Brace was waiting. Karen stumbled through the introductions, then left her mother with Michael and Richard, while she and Brace joined Claire and Carl in the den.

Brace was all business. "We've just received the results of the autopsy. Everything confirms that Senator Jameson shot himself. The M.E. found no evidence of foul play. No drugs of any kind, either."

Claire jammed her fist against trembling lips, and Carl pulled her to the sofa beside him and draped a comforting arm around her shoulders. His eyes met Karen's with a glance that promised he'd do his best to keep her sister-in-law calm.

"Didn't you say he had migraine headaches?" Brace asked.

Karen nodded.

"Initial tests indicate he didn't have so much as an aspirin in his system, so a migraine couldn't have been bothering him at the end. No trace of cancer either. Whatever was bugging the senator had nothing to do with his *real* physical health, so we're marking the case as 'suicide, reasons unknown.' " Brace looked at Claire. "Unless there's something you'd like to tell us."

"There's nothing I *can* tell you," Claire said.

Karen held a neutral expression. That much, at least, was true.

"I have no idea what was troubling Robert," Claire continued. "He was rarely home the last week, and withdrawn the little time he was here. I knew he was depressed, but he refused to talk about it. Believe me, I'd like to know."

Brace stared at her a moment, then sighed. "I guess we'll never know. In any event, the body has been released to you."

Karen spoke before Claire could reply. "We'll make arrangements for Robert's body to be shipped to Florida."

"Just one more question for Mrs. Jameson." Brace pulled out his notebook. "The suicide note. He referred to something being untrue. Any idea what that might be?"

"None whatsoever," Claire said, managing to hang on to her control. Carl's strong presence must have helped.

Brace looked at Karen.

"I wish I knew," she said.

Brace turned his attention back to Claire, and she flinched slightly beneath his scrutiny.

"I'm not trying to stick my nose into your personal affairs," he said, "but this is an official investigation. The FBI is going to take one look at my report and throw it in the trash. If you'll just tell me what the senator meant, it'll save us all a lot of time."

Claire's eyes were like lasers. "If I knew, I'd tell you."

Brace stared at her a moment, then nodded. "I guess it's enough there was no one else involved, no foul play." He extended a hand to Claire. "I'm truly sorry, Mrs. Jameson."

Karen showed Brace to the door. "I'd like a copy of that autopsy report."

Brace gave her a curious look. "You're sure about that?"

"I'd also like copies of the crime team report.".

Brace looked quizzical. "Crime team?"

"They were here, weren't they?"

"Not exactly. Just some cops and the doctor, that's all."

"Did you take photos?"

"Yes."

"I want copies of everything."

"Do you mind if I ask why?"

Karen shrugged. "I guess it's habit. The suicide, notwithstanding the fact he was my brother, there seems to be no logical reason. I'm hoping for an answer. That's why I want the reports."

Brace dropped his steady gaze. "Come by my office. The copies will be waiting for you."

Karen returned to the den where Carl still sat with Claire. "I'll look after the travel arrangements. Carl, maybe you can keep Mother occupied."

Carl grimaced. "I'll do my best."

"If she gives you a hard time," Karen said, "let me know. I threatened to ship her back if she's not on her best behavior."

Claire laughed for the first time. "You know she didn't believe you for a minute."

"One can always try," Karen said.

Seven

During the next few days, Karen left the house only twice. She held one more press conference at the front gates, at which time she released details of the medical examiner's report, answered no questions, and retreated to the seclusion of the house.

She left the house a second time to drive Claire to Lt. Brace's office, where Claire gave a formal statement, waited patiently for it to be typed, then signed it. While there, Karen was given a copy of the reports she'd requested. She studied them carefully, made some notations on a legal pad, then tucked them in her attaché case. Claire, understandably, wanted no part of the official documents or photographs.

Then, joined by Richard and Michael, they drove to Washington to Walter Reed Hospital, where they briefly viewed Robert's body, said their good-byes, and made arrangements for Robert's remains to be shipped to Florida. Karen was given a copy of the autopsy report. They stopped at the airline office to make travel arrangements before returning to the house.

On Tuesday, four days after Robert's suicide, it was time to return to Florida and bury her brother. The casket bearing Robert's body had been loaded aboard the commercial aircraft to Miami. As the family entered Dulles Airport and made their way to the gate, a small group of television people descended on them.

The bright lights from a single camera stung Karen's eyes.

She was surprised to see them. Two days after her final press announcement Saturday evening, the media mob at the house had finally left them alone, and no one, to her knowledge, had seen the family leave for the airport. These people seemed to have been waiting to spring into action as soon as the family entered the airport.

A wide-eyed young woman with a surfeit of makeup and a too-short skirt stuck a microphone in Karen's face. "I'm Melony Crisp with *American Exposé.*"

Karen ignored her impertinence. She'd heard of the program, a syndicated television tabloid show, an electronic version of the newspapers found at the checkout counters of every supermarket in America. Karen strode on purposefully, but the reporter ran beside her and the cameraman crabbed backward, working hard to keep them both in the frame.

"Ms. Perry-Mondori," Crisp said breathlessly. "*American Exposé* has information that your brother was involved in pedophilia and that he killed himself because he was afraid his secret would become public knowledge. Any comment on that?"

A sudden rush of adrenaline stunned Karen. She stopped in her tracks and stared at the woman. Crisp was actually smiling.

"What are you talking about?" Karen blurted.

"Is it true?" Crisp persisted.

"Of course not," Karen stammered, her voice

barely above a harsh whisper. "How dare you make such an unconscionable charge?"

"We're not saying it's true, just that we have information relating to the possibility. We'll be broadcasting that information tonight at eleven. Are you saying you have no knowledge of your brother's sexual deviancy?"

Karen wanted to drive her fist into the woman's face, but prudence prevailed. Fighting to control her raging anger, she pressed forward, her lips tightly sealed.

"Perhaps," the woman said sweetly, "you'll give us a comment after you've seen the show."

In spite of Carl's restraining hand on her arm, Karen, the inner struggle almost lost, whirled, partially rising to the bait. "Robert Jameson was one of the most respected men in the United States Senate. His record is unblemished by scandal of any kind. What you have suggested is obscene and a damnable lie. I warn you, Ms. Crisp. Tread carefully, for I will not see my brother's reputation despoiled in some sleazeball attempt to boost television ratings."

"Are you threatening to sue?"

Immediately realizing her error, Karen snapped, "I have nothing more to say."

"I thought not." Crisp sounded triumphant.

Karen felt her heart leap to her throat. Her worst fears were being realized. She glanced at Claire and Mrs. Taylor and saw the immediate impact of the exchange. Claire seemed about to faint. Richard and Michael were visibly shaken and angry. Only the latter's restraint kept Richard from lunging at the reporter. Martha Perry looked ready to strangle the reporter with her bare hands. And Andrea appeared both puzzled and a little frightened. Carl flashed his daughter a reassuring smile and pulled her closer to his side. With Carl's help, Karen corralled the family group through the gate and onto the airplane.

They were barely seated when more questions were thrown at Karen, this time by Michael, leaning over the back of the seat in front of her.

"What the hell was that woman talking about?" he asked.

"I have no idea," Karen said. "Have you ever seen that program?"

"A couple of times. Kinda vulgar stuff."

"Then you know they're prone to say whatever they feel like," she said. "Pay no attention."

"But they said they had proof," Michael insisted. "They can't broadcast something that isn't true. Can't we stop them?"

Richard leaned forward. "Probably not. I've learned that much in law school. In the first place, you can say almost anything about a dead person because the dead can't sue. In the second place, freedom of speech precludes prior restraint, which is to say you can't—in most cases—stop someone from printing or uttering a lie. You can take action afterward, but not before."

"You're right," Karen said. "As for *American Exposé*'s proof, that's probably nothing but innuendo. That's how those people operate. Until we know what they have, there isn't much we can do."

"Why would they want to trash Dad?" Michael's face was a picture of astonishment and pain. "He's gone. He's no threat to anyone."

Karen took a deep breath. "They don't need a reason. Television tabloids say whatever they think will get them rating points. Truth means nothing."

"But—"

"We'll watch the program in Miami," Karen said, "and see what they're saying. I'm sure you'll find it's nothing to be concerned about."

Michael reluctantly sat down. Exhausted by the exchange with Crisp, Karen leaned her head on Carl's shoulder.

"What can you do?" he whispered.

"I think we'd better be prepared for the worst." She could almost hear her heart pounding.

"You think they have a copy of the tape?"

"It sounds like it, but there's nothing we can do at the moment. As soon as we arrive in Miami, I'll get on it."

"Can't you get a court order or something?"

"I doubt it, but I'll think of something."

As she waited for takeoff with her seat belt pulled tight around her waist, she realized the next few hours would be critical. The aircraft felt like a personal prison, as if its tubular shell were closing in on her. This couldn't wait until Florida. She released her seat belt and moved down the aisle to where Claire sat.

"I have to call in the FBI," Karen whispered. "We'll have to turn over the tape, but it can't be helped."

Claire's jaw dropped. "I don't understand."

"I don't have time to explain. You'll have to trust me. After what that *American Exposé* reporter said, we don't have much choice."

Claire gripped Karen's arm with the strength of a steelworker. "You can't!"

"I'm going to make a phone call. There's still time."

Claire simply stared, too distraught to speak.

Karen returned to Carl, explained quickly, then

spoke quietly to one of the flight attendants. She ignored the stares of her nephews and their grandmothers and left the plane. Satisfied that the television crew had departed, she headed for the nearest pay phone.

A call to a New York contact obtained the name and telephone number of the producer of *American Exposé*, a thirty-one-year-old television wunderkind named Philip Toth. Karen was put through to him immediately.

"Ms. Perry-Mondori," Toth said right off, "I want to advise you that our conversation is being recorded."

"Turn the recorder off. What I have to discuss is confidential."

Toth chuckled. "Sorry, but it's policy. Prevents a lot of unnecessary lawsuits."

"I insist."

"Give me a hint of what's on your mind. I promise I won't tape you unless I have to."

Karen slammed the phone back in its cradle. She was operating under intense pressure and loath to make an irreversible mistake. What she needed was a second opinion, an exercise she'd performed often in times of extreme stress.

"Karen," Carl called from the gate, "you have to board now."

She hurried to him. "I can't. I have other calls I must make first. Tell Andrea I'm taking a later flight and will join you at Robert's Miami house this evening."

He raised his eyebrows as if to disagree, then seemed to change his mind. "Let us know when to meet you."

He kissed her, then turned and loped along the passageway toward the plane.

Karen returned to the pay phone, called the Clearwater office of her law firm, and asked to be put through to Brander Hewitt immediately.

"My deepest condolences, Karen," he said when he came on the line. "It must be terrible."

She pictured Brander, his thinning white hair carefully coifed, his soft face majestically solemn, his gold cuff links gleaming as he leaned back in his highbacked, brown leather chair.

"It is terrible, but what's about to happen may be more terrible." Karen took a deep breath. "Brander, I speak to you now as client to his attorney. You understand?"

Brander had hired Karen into his firm as his protegée, served as her mentor, and presented her as a candidate for partner. An illustrious attorney with a distinguished career both in criminal and civil law, he was always gracious, consistently brilliant, and immediately grasped that Karen wished to invoke lawyer-client confidentiality.

"I understand," he said. "How can I help?"

Careful not to be overheard, Karen told him everything. As he listened, Brander asked a few questions, and when Karen finished, didn't hesitate to offer his advice.

"You've seen a copy of the videotape. Do you believe it could be genuine?" There was no change in his voice, no judgment regarding Robert's alleged aberrant behavior. Brander dealt only with facts.

"Yes, but it's equally likely it's a fake."

"And you believe the television program is about to broadcast excerpts from a duplicate?"

"Exactly."

"In that case, there's nothing you can or should do prior to the tape's being aired, relative to the television program itself. You have no grounds, since the truth—if the tape *is* genuine—is a defense. To attempt to prevent the airing would be counterproductive and give the event increased credibility, not to mention publicity.

"Under the circumstances," Brander continued, "I would contact the FBI immediately and turn the tape now in Bill Castor's possession over to them. The people who provided the tape to Robert have attempted extortion, and the FBI may be able to seize the tape now in the hands of the program's producers as additional evidence, perhaps faulting them for being accessories before the fact. The tape could be held and an investigation begun to determine exactly when they received a copy—and how.

"I suspect, however, that this would be a delaying action at best, for the courts are usually rigid in their desire to uphold First Amendment rights in matters such as these."

"I'm worried," Karen said, "that the FBI's seizure of the tape might do more harm than good."

"Yes, it's possible the television people don't have a copy of the tape, but are planning to broadcast something based solely on gossip and innuendo."

"Melony Crisp said she had proof."

"You can't take her word for it, and to press the issue smacks of prior restraint."

Karen leaned her throbbing head against the cool metal of the pay phone. "So what do I do?"

"My initial reaction is that the FBI would be unsuccessful, for a variety of reasons, in preventing the tape—even if it is identical to yours—from being shown. In the event that it *is* identical, the seizure could certainly come immediately after the showing, but not before. No probable cause. Still, without the Bureau's cooperation, you have no chance for rebuttal, and once the tape airs, you'll have gained the FBI's enmity for withholding evidence."

Karen sighed. "I'm between the proverbial rock and a hard place."

"I maintain that you should contact the FBI immediately and be completely forthcoming, but that's a decision only you can make, Karen."

"Thanks, Brander. I appreciate your counsel."

"I wish I could be more helpful."

"You can." Karen's mind churned. "Call Bill Castor and ask him to bring the tape I sent him and meet me at the Tampa airport this afternoon. I plan to take the next available flight out of Dulles."

"I could send Bill to Washington with the tape, if you want to deliver it to FBI headquarters."

"No, I don't want it here. I have my reasons, but I can't take time to explain now. Thanks again, for everything." She hung up the phone and hurried to purchase a ticket to Tampa before catching a cab back to Robert's Virginia house.

Two hours later, ensconced in first class on a direct flight to Tampa, Karen leaned back and closed her eyes. There was always a chance that the reporter for *American Exposé* had been lying, feeding her a line to elicit a reaction. The program was famous for its ambush interviews, often shocking a victim into blurting embarrassing comments. But, in her heart, she knew she was kidding herself. As she had feared, Robert's death had put a crimp in the blackmailer's plans, and now they were doing what she'd expected them to do—laying a foundation for future extortion.

Brander Hewitt, a man she respected and admired, had given her good advice. As much as she feared the repercussions that taking his advice would bring, she couldn't escape the wisdom of Brander's counsel. Especially when it confirmed her own instincts. To ignore Brander's advice *and* her instincts would be foolish.

She dug a small black notebook out of her attaché case, looked up a number, and reached for the phone on the back of the seat in front of her.

"Federal Bureau of Investigation, Tampa office," a woman's voice answered.

"May I speak with Linda Holt? This is Karen Perry-Mondori calling."

"I'm sorry, Ms. Mondori, but Agent Holt is out of the office until two. May I have her return your call?"

Karen looked at her watch. Her plane would touch down in Tampa a few minutes after two. "Could I meet with her in her office at three o'clock?"

The receptionist paused and rustled pages. "She has that time free. I'll schedule you in, Ms. Mondor—"

"Perry-Mondori, Karen."

"Right, Ms. Mondori. Special Agent Holt will see you at three."

With a frustrated sigh, Karen hung up the phone and flagged down the flight attendant to request aspirin for her headache.

Bill Castor, short and thin, his face with the perennial youthfulness of Dick Clark belying his forty-plus years, was waiting for her when she disembarked in Tampa.

"Do you have it?" she asked.

He patted a manila envelope tucked under his arm.

"Right here. I have something else, too, but I'll wait until we're in the car to explain."

Karen nodded and glanced around the concourse. She wouldn't have been surprised to see Melony Crisp and her camera crew leap out from behind a phone kiosk. Even without a bevy of reporters in evidence, she had no desire for Bill's information to be overheard. He had worked as her private investigator for many years, and although he'd had only a few days to track the source of the tape, knowing Bill's expertise, she was certain he'd made progress.

They passed silently through the airside building, boarded the shuttle for the main terminal, then took the elevator to the parking garage. Safely ensconced in Bill's car, Karen turned to him. "What have you got?

Bill handed her a computer printout. "There are two lists on those sheets. The first is all the companies known to have equipment capable of producing a falsified tape."

"How many?"

"Should be a breeze," Bill said with a boyish grin. "Only 194, including NBC, CBS, ABC, CNN, UCN, most large advertising agencies and production companies, and every major movie studio in the country."

Karen groaned.

"The short list," Castor continued, "gives you the names of those who've purchased a massive parallel computer since they were invented."

"Massive parallel?"

"State of the art in computer manipulation. Super speedy and unbelievably real."

"How many on the short list?"

"Twenty-one, including the FBI, CIA, the Pentagon, Navy, Air Force, Army—"

"All of whom Robert probably antagonized at some time or another," Karen said with a grimace.

"—plus six other government agencies and eleven obviously wealthy corporations, including some from the first list." His boyish grin turned wry. "I'm sure they'll be falling all over themselves to tell you what they know."

Karen looked over the lists for a moment, then sighed. "Somebody produced that tape, and for a reason."

"I kept a copy. Do you want me to start checking them out?"

Karen shook her head. "Let's see how the FBI responds. If they pick up this ball"—she indicated the lists—"I may need you to move on something else."

"Just say the word." His expression sobered. "I'm sorry as hell about your brother."

The private investigator's gruff kindness made her want to cry again. She slipped on her sunglasses as they drove out of the parking garage and headed for the long-term lot where she had parked her Beemer.

Just before three, Karen entered the downtown Tampa office of the Federal Bureau of Investigation. As soon as the receptionist announced her arrival, Linda Holt, a petite woman in her late thirties, hurried out to the front office.

"I was so sorry to hear about Robert."

Karen greeted her study partner from her law school days at Yale with a hug. "Thanks. We're all still in shock."

"According to the news, I thought you'd be in Miami by now."

"I was supposed to be, but I need your help with something."

Linda's face lit up with curiosity. "Come into my office."

Moving with her characteristic quickness, Linda stepped into her office and motioned Karen to a chair. The special agent, as always, was dressed conservatively and wore little makeup on a face agreeably framed by straight black hair, slightly streaked with gray, and tucked gently behind her ears. In all, she looked like anything but an FBI agent who had been promoted to head the Tampa office a year ago, but more like a dedicated high school teacher.

Karen assessed her friend's appearance and smiled. If Linda's careful attention to detail was employed to lessen the impact of her attractiveness, it was a complete failure. Linda had an inner beauty that emphasized her obvious physical endowments. And a heart to match.

While Linda settled behind her desk with its view of the Tampa skyline behind her, Karen reviewed the plan she'd formulated during her flight. Ever since law school, she and Linda had been as close as sisters, but Karen wouldn't burden her friend with the total truth, wouldn't ask her to perjure herself to protect Claire. With Robert gone, protecting Claire had become Karen's responsibility.

"What can I do for you?" When engaged in discussion, either business or personal, Linda never seemed to blink her large brown eyes. Her brow furrowed and her jaw set, she leaned slightly forward, as if trying to speed things up. Karen, used to her friend's intensity, felt no pressure.

"Claire, my sister-in-law, has been a basket case," Karen explained.

Linda nodded. "That's understandable. I can't

begin to imagine the shock and grief she must be experiencing."

"She's not thinking straight. I found that out this morning when the family was boarding the plane for Miami and Melony Crisp from *American Exposé* confronted us."

Linda uttered a sound of disgust. "Trash TV. Almost makes me wish they'd repeal the First Amendment."

"Crisp claims possession of a video of Robert that will damage his reputation. Claire was frantic. Between the heavy sedation she's been under and the shock of Robert's death, she initially failed to tell anyone about a video that arrived the morning of Robert's death."

"So Crisp *does* have something on Robert."

Karen nodded. "I put the family on the plane in Carl's care and rushed back to the house. When I saw the tape's contents, along with a blackmail message, I knew immediately it was the reason for Robert's suicide. I've brought the tape to you."

Karen had framed her explanation with care. Not a single sentence was untrue, although their sequence was misleading.

"You didn't take it to the Bureau in D.C.?" Linda spoke rapidly, with passion and much waving of hands—a habit, Karen recalled, her friend had found impossible to break. "Don't they have an agent on the case?"

"You remember what went down during the Uccello case," Karen reminded her. "Robert and his Senate investigative committee left a lot of folks at the FBI with egg on their faces. I'm afraid the Washington hierarchy will see this tape as a chance to get even. Claire and her sons couldn't survive that. And

Robert was a good man. He doesn't deserve having his reputation besmirched. That's why I came to you. I know you'll treat this fairly."

"What's on the tape?"

"Robert having sex with a ten-year-old girl."

Her words shocked the animated Linda into stillness. "My God, did Claire see it?"

Karen nodded.

"Is the tape the real thing?"

"Claire believes it is. It's very convincing. But with the phenomenal advances in computer technology, who knows? It could be a frame-up."

Linda leaned back and combed her fingers through her hair. "If Claire gave a statement to the police, under oath, and didn't tell them about the tape—"

Karen threw her hands in the air. "For God's sake, think of what she's been through. She can barely function. She's not responsible for her actions."

"That's not for me to decide. You were acting as her attorney?"

Karen nodded.

"You should have made certain her statement was truthful and complete."

Karen's face reddened. "Come on, Linda, you're deflecting the issue. Claire isn't a criminal. The people who tried to extort money and caused my brother to kill himself, *they* are the criminals."

"The tape contains kiddy porn scenes involving your brother?" Linda's eyes mirrored her disgust.

Karen slipped the tape, still in the cardboard package in which it was delivered, from her attaché case and laid it on Linda's desk. "It's all there, plus a request for a million dollars to keep it from the public."

"Has anyone in the family been contacted since?"

"No."

Linda removed a large glassine bag from the bottom drawer of her desk and, using her thumb and index finger, placed the videotape inside. "Who has handled this besides you and Claire?"

Karen thought back to the evening Carl had viewed the tape. He hadn't touched it. Her instructions to Bill Castor about leaving no fingerprints had been specific. "Just Robert, as far as I know."

Linda grimaced. "This isn't my case—"

"Please, see what you can do. If that tape becomes public, all hell will break loose. I'm going to ask Claire and the boys to move into seclusion near me after the funeral. If the whole family's here, we'll be in your jurisdiction. As I said before, I know you'll treat Robert's memory with fairness."

Linda hesitated, but only briefly. "I'll have to send the tape to Washington for the lab to examine it. And I'll need a written statement from you and Claire, confirming what you've just told me."

"My plane leaves at five. Can't statements wait until after the funeral?"

"Claire's can, but I'll need yours now if you want me to act." Linda turned to her computer. "You dictate, I'll type."

When the statement was complete, Linda printed it.

Karen read the statement quickly and signed it. "You'll have your people in New York grab the tape the TV people have?"

Linda looked doubtful. "I'll do what I can."

"Robert was a United States senator. He's entitled to protection from the likes of the people who produced this tape. Notwithstanding the slim possibility that Robert could be an actual participant in those disgusting activities, the tape is an article of black-mail. The duplicate in New York could have come from the blackmailers and, as such, it's evidence."

With a smile, Linda raised her hand to interrupt. "You don't have to convince me, Counselor. How that copy came into the possession of *American Exposé* may be a significant clue to who's behind this scheme."

"Then you'll confiscate it?"

"As I said, I'll do what I can."

"Please, move fast. The tape's scheduled to air at eleven tonight."

"I have to work through proper channels and the chain of command. I can't promise anything except to do my best."

"I know," Karen said quietly. "That's why I came to you. Will you contact me in Miami as soon as you hear something?" She gave Linda Robert's Miami phone number.

Linda rose from her desk and hugged Karen once more. "You'd better get out of here. You have a plane to catch, and I need to contact Washington and New York."

Eight

The much-awaited call from Linda Holt came at ten-thirty.

Karen sat with the family in the Florida room of Robert's Miami home, located on a canal leading to Biscayne Bay. The modern house, more masculine than the Virginia one, was decorated with leather, chrome, richly finished hardwoods, contemporary art, and thick carpets. A stucco-over-block rancher, with high ceilings and wide expanses of tinted glass overlooking the swimming pool, it had its own ambience. Claire's touch was visible here, too, but less so. Here, she'd given Robert full decorating rein, and the furnishings reflected a different taste from the Virginia farmhouse.

Karen shooed everyone out of the room as the phone rang and she picked up the receiver.

"I'm afraid I have bad news," Linda said.

Karen's heart sank. "I can't believe the FBI couldn't get the tape."

"We have the tape and a full statement regarding its acquisition. According to the producers, nothing on the tape they received indicated blackmail. Just the . . . activity."

Karen felt a surge of relief. "At least you have the tape."

"Two of our New York agents made the call, and they did get the original."

"Then what's the problem?"

"The producers made a copy, and we've been unable to find a judge willing to sign an order preventing them from airing it. I'm sorry, Karen. We did what we could."

"I know, Linda. Thanks for trying."

"I'm calling from Washington. I brought the tape with me, and the lab's already examining it. We'll be launching an investigation immediately. And we'll find the people responsible, I promise you. The FBI has acquired jurisdiction in this case. The Virginia authorities are out of it."

"Is that supposed to cheer me up?" Karen groused, disturbed at the terrible news concerning the tape.

"I'll keep in touch," Linda said, sympathy evident in her voice.

Less than a half hour later, Karen and Carl, Claire and her sons, Martha Perry, and Mrs. Taylor watched the airing of *American Exposé*. Karen had sent Andrea to bed hours earlier.

A still breathless, electronically reproduced Melony Crisp gazed into their eyes. Her high-pitched voice uttered words with the staccato rhythm of a machine gun.

"We should be used to disappointment by now," she began, "accustomed to the shortcomings of those in public service. Tonight, however, we have evidence of a major character flaw in a man who, until his death a few days ago, had been a respected member of the U.S. Senate.

"We wondered why Robert Jameson killed himself, suddenly and violently, on a sunlit October day last week. Now, we think we have the answer. He was about to be exposed as the sicko that he was, as a man engaged in one of the most repulsive of sexual activities—pedophilia—sex with little children.

"We have irrefutable evidence of his depraved behavior, but first, we implore you to remove your children from the room. Unfortunately, the material is distasteful, but we feel, in the interests of honest journalism, you are entitled to know about Robert Jameson."

Five minutes later, after several commercials and additional hyperbole, the program ran parts of the tape. Black rectangles inserted on the screen covered strategic parts of both bodies, including the face of the child. Robert's face was clear and crisp. It was also abundantly clear exactly what was taking place in a nondescript room in an unknown building.

Karen and Claire had debated whether the boys and their grandmothers should see the program and had decided they must, if only to prepare themselves for the next wave of media attention. But now, as Karen watched their faces, she wondered if they'd made the right decision.

Michael and Richard both looked as if someone were stabbing them repeatedly in the heart, so strong were their expressions of pain. And Claire, seeing it again, looked even worse. Only Karen's mother failed to appear wounded. She looked angry. When the program segment was over, she expressed her outrage.

"That's a goddamn lie," she screamed and pointed a finger at Karen. "And you, Karen Perry-Mondori, had better spend the next few months of your miserable life proving it's a lie. For if you don't, your brother will haunt you from his grave for the rest of your life. And so will I."

Martha's stare was withering as she looked at the others, especially Claire. "And a curse on all of you who would even consider believing such a thing. Have you no faith in Robert's humanity? Do any of you really believe he could do such a thing?"

"Mother—" Karen began.

Martha whirled and stared at her daughter with eyes as cold as liquid nitrogen. Never in Karen's experience had she seen her mother express such pure, primitive hatred. "Don't speak to me again, Karen. Or any of you. Not until you've totally rejected what you've seen this day. It's a lie, and anyone who accepts such blasphemy no longer exists in my life."

She turned on her heel, stormed out of the room, and slammed the front door as she left the house.

Richard turned to Karen. "I think Grandmother's right. The tape was faked."

Karen fought back the urge to scream. "It's possible. We won't know until the tape's been examined by experts. There's a copy at the FBI lab now."

Michael spoke up. "There's no way Dad could have been a pedophile. I did a paper on them for one of my psychology classes. Pedophiles follow accepted patterns. Dad didn't. If he'd been a true pedophile, he would have exhibited tendencies long ago. He never did."

Claire curled her legs beneath her in her chair, almost in a fetal position, and said nothing. She didn't have to. The horror on her face said it all.

"The film can't be real," Michael continued. "If it was, it was obvious Dad knew the camera was running. No pedophile would ever *allow* himself to be videotaped. They do their stuff in secret, not in front of a camera, not unless they're exhibitionists as well, and Dad was no exhibitionist.''

Karen experienced a brief flare of relief. The boys, at least, were handling the disclosure of the tape well. But her relief was short-lived.

"No matter what we believe," Michael said, "the entire country thinks our father was a pervert. Dad's gone, and now *American Exposé* has killed him all over again."

He collapsed onto the sofa, his broad shoulders shaking with gut-wrenching sobs. At the sight of his twin, Richard's composure cracked, and tears coursed down his handsome face.

In her chair in the corner, Claire seemed to crumble to dust before Karen's eyes.

A crowd of five hundred had been expected to attend Robert's graveside funeral. Aside from family, only forty brave souls, close friends, had courage enough to remember a man they'd cared for, even if they looked shamed and embarrassed as they quietly witnessed the ceremony and burial. They were out-numbered by the media.

Karen delivered the eulogy, a short speech, per-haps three minutes. She'd planned a much more elo-quent oration emphasizing Robert's many qualities and contributions to society, but as she spoke, she sensed signs of discomfort and impatience among those in attendance, so she cut her remarks short. As she walked back to join Carl and Andrea, her mother glared at her.

Later, back at the house, Karen read her brother's will, a remarkably simple document, including some small bequests to charitable organizations, but the bulk of the estate stayed close. Richard and Michael were each to receive fifty thousand dollars immediately, plus trusts worth a hundred thousand each, payable when they reached thirty. Robert had bequeathed Karen his rare book collection, and Claire the remainder of the estate. Claire would also receive Robert's pension and the proceeds from a long-existent and significant life insurance policy, more than enough to carry her through. Her husband, like many, had been worth more dead than alive.

Robert had left his mother nothing, a stinging rebuke, but not unexpected. Martha hardly blinked an eye.

As the will was read, Michael and Richard went to pieces again, their behavior so uncharacteristic, in spite of their stress, that Karen's concern for her nephews mounted. When she finished the document, everyone drifted to the early luncheon buffet family friends had prepared in the dining room, and left Karen alone with a desolate Claire.

"I think we should cancel the memorial service in Washington," Claire said. "I've had about all the humiliation I can handle. The boys have, too."

Karen couldn't disagree. The devastation visited upon Richard and Michael had left them limp, their expressions hollow, their voices but whispers, their movements like those of old men. They seemed lost, adrift, their lives disconnected from the world around them. They were young and strong, and Karen knew their depression would lift, but not for some time, and never completely. Last night, she'd offered words of encouragement, but they had received them with blank stares, because her message had lacked what her nephews needed most, incontrovertible proof of their father's innocence. Robert had been damned before the world, and his sons blamed themselves for being unable to right the terrible wrong done to him.

Karen put the will back in its folder and slumped in a chair. "You're right, Claire. A memorial service right now will serve no purpose."

"In fact," Claire said, "I don't want to go back to Virginia—ever. Will you help me sell the house and cars?"

Karen rubbed her temples. "I think you're being hasty."

"I'm not," she insisted. "I could never show my face in Washington again. And there's no reason now for me to be there. We only bought the Virginia house because of Robert's work. Now that he's gone, so's the need. Please, will you help me get rid of the place? Right away?"

Karen sighed. "If that's what you really want."

"I do. The mortgage papers are in the den safe along with the titles to the two cars. I'll give you power of attorney so you can do what you feel is necessary."

"What about the furniture? Your roses?"

Claire shook her head. "Sell the contents. I don't care about any of it. I want to put all of this behind me as soon as possible."

Karen gave one last effort at dissuading her. "You worked the skin off your hands remodeling that place. And now you want to throw it all away?"

Claire glared at her. "Will you just do as I ask?"

"All right," Karen said, "but only if you'll promise to consider professional counseling. You and Richard and Michael. You've had a very bad shock and your emotions are confused. Before you make too many snap decisions, it would be wise to talk things over with an expert."

Claire gave her a rueful smile. "And just what would a headshrinker say to any of us?"

"I don't know. That's the point. You're not the only people in the world to have suffered a shock like this."

Claire shook her head. "I know what he'll say. He'll say our pain will diminish over time. What a revelation."

"It's not that simple."

Claire was resolute. "I see my face and hear my name on television and in newspapers. I've become a public commodity, for a while, at least. Absolute strangers know all there is to know about me. I'm not ready to pour out my soul to yet another stranger. I may be depressed, but I'm functioning, and that's what counts."

"But Richard and Michael—"

"The boys are stunned, but they'll bounce back. Other young men have lost their fathers. The world doesn't stop."

Claire suddenly burst into tears and wet mascara blackened her cheeks. Karen slipped out of the room and left her sister-in-law alone with her grief.

"You have to eat something or you'll make yourself ill." Carl joined Karen a few minutes later in the shade of a huge ficus tree on the patio and handed her a plate from the buffet filled with her favorite foods.

Karen took the plate. It was easier than arguing. "I'm going back to Washington this afternoon."

Carl almost upended his own plate in surprise. "Why?"

"Claire wants me to sell the Virginia house and cars. Immediately."

"She's still in shock. She shouldn't be making those kinds of decisions yet."

"That's what I told her, but she insisted."

"It's not like you to support Claire's rashness. Why are you really going?"

Karen picked at the potato salad on her plate. "I want to ask some questions, find the answers to why someone was blackmailing Robert."

"Why not send Bill Castor?"

"Because as Robert's sister, I'll be less likely to raise suspicions. People Robert worked with may open up to me, where they'd close up like a clam around a private investigator."

"You don't think he killed himself, do you?"

It was Karen's turn to be surprised. "How did you guess?"

"You've never been able to hide anything from me," Carl said with a smile.

"I've never had a reason to. I haven't voiced my suspicion because it flies in the face of the evidence. Maybe if I can determine why Robert was depressed, I can accept his suicide."

Carl slid his arm around her shoulders. "You've been so busy taking care of everyone else, you haven't done your own grieving."

"I like to keep busy."

"Eat," he ordered, and she obliged him by taking a bite.

"I need to move Claire and the boys out of the limelight," Karen said. "When you get home, would you have time to call a realtor to find a furnished house for them to rent?"

"I can do better than that. Do you remember Steve Betz?"

"The anesthesiologist?"

"He's moving his practice to Spokane. He told me just a couple days ago that their house in Cobb's Landing is on the market, fully furnished."

"On Lake Tarpon? That would be perfect, about as secluded as you can get."

"I'll make the arrangements," Carl offered. "How long will you be in Washington?"

She sighed. "As long as it takes."

Karen flew to Washington early that afternoon. Immediately after lunch, when Carl and Andrea had left for the airport for their flight home, she'd been eager to distance herself from the intense gloom generated by those around her. The remnants of Robert's family were disintegrating before her eyes, and she, helpless to stop it, wanted escape.

There was no escape. Newsstands at Dulles held the latest editions of the *Post* and the *Times*, their front pages replete with stories and photographs of Robert. She bought copies of both and glanced through them, wincing at a photo taken from *American Exposé*'s broadcast.

From a pay phone, she called Linda's Tampa office to learn how the investigation was going. Karen told Linda's secretary that she was back in Washington and would be at Robert's Virginia house later. Linda could call her there.

Then Karen phoned Robert's office and a staffer passed her call on to Robert's chief of staff, Marie Morley, an experienced political aide whom Karen had met before.

"I was hoping you'd call," Marie said.

"I wanted you to know that Claire has decided to cancel the memorial service."

"I'm sorry to hear it, but I can appreciate why. We heard about the Florida funeral."

Amazing, Karen thought. The Washington grapevine was like no other, the most efficient communication channel in all of government.

"Yes," Karen said. "It hasn't been very pleasant."

"We still can't believe any of this."

"What will you do now?" Karen asked.

"Someone will be appointed to fill out the senator's term. We're just going to stay put until that happens. Whoever it is will need help with the transition." Marie sighed deeply. "Robert was a member of three committees. Of course, whoever they choose won't get those assignments, but these files will have to be turned over to somebody. Which reminds me. What should I do with the senator's personal effects?"

"Ship them to his Florida address."

"We would have come for the funeral had we known the memorial service would be canceled. I'm sorry now we weren't there. How's Claire?"

"As well as can be expected."

"And Richard and Michael?"

"Not good."

"You don't sound so hot yourself," Marie said.

"It's tough. Like you, I have trouble believing any of this really happened."

"I hope you'll come by when you have a chance. I'd like to discuss some things with you."

"Like what?" Karen asked.

"It's just . . . I'd like to talk to you for a bit, if that's all right."

"Were you aware of Robert's recent depression?"

Marie paused. "That's one of the things I want to

talk about. But not on the phone. Could you come to the office at seven?"

"I'll be there."

On the way to the Virginia house, Karen stopped in Warrenton and listed the house with a real estate broker. The agent took Karen's key and had a duplicate made while they discussed the terms. Karen asked the agent to attempt to sell the house furnished and to arrange for someone to paint the garage where Robert had died.

When Karen arrived at the house, she wandered around for a few minutes, taking a rough written inventory. The house was supposed to be protected by a security service, but the relentless press reports had included the address, an invitation to burglars undeterred by the sophisticated alarm system. In case of theft, Karen wanted a record of the contents and made a mental note to buy an inexpensive camera and photograph each room. Insurance companies were more impressed when physical evidence of loss was available.

She still had the cars to dispose of, and Robert's horse at the stables in town, but she left those for the next day. She went to the den and poured herself a brandy. Her gaze fell on a drawer adjacent to the television, the drawer that Claire had said had held the gun that Robert used to kill himself.

Inside the drawer were various papers, neatly arranged, and an old linen cloth, soiled by oil. She noticed beneath the cloth an inch-wide stain on the cover of a writing pad, a stain obviously caused by the oil on the cloth. Just as Claire had said, the storage place for the gun had been changed from the bedroom to the den.

Karen walked through the house, its carefully
tended rooms once warm and cozy, now cold and
forbidding, and sat at the kitchen table, staring out
at the slate-gray sky. She removed the autopsy report
from her attaché case and read it again. This time,
she was more dispassionate, her lawyer's trained eye
seeing more than before: not Robert's report but that
of a stranger's. In that light, the facts were easier
to assimilate.

She looked at the black-and-white police photographs of the body, stark, yet vividly real two-
dimensional images of violent death. She saw the
blackness that was blood, the vacant-eyed tilt of the
head, one leg akimbo, the other extended straight
out, as if reaching for something. One arm hung life-
lessly at Robert's side, the other rested in his lap, the
fingers of his right hand still clutching the weapon
that had ended his existence.

In one photograph, the sole of one shoe, obviously
a new pair, reflected the light from the photogra-
pher's flashgun, making it appear as if a silver dollar
were attached to the bottom of the shoe. In another,
a closeup, the body was tilted forward, affording a
view of the exit wound in the back of Robert's head.
In still another, the body had been removed, the
space Robert had once occupied outlined in chalk.

Karen put the photos down and wept.

At seven Karen arrived at the office once occupied
by her brother. It was a familiar room, unlike most
other business offices Karen had ever seen.

Robert Jameson had a rare reputation for thrift
when it came to the expenditure of public funds, and
that quality was reflected throughout. The walls were
painted, not paneled, and the desk, while large, could

have been purchased from the nearest office supply store. Prints, not originals, covered the walls, and the furniture was upholstered in Naugahyde instead of leather. Here had worked a man with other than the accumulation of wealth on his mind.

Marie offered her a drink, which Karen declined, then poured one for herself and slipped into the big chair behind the desk. She was an attractive, dark-haired woman of about thirty-five, tall and thin, carefully groomed, the senator's chief aide, a woman highly respected for her well-rounded intelligence and political acumen.

During the last election battle, she'd acted as Robert's campaign manager and had proved a formidable adversary for those planning the campaign of the man running against the incumbent senator. Robert had won in a landslide. Karen imagined that the lineup of those seeking Marie's future services was growing daily.

"Thanks for coming," Marie said. "It's all so awful."

"Yes," Karen agreed and settled in a chair in front of Robert's desk.

"I wanted you to know . . . this had nothing to do with Robert and me."

"What?" After all that had happened, Karen had thought herself incapable of further surprise, but the implication in Marie's statement stunned her.

"It was over long ago. Simply a case of two people being shoved together inside the pressure cooker of political stress. It was just sexual release, nothing else. The fact that we were able to work together for years afterward, never allowing it to be repeated, should be proof of that. Robert loved his wife, not me. Claire never knew about me."

Karen, remembering her conversation with Claire the morning after Robert's death, wasn't so sure.

Marie sipped her drink. "He was truly an exceptional man."

"You were in love with him."

Her face reddened. "Does it show?" she asked quietly.

"No," Karen lied. "A lucky guess."

"Robert was a practical man. He needed me in his work. I mean, he *really* needed me." She sighed.

"You said you were aware of his depression."

"I was, but he never discussed it. Funny. Now that I think about it, it's one of the few times he ever kept something from me. He did say he was concerned about a bill he wanted passed. He wasn't getting much support, but he'd been through that so many times, it's hard to associate his depression with that. I thought it had to do with Claire, but I was simply guessing. I was hoping you'd know."

"I don't," Karen said. "Claire maintains she was aware of his depression and alluded to the same thing, the legislation. But she noticed nothing else."

Marie shivered. "It's so grotesque, this tape business. It's just not Robert. People look at me as if I knew, and I knew nothing. None of us did. Is the tape real?"

"I don't know," Karen said. "Instinct tells me it's a fake, but that may be wishful thinking."

Marie got up from the chair, went to a closet, and removed a cardboard box. "These are some of his things. I'll have the rest ready by tomorrow. I really hate to ship them."

"I'll drop by and pick them up," Karen said.

Nine

Linda Holt, a file folder tucked under her arm, took the elevator to the seventh floor of the J. Edgar Hoover Building and walked purposefully down the hall to the office of George MacLean, one of many assistant directors of the FBI. Her eyes gleamed with exhilaration.

She entered the outer office, was immediately waved through by MacLean's secretary, and went into MacLean's austere office. Special agent Donald Tucker, young in years but a Southern Old World gentleman, stood up.

"Sit," she said.

MacLean gave her a baleful stare. "Tucker is almost finished. Have a seat yourself."

She had left Tampa a little over twenty-four hours ago, right after Karen Perry-Mondori's visit, and had personally delivered the tape of Senator Jameson directly to the FBI lab for analysis. Their initial report lay in the file folder on her lap.

With her eyes on MacLean, she waited. He was a reformed smoker, but he'd picked up a replacement habit, one almost as disgusting. He chewed his nails incessantly, halting only in the presence of his superiors.

Tall and muscular, with close-cropped, dirty-brown hair, he always wore a starched white dress shirt with one of his small selection of suits, all of which were blue. He'd once been told he looked good in blue and took it to heart. His ties were the same, royal blue with a small embroidered FBI insignia in red. Those who knew him called his apparel "the uniform." None had ever seen him wear anything different.

Usually cool and calm, MacLean could erupt in sudden anger when he beheld incompetence, but Linda liked him for his vast store of experience, his willingness to share it, and especially for his propensity to treat all underlings, male or female, alike. Unlike most senior FBI officials, MacLean accepted women as equals in almost all respects. Linda imagined J. Edgar Hoover rolling over in his grave.

Tucker was finishing his verbal report. "Forensics says there are two sets of prints, besides the senator's, on the tape's cardboard box, and they expect to match them. Ms. Perry-Mondori stipulated in her statement to Special Agent Holt that she and the senator's wife touched it, so my guess is the prints belong to those two. Obviously, the tape was hand delivered by people who were very careful."

"The laser showed nothing?" MacLean asked.

"Zip, which means no human hands touched the cardboard at the factory. That's not unusual, but the people who made the actual package wore gloves."

"The package was handmade?"

"Yes, with an X-Acto knife or something similar," Tucker said. "As for the cassette, same two sets of prints plus the senator's."

"What about the tape delivered to the TV people?"

"Toth says it was dropped off at the reception desk, addressed to him. An assistant screens his mail, so she looked at the tape before Toth even knew it existed. The assistant contacted the two people who'd delivered the tape by telephone, got them to come in and sign statements, and then took the tape to Toth."

MacLean raised his eyebrows. "Are they always that careful?"

"Uh-huh, too many lawsuits. Unfortunately, the assistant threw away the envelope the tape came in. At least ten people have handled the tape since. The prints are all smudged."

"Wait a minute." MacLean stopped chewing his nails. "*Two* people delivered the tape?"

Tucker nodded. "Names and addresses are in my written report. One was the camera operator and the other worked the lights and sound. Both are from Vegas, associates of some porno producer named Kraven. They claim the tape was shot in a Vegas motel and Jameson was too bombed on drugs to care."

Linda fidgeted at Tucker's statement, but said nothing. Her turn would come.

"How did Toth's assistant know where to contact these two for a statement?" MacLean asked.

"A note inside the package gave their names and hotel room number. They must have known the drill. Copies of their written statements for *American Exposé* are in the file I just gave you. Toth's is in there, too."

"How would they know the drill?" Linda asked.

"I have no idea," Tucker said.

MacLean glowered. "Then I'd say you have a lot of unfinished business. I don't like incomplete investigations, Tucker."

"Sorry, sir."

"Don't be sorry, be thorough." MacLean turned to

Linda. "And what little pearls of wisdom do you have for me? You sounded very up on the phone."

"The lab has compared the three videotapes," she began. "All were produced on virgin tape, VHS, regular format, standard speed. The one delivered to Senator Jameson was a second-generation copy. The one our people picked up from *American Exposé* is also a second-generation copy, and the copy Agent Tucker just confiscated from the television people is third generation."

"So," MacLean looked thoughtful. "Two of the tapes were copied directly from the master, and the third was a copy of a copy. The tapes delivered to the senator and *American Exposé* were made from the same master."

Linda nodded. "Which directly ties the extortionists to the people who delivered the tape to Toth."

"Good," MacLean said. "Anything else."

Linda was beaming. "I didn't tell you this on the phone for fear you'd have a stroke."

MacLean gave her a piercing look.

She took a deep breath. "The lab's convinced the tapes have been manipulated. I'm prepared to state that Senator Jameson was not the person originally taped with that child."

Tucker looked incredulous. "Are you serious?"

"Very," she said.

"How convinced?" MacLean asked.

"First," Linda said, "the lip synch is off just a hair. Not every word, just a few of them."

"So?" Tucker said.

Linda turned to him. "If it was mechanical error, the entire audio would be out of sync, so the lab maintains the audio was dubbed."

MacLean shrugged. "So the audio was dubbed. It's the pictures that prove the evidence."

Linda shook her head. "There's no point in dubbing the audio if the tape's legit."

MacLean remained unconvinced. "That's it?"

"No," she said. "The tape was made professionally. Professional grade cameras and tape, not the home stuff. That's why the second-generation copies look so good. They used at least four sets of special lighting with bounce umbrellas. The editing is first rate, another mark of people who know what they're doing."

She took another deep breath. "This means at least two technicians had to be in the room."

"The two who showed up at Toth's studio," Tucker said.

"But there were more than two, at least four. The camera *moves*. Some home electronic devices prevent images from jiggling, but this camera was mounted. Somebody had to work the dolly. Somebody else had to work the audio boom. Which brings me back to the question of dubbing. Why was it needed?"

MacLean looked mildly interested. "Go on."

"When one looks at this tape objectively," she said, "one is required to accept the theory that Robert Jameson would willingly allow professional filmmakers to include him in some pornographic video. Not just pornographic, but a movie that shows him committing a felony. That's political suicide and an utterly impossible activity for a rational man."

"Speculation," MacLean said crisply.

"Excuse me," she said, "but I think it's more than speculation. The man cannot possibly have been that stupid. Some other politicians, yes, but not Robert Jameson. He was a famous senator with a high recog-

nition factor and well-known for his levelheadedness
and pragmatism. He wouldn't have allowed himself
to be part of this. Which leaves us with three options:
one, he was forced to do it; two, he was drugged; or
three, it never happened."

"If he was forced or drugged," Tucker said, "it's
still him on the tape, right?"

"His facial expression," she said, "gives no indica-
tion of stress. So we can rule out force. As for drugs,
I checked with Dr. Stafford on that issue. He says
Jameson would have been unable to maintain an
erection if he was drugged to the point of being completely unaware of his actions. Drugged just enough
to agree to this? Not on your life. No, this tape is a
complete fabrication."

"You're that sure?" MacLean seemed unconvinced.

"I'm positive."

"But you have no *real* proof," he said.

"Not yet."

"I thought we had equipment capable of determin-
ing if a video has been doctored."

"We do," she said, "but it's rudimentary. The lab
ran the tape through. It seems legit, but they know
it isn't. Harper in the lab thinks it was done with new
equipment that leaves no trace. The makers were a
little sloppy on the audio, that's all."

MacLean flashed a tight smile. "So all you have is
a theory?"

"An informed theory."

"Don't use that expression with me," he snapped.
"It makes you sound smug."

Linda simmered in silence.

"Will you be able to prove it?" MacLean asked,
pushing hard.

"I think so."

"You *think* so?"

For a moment they simply stared at each other, while Tucker waited for the inevitable explosion.

Linda finally nodded. "Given access to the right technicians and equipment and enough time, I can prove it. I need your okay."

MacLean said nothing.

Tucker changed the subject. "By the way, I looked over Perry-Mondori's statement. I think she lied. I talked with our resident shrink and he agrees. I think Claire Jameson showed her sister-in-law the tape immediately."

Some of the redness left MacLean's cheeks. "What makes the psychiatrist think she's lying?"

"Perry-Mondori flew to Virginia as soon as she heard about her brother's death. She's a criminal attorney and a good one, from what my sources tell me. She'd want to know why her brother killed himself. Claire Jameson would be hell-bent to tell her."

"Why?" Linda asked.

"Because of the suicide," Tucker said. "How could Mrs. Jameson explain the suicide without telling her sister-in-law about the tape?"

"The existence of the tape," MacLean added, "not to mention lack of autopsy evidence, proves the brain tumor theory was crap."

Tucker nodded. "Our lady lawyer was trying to stall for time, trying to keep the tape a secret. Then she got nervous when the TV people revealed the existence of another copy, and she decided to tell us about it."

Linda kept quiet. She'd guessed as much herself, but had no hard proof. And she had refused to put Karen on the spot by asking her point-blank.

"It all fits," Tucker continued. "The suicide note

alludes to his wife's failure to accept his word that 'it' never happened. 'It' has to be what's on the tape."

"Back to the tape." MacLean turned to Linda. "You're saying it was all computer manipulation?"

"Yes, but, as you said, I have no proof. In order to próve it's fake, I'll need help."

Tucker looked at Linda in awe. "Can they really fake a tape and make it that realistic?"

Linda nodded. "It's called morphing. They've been doing it for years in commercials and films, using models or people in costumes. These days, they use models and computer imaging. Not too long ago, it would have taken weeks to 'morph' a scene. Now, with the equipment available, that same scene can be done in a matter of hours."

"How do you know all this?" Tucker asked.

"I do my homework," she shot back. "In addition to increasing production speed, they've found a way to get the flesh tones right. They've conquered the technical problems and now they've got the cost down, which means that anyone with a couple of million bucks can make completely undetectable fake videos."

"Big deal," MacLean said with a grunt. "Apart from creating monsters and cute animals that talk, what good is it?"

"In the near future," Linda said, "all movie stars could be computer generated. The ultimate animation. No people, no buildings, no sets to pay for, just computer-generated images, and you'll never know the difference."

"Yeah," Tucker said, "they've already resurrected long-dead stars like John Wayne and Fred Astaire."

Linda nodded. "It's great for the studios. No big salaries, no temperamental stars, no expensive locations or sets, just creations that look, act, and talk like the real thing. Should shake the entertainment business to its very foundation."

"You're talking years in the future," Tucker said.

"In just a few years, men will be falling in love with some bimbo on the screen who doesn't even exist, and women will be drooling over some great-looking Italian hunk produced by someone's imagination. Hi-tech cartoons, indistinguishable from real life. Fantasies come true. That ought to keep the shrinks busy."

"The unions will be upset," MacLean said dryly.

"Entertainment unions—except those for computer technicians—will be finished," she said. "Who needs people when you can create them in a computer?"

MacLean rubbed his jaw. "Things are getting out of hand. The treasury had to change all the paper money because laser copiers are too damn good. Then they ordered copiers detuned. With this new technology, we'll have to treat every photograph, video, every piece of film as suspect, especially if there are breaks in the chain of evidence. Once this new technology hits the fan—"

"It already has," Linda interrupted.

"—every defense attorney in the country will scream 'fake' the moment photos, tapes, or films are introduced as evidence. Do you have any idea how heavily this impacts law enforcement?"

Linda grimaced. "More work for the labs."

"More work for everyone," MacLean said. "Inventions are supposed to make life easier, but this makes it tougher. I predict this morphing stuff will be outlawed in five years."

"I want to head the Jameson investigation," Linda said, catching her boss off-guard.

MacLean scowled. "Why am I not surprised?"

"Who better? Jameson was a senator from my state, and according to his sister, his family will be moving close to the Tampa office—"

MacLean looked dubious. "I don't know—"

"—and the film industry in Orlando, one of only a handful of places this film could have been produced, is in my back yard."

MacLean pushed his chair back. "If I put you in charge, where would you start?"

She stood up and leaned on his desk. "About five places at once. With the senator's speeches, for one. I'd search for words that match the audio on the tape and proof them with the stress analyzer. I'll also start looking for the original video."

"The master?" MacLean asked.

"No, the one with the girl."

Tucker frowned. "She could be the same as the senator, a fake, if what you think is true."

"Maybe," Linda said, "but I don't think so. Once we find her, we check the link and start to put it together."

Tucker stood with a smirk. "Should be easy. Can't be more than three or four hundred million ten-year-old females in the world. My gut tells me money is not the real motive behind the tape. I say we interview every senator and representative, instead of putting an entire task force on the girl. Jameson might not be the only one blackmailed."

"You're right on the motive," Linda said. "If the Jameson tape was done on last year's equipment, the makers spent a half million in pure labor to produce it. If it was done with new technology, which I suspect is the case, they spent much less on labor, but the equipment required an initial investment of at least two million. Either way, it's unlikely a million-dollar extortion was the real goal."

"This can't be about money," MacLean said. "Much too sophisticated."

"So we have a starting point," Linda said. "Find out who has this equipment and who among them has a reason to either blackmail or destroy Robert Jameson."

MacLean threw a pencil at the wall. "Just what we need, another goddamn conspiracy. And another goddamn task force."

Tucker grinned. "Look at it this way. When it comes to protecting politicians, cost is not a problem. They'll spend billions to cover their asses. We'll have full support on this one."

MacLean rubbed his eyes. "Good point. All right, Linda, you're in charge. You can discuss this with Jameson's sister, but no public statements from us until we have irrefutable proof. That means when we lay charges and have people in custody. We learned our lesson on premature statements with the suspect in the Olympic bombing."

"Once I've talked to Karen," Linda said, "and the cat's out of the bag, she might call a press conference. I wouldn't blame her if she did."

"We can't control Karen Perry-Mondori," MacLean said. "I don't care what *she* says, but *we* don't make any statements until this is wrapped tight."

Linda frowned. "What am I supposed to do if she holds a press conference and says I talked to her?"

MacLean leaned forward. "Let me make this clear. You make *no* statement."

"That hardly seems fair," she protested. "The woman's brother has been savaged by *American Ex-*

posé, and it's all a lie. When she says it's a lie, someone should support her."

"I realize the senator's sister is your friend,"
MacLean said, "but you still have no hard evidence
the tape's faked. I don't want this to look like the
Bureau is covering up some senator's deviant behavior. Until we have more than an 'informed theory,'
a cover-up is exactly what any support from us will
look like."

The room was silent save for the hum of
MacLean's computer.

Finally, Linda said, "Our lack of support could also
be interpreted as payback time for Jameson's fer-
reting out bad apples in the Bureau two years ago."

MacLean threw another pencil. "Don't remind
me!"

Linda backed off the obviously touchy subject.
"How many people can I have?"

"Donald and three others. That's all I can spare.
And you've got a month."

"A month? That's not enough."

"The budget's tight. It'll have to do."

Linda nodded. "According to my office in Tampa,
Karen Perry-Mondori is back in Virginia. Can I tell
her what we've found so far? She deserves the
truth."

MacLean nodded. "But make it quick. You've got
a plateful."

Linda nodded and hurried from the office, her excitement tempered by a small fear. The fear of screwing up.

At nine o'clock, Karen opened the door of the Virginia house to Linda and led her into the den. "Want
a drink?"

"No, thanks," the agent said. "I'm on duty."

Karen handed Linda a file folder. "It's Claire's official statement. You'll also find a doctor's note to the effect that her original statement was made under extreme stress, hence her exclusion of any mention of the tape. I hope you're not going to make an issue of it. Claire's suffered enough already."

Linda took the folder and placed it in her attaché case. "Under the circumstances, I don't think there will be a problem."

Karen felt a wave of relief. She settled into a wingback chair while Linda sat on the sofa. "Any leads on the blackmailers?"

"Not yet, but I have news of another kind."

Karen lifted her eyebrows. "Good news, I hope."

Linda nodded. "I've read the suicide note Robert left. In it, he referred to something as having never happened. Do you think he was referring to his actions depicted in the video?"

Karen took a deep breath. "It's all there in the statement. Robert showed the tape to Claire and claimed he was either suffering from hallucinations or a victim of forgery. Claire ruled out both explanations, and they argued. Shortly after that, Robert killed himself. Clearly the reference in the note was to the tape."

"There's a *very* strong possibility," Linda said, "that your brother was right about the tape being fraudulent. The lab's examined it several times and will need more extensive experiments, but at this moment, the technicians are convinced the tape is a complete fabrication."

Karen found breathing difficult. "What convinced them?"

"You've seen television commercials where certain

objects dissolve slowly, then reform as different objects? The same technique was used in the production of the tape involving your brother."

"So the tape *was* altered," Karen said, "manipulated, whatever you want to call it."

Linda nodded. "Unless there is some other evidence to the contrary, your brother was never a pedophile."

"If the tape was altered, exactly what images were there to begin with?"

"Maybe if I explain it as the lab technicians told me, you'll understand better. A very fast computer, known as a teraflop—sometimes called a massive parallel computer—and a digital image manipulator were used. With these two machines, an experienced technician can change any and all frames in either a videotape or film strip to whatever is wanted."

Karen remembered the lists Bill Castor had given her. One had the names of twenty-one agencies or corporations who had purchased massive parallel computers since their invention. She itched to share the list with Linda, but doing so would validate any suspicions that Karen had viewed the tape sooner than she'd claimed. Giving the list to Linda would have to wait.

"In the case of the video in question," Linda continued, "we think the tape was originally a pornographic video involving some other man, whose image was replaced by that of your brother's."

"Can you be more specific?" Karen asked.

"Someone, using the equipment I've described, freeze-frames the image from a single frame of videotape. That single frame is comprised of thousands of little dots called pixels. You can see them when you look through a magnifying glass at a color photo in a magazine."

Karen nodded. "What next?"

"The frozen frame is fed into a computer, which scans the frame, assigns a series of numbers to each individual pixel, and stores the information in its memory.

"For example, say that a single pixel within the eye represents a blue tone, and it's given number values ranging from 100 to 150. The pixel next to it might be slightly different and given number values 151 to 200. The computer is told that the first series of numbers relates to a certain pixel in a specific section of the frame. With me so far?"

"I think so," Karen said.

"Assume you want to substitute another color, say brown. The technician enters the numbers for a certain shade of brown already stored in the computer memory. He then orders the computer to replace the first pixel number values with the second. That procedure is repeated with every pixel in every frame. Eventually, you have a complete change."

Karen held up her hand. "So you're saying, to start with, they had to have had videos of Robert in the nude?"

Linda shook her head. "All they needed were videos of Robert's basic skin tones, features, and general body shape. The rest is created. The technician takes a tape, say of Robert delivering a speech, and assigns number values to each pixel in each frame. Once that's been accomplished, he orders the computer to make the changes required.

"The computer operator can electronically remove Robert's clothes, remove the background, paint in the skin, and Robert is now standing in the middle of nowhere, nude. Then the operator instructs the computer to replace the original numbers on the porno tape with the new ones of Robert. If the original participant was short and fat, other changes are made, putting in the background previously hidden, for example. Short and fat becomes tall and muscular. Mr. X becomes Robert Jameson."

"How long does the procedure take?"

"Months," Linda said, "before the invention of massive parallel, or teraflop, computers. Now they can do the job in days, even hours, depending on the power of the teraflop."

"My God," Karen said. "It's that fast and that simple?"

"The equipment," Linda said, "is so sophisticated, a tape could be made showing the President of the United States making love to Madonna in that very same room, when, in fact, neither person had ever been near the place. No one would be able to tell it was faked."

"Wait a minute. If no one could tell, how can *you* tell it's not Robert?"

"The FBI technicians go by experience and instinct," Linda said. "They will still have to actually *prove* it's a fake. That task will be daunting, but not impossible, and it will take time. You'll have to be patient."

Stunned, Karen ran a hand through her hair. "So someone sat down at a computer, took existing video images of Robert and inserted them into an existing pornographic video, making it appear he was fornicating with a child. Do you realize what this means?"

"The implications are legion."

"I was thinking of Claire. When she hears this, she will feel completely responsible for Robert's death because she didn't believe him when he said the video was faked."

"I'm sorry."

"God!" Karen ground her teeth in rage. "How can I help find these bastards?"

"In the statement you gave me, you mentioned that Robert kept tapes of his speeches. Do you know where those are?"

"They're here," Karen said, "some of them. There're others in Florida."

"Good. I'd like to take the ones here. You can give me the copies in Florida later. I plan to examine each one for specific word matches. If I find one, the lab will do an audio stress analysis, comparing the original in the speech to one in the forgery. An exact match will tell us that word was dubbed into the forgery."

"That's fine," Karen said, "but how does it prove the video was faked?"

"It proves that the audio portion was dubbed. If the tape was genuine, there'd be no need to dub the audio. To *prove* the video was faked, we'll have to find the original porno tape and the people who produced it. We'll need their testimony."

"Do you have any leads?"

Linda nodded. "Names and addresses of a couple from Vegas who delivered a copy of the tape to *American Exposé*. They checked out of their New York hotel right after *American Exposé* paid them for the tape. But following through will take time. And my resources are limited."

"Give the names and addresses to me. I'll put my private investigator on it."

Linda looked doubtful. "I shouldn't, but I'll need my other agents to analyze the tape and track down the little girl. My boss only gave me a month on this."

"The little girl? The one in the video with Robert?"

"Her image could have been forged as well, but I doubt it. Even if it was, she's still a lead. Proving the tape was manipulated is possible, but it isn't going to be easy."

"Will you do something right now?" Karen asked.

"What?"

"I'd like to call a press conference and have you—"

Linda shook her head. "Until we have hard evidence, no one will believe us. Even when we do present our case, you can be sure there'll be doubters."

"I want the media to know you're investigating. That's all I ask at this point."

"I'm afraid I can't help you."

"Why not?" Linda's refusal caught her by surprise.

"Let's just say . . . policy."

"Policy? It's the policy of the FBI to let a member of the United States Senate be depicted as sexually depraved when it isn't true? We've been friends too long for you to give me that kind of nonsense, Linda."

"I'm sorry." Her friend squirmed in her seat, obviously uncomfortable.

Karen's face flushed with anger. "Sorry doesn't cut it. The fact is, you *are* investigating. You have leads. My brother doesn't deserve to have his tarnished image perpetuated for another second! The country should be told."

"I can't help you." Linda's face reddened.

"Who's responsible for this asinine policy?" Karen screamed.

Linda stood, her body rigid. "I can't answer that."

Karen moved to the telephone, picked up the receiver, and held it in the air. "You call him right now. I'm your friend, Linda, but I'm also an attorney, and right now, a very angry attorney. If you don't allow me to talk to your boss, I'll build a fire under you so hot, you'll not sit down for eternity."

"Don't threaten me," Linda snapped.

Fury swept through Karen. "Call him. I won't ask you again."

Linda hesitated. Then her posture slowly relaxed, and she reached for the phone. She flashed Karen a weak smile. "I'm doing this because I *am* your friend, not because you threatened me."

Karen's anger ebbed and her shoulders slumped. "I have to do this. If it causes you problems, I'm sorry."

"I understand." Linda took the receiver from Karen's shaking hand and punched in numbers. "George, it's Linda. I'm with Karen Perry-Mondori, and she wants to talk with you."

Linda was silent, listening to the man on the other end. Whatever he was saying made her wince. "George—"

Karen ripped the receiver from Linda's hand. "To whom am I speaking?"

"Assistant Director George MacLean. Ms. Perry-Mondori, I presume?"

"Yes, and I understand you are responsible for this ludicrous policy of official silence."

"I am."

Karen's anger returned in a rush. "Let me explain something to you, Mr. MacLean. The entire country is of the opinion that my late brother was a sexual deviate. According to Agent Holt, you suspect that the video was fabricated through some kind of electronic witchcraft. I want the world to know the truth, and I want it to know immediately."

MacLean inhaled sharply. "I understand your eagerness to make a public statement, but the fact is, without hard evidence, it will appear that—"

"Don't give me that! You *have* evidence. Without evidence you wouldn't be conducting this investigation. Do you seriously believe there can be anything worse than the prevailing public opinion?"

"That may be so, but—"

"I'm not arguing with you. I'll be holding a press conference within two hours and telling the world what Agent Holt has told me. I want her at my side. You either back me up or face the consequences."

"Consequences?" MacLean sounded amused.

"If you don't back me up, I'll declare in my press conference that the FBI is dragging its feet in this investigation in order to retaliate against Robert Jameson for revealing the complicity of FBI agents in drug-trafficking during the Uccello hearings."

There was a moment of silence on MacLean's end before he spoke. "Do you always play hard ball, Ms. Perry-Mondori?"

"I'm not aware of any other kind."

MacLean paused again. "Let me talk to Agent Holt."

Karen handed the receiver to an ashen-faced Linda.

"Yes?" Linda said.

"Nice going," MacLean shouted, so loud that Karen heard every word. "You've managed to put our backs against the wall. No matter what we do, we lose."

"George—"

"Save it. I don't give a damn what you do now, but I want you in my office by midnight tonight."

Before Linda could answer, he hung up.

Two hours later, the press conference was held in Washington at the offices of the local NBC affiliate.

Karen, her voice trembling at times, announced that the FBI had determined that the videotape shown on *American Exposé* was a complete fabrication, that it had been produced for the purposes of extortion, and that she personally was offering a reward of one hundred thousand dollars to anyone providing information leading to the arrest and conviction of those responsible.

Linda Holt took her turn in front of the microphone, explained her reasons for believing the tape was a computer-generated image rather than reality, and cautioned that the case was in its infancy. It would be some time, she said, before the evidence needed to prove her contention was found. Nevertheless, she was sure it *would* be found.

She explained, in the kind of detail she'd used with Karen, how it could have been done, then left Karen to face the many questions proffered by the media. As Karen spoke, Linda left the room and raced down the hall to the elevator.

She knew George MacLean would be waiting in his office. She also knew she was in for a tongue-lashing. She shivered as the elevator started down.

Ten

It was raining hard the next morning when Karen parked her car and hurried across the wet expanse surrounding the Senate Office Building. Despite her umbrella and raincoat, she felt as damp as her spirits as she headed to her brother's former office.

The receptionist, a woman in her sixties, told her to take a seat. "Miss Morley is with someone else just now. She shouldn't be much longer."

Normally, when forced to wait—a regular occurrence for a criminal defense lawyer—Karen used the time to advantage, either by holding conversations on her cellular phone or preparing handwritten notes for later attention by Liz Walsh, her secretary. Today, she simply sat, slumped in a chair, her thoughts a whirlpool of unanswered questions as she empathized with those for whom personal dilemmas dulled normally trenchant minds.

Linda's theory regarding the counterfeit video had been both a blessing and a curse. While the ramifications of the curse were still in evidence, the benefits of the blessing were yet to be realized.

Karen had called Claire prior to the press conference, then again at its conclusion. Her sister-in-law's initial reaction had been relief, but it wasn't long before she collapsed in a paroxysm of sobs. The sudden revelations, while welcome, had only bolstered Claire's feelings of guilt for not having believed her husband's frantic denials. While Robert's reputation was in the process of being resurrected, Claire was forced to confront a new legion of personal demons.

Karen had also talked to Richard and Michael after the press conference. While they expressed relief that their father was to be exonerated, the tone and timbre of their voices revealed their underlying concern. Where was the evidence? they'd asked. And once it was found, what would be done to the people who had caused their father's suicide? Karen hadn't been able to provide answers that satisfied them.

As for the press conference, Karen had hoped it would be a boon and, awash in anger and grief, had rejected Linda's objections to it without really listening. Now, having had the chance to digest many of the media reports on the press conference, Karen saw clearly that Linda had been right in counseling caution.

The media response had been carefully moderate, a thick cloud of cynicism blunting the impact of the revelation. Some politically partisan observers had come perilously close to blatantly accusing the FBI of cooking up the story to whitewash the alleged sins of Robert Jameson. Others had leapt wholeheartedly to the senator's defense.

They were the extremists on both sides.

The large majority of pundits, most of them respected for their balanced views, were simply skeptical, sitting on the fence, waiting to see some actual evidence, proof that was not yet available, before commenting in depth.

So the tormenting questions whirled in Karen's mind. How could the FBI find such evidence and when? Who had done this and why? Would they all be caught? And if they were, what would be the charge? All the questions were important, but the last was particularly worrisome. Intimately familiar with criminal law, she knew punishment could not be taken for granted.

For a moment, she placed herself in the position of defending those responsible for the tape's production. While lacking the strength of thorough research, her off-the-cuff analysis was chilling. She could think of a dozen semiscurrilous but effective defenses. In the hands of a competent defense attorney, the perpetrators of this vicious lie were unlikely to serve jail time if convicted, and even a conviction was no cinch. No one brilliant enough to conceive such deceit would be so reckless as to leave all escape hatches locked.

She sat there, her rage building anew, and turned the various aspects over and over in her mind. Someone had created this tape in an effort to destroy Robert. They had succeeded, perhaps beyond their dreams. The perpetrators might be found, and if convicted, could be jailed. The odds on the latter were slim. Linda had explained on the way to the press conference the money and expensive equipment needed to produce the tape. If Karen couldn't assure the perpetrators' loss of freedom, she would damn well guarantee their loss of fortune. She'd hit them with a wrongful death suit that would leave them destitute.

What she really wanted was to kill the bastards personally.

But first she had to find out who they were. If anyone knew who had the motivation to blackmail Robert, it was Marie Morley, his chief-of-staff. Politics had been Robert's whole life. He'd made no personal enemies. His adversaries were all political.

"Miss Morley will see you now, Ms. Perry-Mondori," the receptionist announced.

The door to the inner office opened, and Marie Morley emerged and escorted Karen into Robert's office. The former aide sat in one of the two chairs before the desk, Karen in the other.

"Did you see the press conference?" Karen asked.

Marie nodded. "It was like a weight being lifted from my shoulders. At the same time, my mind started functioning again, because it all—finally—made grotesque sense. I was about to call you when you called me this morning."

Karen leaned forward, intensely interested. "You were?"

"This was no blackmail scheme. This was politics of the worst kind. This was *evil.*"

"Why do you say that?"

Marie hesitated a moment, smoothing the skirt of her red wool suit. "Ever since last night, I've been racking my brain, trying to think of someone who might have had a reason to do such a terrible thing to Robert. He was a good man, but the list is long, because he was, after all, a senator. Perhaps even worse, he was a senator with conviction and values and ethics. You can make a lot of enemies with those qualities, and Robert had his share of enemies, believe me."

"Did you reach any conclusion?"

"I made a rough list, but one name keeps popping to the top, and I'm forced to consider it seriously. I'm not making any accusations, but if you're looking for a possible suspect, there's someone you should check out before all others."

"Who?"

"Walter Stockman."

Karen felt a tremor run down her spine. Walter Stockman was a legend, either a bastard or a genius, depending on which side of the legend—and the poverty line—you were standing. Chairman of one of the nation's largest communications conglomerates, he'd started with three thousand dollars at age twenty-two, bought into a failing newspaper and turned it into a profitable supermarket tabloid within five years. From there, he'd branched into radio and television stations, more newspapers and magazines, a movie studio, three book publishers, and eventually, the second largest cable network in the country.

In 1981, pressed for cash by that year's recession, he'd taken his privately held company public by offering to sell twenty percent of the common stock. The offering was sold out in less than an hour.

Then, just three years ago, Stockman, at the age of fifty-seven, had sold another twenty-five percent interest in his empire for the astonishing sum of five billion dollars. The sale had been made to buyers thought to be fronts for Japanese business interests, but a proposed Congressional investigation had been quickly squelched. Stockman still retained fifty-five percent of the company, which allowed him to do what he pleased.

He was a man of enormous power, a confidante of many in Congress, a friend to powerful people all over the world. He employed the three most respected and influential lobbyists in the country. He had clout and was unafraid to use it.

But what sent shivers down Karen's spine was the fact that two of the corporations Stockman controlled were on the long list Bill Castor had given her at the

Tampa Airport of companies known to have equipment capable of producing the tape. And one of those was also on the short list of twenty-one who had purchased a massive parallel computer, a teraflop.

"Was Stockman an enemy of Robert?" Karen asked.

"On the surface, no, but I expected him to become one. Big time."

"Why?"

Robert's former aide leaned back in the vinyl-covered chair. "Stockman has been diligent about ingratiating himself to politicians. With his money and influence, that hasn't been difficult. He spreads his largess around freely, with little concern for party affiliation or personal philosophy. A shotgun approach, but it works."

"I can't see Robert taking anything from Stockman."

Marie shook her head. "Robert was one of the few who refused to accept direct campaign contributions from Stockman, though he had a legal right to, since Stockman pays attention to the rules. Stockman saw Robert as a special challenge and has been unrelenting in his pursuit and attention. Stockman even managed to filter money to the senator through various PACs. You don't always know where the money comes from, and if you cut off the PACs, you might as well fold up the tent."

"Why do you consider Stockman a prime suspect?"

"About three months ago, the senator became especially interested in Stockman after a delegation of men and women arrived here for a meeting. They represented five hundred former employees of one of Stockman's Florida operations, a printing and distribution center for one of his magazines. All five hundred had been fired in a cost-cutting move."

"Downsizing to save the company," Karen said, "the scourge of the nineties."

Marie shook her head. "In fact, while profits of that particular division had declined modestly, the company paid Stockman's manager a bonus of twenty-eight million dollars three weeks after the firings."

"Twenty-eight *million*?"

"Not bad for someone whose only qualification is a longtime personal friendship with Stockman."

"Not bad at all."

"Robert asked his investigative staff to do some digging. They found that seventy percent of Stockman's employees are allowed to work only thirty hours a week, which permits the company to forgo providing medical and other benefits. But to keep their jobs, these same employees are required to *volunteer* as many as twenty additional hours a week. On the books, the employees are paid competitive wages, while in truth, they're sacrificing both income and benefits."

"Nice guy," Karen said with irony.

"As a result of the investigation, Robert began discussing two things with some of his colleagues. One was a proposed Senate hearing to investigate such employment practices, and the other was the feasibility of authoring a bill that would limit the amount of compensation to CEOs of all publicly held corporations under certain conditions. These discussions were held secretly."

"Why secretly?"

"A few years ago, the SEC imposed certain reforms designed to prevent CEOs from financially raping the corporations they manage. The new rules allow shareholders owning at least one percent of a public corporation to vote on executive compensation packages. Previously, boards of directors could block such a referendum, but not anymore. The reforms worked for a while, but now that the pressure is off, things are returning to the way they were. There seems to be no limit to personal greed on the part of corporate managers. In any case, Stockman owns a majority interest in all of his companies, so he can shrug off shareholder revolts."

"That doesn't explain the need for secret discussions," Karen said.

"Congress considered investigating Stockman's business ethics once before, but the inquiry was thwarted by a concerted effort by some special interest groups. Hence, the need for stealth while considering another attack."

Karen nodded. "Now I get the picture."

"So," Marie continued, "everyone involved is walking on eggs. There's Stockman's influence, of course, but let's face it. This is America. Government interference in the operation of major corporations is, if not a no-no, very dangerous ground. Nevertheless, the senator felt strongly that Stockman and his friends were bleeding his corporations dry, and Robert wanted to stop it."

"That sounds like Robert," Karen said with a sad smile.

"And then there was the issue of management-employee relations. The employees and shareholders of Stockman's empire appear to be among the most ill-treated in the country. Some of that mistreatment is, unfortunately, legal, but laws *are* being broken, and no one seems to give a damn. Robert did."

"You think Stockman may have learned of Robert's interest in his companies?"

"I think Stockman knew what was going on. I also think he was responsible for that fake tape."

Karen sighed. As with Linda, Marie had offered only theories. "Do you have any evidence to support that?'

"When Robert returned from a convention in Las Vegas a few weeks ago, he told me that Stockman had threatened to destroy him unless he backed off the legislation. Stockman whispered the threat directly into Robert's ear. No witnesses. It troubled Robert deeply."

"Unfortunately, that threat may not be admissible evidence."

"It's the best I can do. The threat also explains Robert's depression. At the time, the cause didn't register. With so much going on, I had trouble isolating the problem. Now, with the help of hindsight, I can see what created his depression. Stockman is ruthless when it comes to getting what he wants— megalomaniac isn't too strong a word. I've seen him destroy others who've stood in his way."

"Robert was afraid Stockman was out to ruin him?"

Marie shook her head. "Robert wasn't afraid for himself. He appeared to have ignored the threat, but those supporting the bill had become somewhat tepid. I'm sure Robert felt they were being unduly influenced, and he was searching for ways to counteract Stockman's pressure. But he hadn't found them. Stockman is not only ruthless and powerful. He's also cagey. Lots of charges have been thrown at him in the past. So far nothing has stuck. Knowing you were up against Walter Stockman would depress anyone, even Robert."

Karen pulled out her notebook and jotted some notes. "You're very observant."

"That's my job."

"Can you provide me with copies of the documentation relating to the investigation of Stockman?"

"I'll be happy to."

"What about the other senators? Do you have their names?"

"I'll include them with the copies."

Karen smiled, feeling better than she had when entering the office. "Thank you for bringing this Stockman situation to my attention. If you ever tire of politics, you should become a detective. You have an investigator's inquiring mind."

Marie laughed. "Politics can be very challenging. I can't think of anything I'd rather do."

"My challenge," Karen said, "will be tying Stockman to this."

"Will you pass this information on to the FBI, or should I?"

"I'm meeting Special Agent Holt for lunch. If you have time to make those copies now, I'll give them to her."

Marie suddenly brightened. "I just thought of something else."

"Yes?"

"That television tabloid show, *American Exposé*, where the altered tape was shown?"

"Yes?"

"That show is produced by a company called Toth Productions. Toth Productions is owned by one of Walter Stockman's companies."

*   *   *

With the information from Marie Morley tucked safely in her attaché case, Karen drove to the Watergate Hotel where she was meeting Linda for lunch. With time to spare, she found a pay phone and placed a call to Carl's office. He had been in emergency surgery when she tried to reach him before the news conference last night.

"I read a recap of the press conference in the *Times* this morning," Carl said. "Sounds like you're making progress."

Karen savored the sound of his voice and felt a stab of homesickness. "Some progress, but not fast enough. I've sent Bill Castor to Vegas to track down the pair who delivered the tape to *American Exposé*."

"I thought the FBI had launched an investigation."

"They're giving Linda minimal support. That's why I may have to spend a few more days here. How's Andrea?"

"Happy as a clam. She's involved in some special project at school that Rahni's helping her with. By the way, I've lined up that house at Cobb's Landing for Claire and the boys. They'll drive up from Miami today. They should be settled in by the time you return."

"I appreciate all your help."

"You can show me how much when you get home," he said, and she could hear the smile in his voice. "What's your next step?"

"I'm meeting Linda for lunch to pass on a lead on the tape's producer."

"Don't forget to tell her about the electrical outlet."

"What?"

"The European 220 volt outlet in the room where the original tape was made. If Linda's right and a porno flick was used, it was made in Europe."

"Have I ever told you what a marvelous eye you have for details? You should be an attorney."

Carl laughed. "Too bloody for me. I'll stick to back surgery."

"I miss you."

"I miss you, too. I have to go, but I'll call you tonight at the Virginia house. I love you."

Karen placed the receiver in its cradle and turned toward the restaurant.

After lunch, Linda headed straight for MacLean's office to tell him about Carl's discovery. The veteran FBI administrator looked at a freeze-frame photo she had picked up from the lab on her way in, saw the circled electrical outlet, and shook his head. Without a word to Linda, he picked up the phone and punched three numbers. "This is MacLean. Let me talk to Windon."

Linda had spoken to Wallace Windon three times in the past twenty-four hours. A sociologist by training, he was the resident FBI expert on all aspects of the still-burgeoning business of pornography. Unlike some of his associates, his attitude toward pornography was impersonal, his interest almost academic. His fascination and expertise lay with the details of production and distribution of the material rather than the wild assortment of activities depicted in such tapes, films, books, and other assorted paraphernalia.

"Wallace? I have Linda Holt in the office. I'm turning on the speaker phone."

"Hi, Linda," a deep voice rattled from the small speaker. "What's up? I just talked with you before lunch."

"Sorry to bother you again," Linda said. "I've just

discovered that the original version of the tape was produced in Europe."

"How'd you determine that?"

"The electrical outlet. It's 220."

"Jameson ever go to Europe?"

"At least twice a year," she said.

"So they probably figured it didn't matter. Then again, they might have left it intact deliberately."

"Maybe. Either way, can you give us a starting point?"

"Sure. Don't change what you've done, though."

"You mean the photos of the girl?"

"Don't pull them back. A lot of this stuff is imported. Las Vegas is still your hot tip. Besides, I seriously doubt the manipulation was done offshore."

"I agree," Linda said, "but I'd still like to broaden the scope of our investigation."

"Europe is swimming in porno stuff. Attitudes are different there and it's sold more openly. The child was blond, so I'd say Germany or the Scandinavian countries. The man to talk to is Kurt Gustavson in Stockholm. He's with the Swedish National Police. His number's in the international book."

"He's the Swedish expert?" MacLean asked.

"One of them, but he's the best. Most of the kiddie stuff originates in Stockholm or goes through channels there. Even the German stuff is distributed through Sweden. Kurt's your best bet. If he doesn't recognize her, he'll know where to look."

"Does this Kurt speak English?" MacLean asked.

"Probably better than you or I. He was educated at Oxford. Majored in languages."

MacLean thanked him, hung up, and turned to Linda. "I'll have a cover letter prepared. We'll fax it and the child's photo, but not before I talk to Gustavson. How many hours ahead of us are they?"

"Six."

MacLean looked at his watch. "I'd better call him now."

He consulted a thick directory, found the number he was looking for, and placed a call. In less than a minute, he was explaining the problem to Kurt Gustavson in Stockholm.

"I'll be delighted to help you in any way I can." Gustavson's accent was a peculiar convolution of Swedish and U.K. English. "You say she's about ten?"

"She was when the film was shot. It could have been years ago, for all we know."

"We have an extensive collection in our archives. We've cataloged thousands of faces. If the film was ever circulated here, I'm sure we'll find her."

"Thank you, sir. I'll have the fax out within the hour." MacLean hung up the phone. "How's it going with the videos of the speeches?"

"Nothing so far," Linda said. "We've reviewed six, only three hundred to go."

MacLean grinned. "Only three hundred? Jameson wasn't much of a speechmaker, was he?"

"Voluble enough to keep us busy for God knows how long. Harper is practically falling asleep."

"Stick a tack under his ass."

"I will." She stood up to leave. "Look, I know you're upset about that press conference. You made that pretty clear last night. I—"

MacLean held up a hand. "I was thinking about that. I owe you an apology."

She almost fell down. George MacLean had two rigid tenets by which he lived: never admit a wrong, and never apologize. For him, the Golden Rule was but a childhood inculcation. This two-part doctrine, his personal stone tablet, was the rock to which he clung.

"You look surprised," he said.

"You could say that."

He sighed. "Why is it you people think I'm such a hard case? It's my job to keep you on your toes."

"I'm aware of that. I just wondered why the change of heart?"

"I have a son twenty-six. Neat kid. Computer programmer over at the Pentagon. I was thinking about him last night, wondering how he'd react if he'd seen his old man on TV like Jameson's kids did. I couldn't really imagine."

Linda nodded.

"When Jameson's sister ripped into me on the telephone, I was ready to tie a can to your tail. That comes from being inside these walls all day. You look at nothing but files long enough and people become just names. Humanity goes. I'm sorry. I was right about the press conference being premature, but being right isn't always what's important. I forgot that."

Linda cleared her throat, unable to think of something to say.

"You read the *Post* this morning?" he asked.

"We made the front page. It could have been worse."

"I agree," MacLean said, "but I got the feeling they don't believe us."

"Me, too. It's just as you predicted. Why do they always believe the worst?"

"Because it sells papers." He grimaced. "And, hell, because they're usually right. Are you aware of the additional pressure their skepticism puts on you, me, all of us?''

"Very."

"They'll be investigating us now, trying to make it look like we're covering up for Jameson."

"But as you said, being right isn't always what's important."

"Touché," he said.

"I could use some additional help. I had no idea there were this many possible leads."

"Forget it." He turned his attention back to the files on his desk and reassumed his man-in-charge persona. "I'm not trying to punish you, but you've got all the help you're gonna get. Make the best of it."

Linda, offering up silent thanks for the assistance of Karen and her private investigator, left the office.

From the front porch of the Virginia house, Karen watched as the moving company loaded the last carton onto their van for shipment to Florida. Claire had insisted Karen sell everything, evidently not thinking clearly enough to remember the number of clothes, personal belongings and mementos she, the twins, and Ursula had abandoned.

After the dealer picked up the cars the next day, Karen could return home, her task here finished, unless Linda discovered some way she could help further with the investigation. If not, Karen would lay the groundwork for the wrongful death suit against Stockman and have it ready to file as soon as enough damning evidence surfaced.

Linda Holt's government-issue vehicle passed the van exiting through the gate, and Karen waited as Linda drove up, parked, and climbed out of the car.

The special agent's excitement was evident in the haste of her approach.

"We're making progress," Linda said.

Karen shivered in the chill of the late October afternoon. "Come in and tell me about it. I'll make coffee."

Linda followed her into the kitchen. "Remember how the girl on the tape kept repeating Robert's name?"

"Yes." Karen filled the coffeemaker with water and reached for the ground coffee. Her gaze fell on two long, black streaks on the tile floor she hadn't noticed earlier. Poor Ursula had been so upset, she'd failed to maintain her usual pristine standard in the kitchen. The cleaners the realtor had hired would scrub the floor, as well as the garage where Robert had died. She turned her attention back to Linda, who had shed her coat and sat at the kitchen table.

"The repetition of his name," Linda said, "was done to give added authenticity, but somebody got lazy."

"Lazy?"

Linda handed her printouts from the audio stress analyzer and pointed to three graphs. "They used the same loop each time. An obvious mistake."

Karen looked at the printouts. "That's great, but is that all?"

Linda's eyes shone with excitement. "You'll also remember that Robert never addressed the girl by name? Look at these other printouts. Harper in the lab has determined that the word 'lovely' was taken from a commencement address given by Robert over a year ago. The word 'delightful' was cribbed from a three-year-old speech. The grunts were lifted from a tape of the congressional softball game last summer.

The stress analysis proves these words to be an exact match. As for the rest of Robert's dialog on the tape, I'm sure Harper will find matching words from his speeches, in time."

"That's good, but I won't be happy until I can tie this to Stockman." Karen dumped ground coffee into the filter-lined basket and wished she could mince Stockman into as fine a powder.

Linda nodded. "I told MacLean what you learned from Marie Morley."

"And?"

"He figures Stockman's a prime suspect. MacLean wants me to lean on the other senators on Morley's list, as well as the people at *American Exposé.* Once you hear back from Bill Castor in Vegas, I'll send Tucker back to New York. Maybe with Castor's info, Toth's answers will be more to the point."

"You're not going to tip your hand to Stockman?" Karen asked, alarmed.

"Not hardly," Linda said, smiling. "However, we can pretend we know more than we really do without mentioning names. Makes people nervous, and nervous people make mistakes. I'll have Tucker tell Toth this is now a murder investigation."

"Murder? That's not a federal crime."

"Toth probably doesn't know that. Since Robert committed suicide as a direct result of viewing the tape, his death could be construed as felony murder by the Virginia authorities. I'll have Tucker work that angle."

Karen frowned. "That's a reach, don't you think?"

"It's worth a shot, especially when you consider what's at stake. Robert was a U.S. senator. You know how those bureaucrats in Congress love to overreact.

Maybe they'll pass a law making this kind of thing a federal crime in the future."

"Too late to vindicate Robert."

"I'm sorry."

"I have my own plans for bringing Stockman to justice." She laughed at Linda's startled expression. "Don't worry. As much as I'd like to blow the bastard away, I'll work through the proper channels."

Linda's face expressed her relief.

"I'll be right back," Karen said and left the room.

When she returned, she handed Linda a copy of Bill Castor's lists. "You may already have this information. If not, these will save you some time."

Linda flipped through the pages. "What are these?"

"Agencies and corporations with the equipment needed to create a phony tape of the same quality as the one of Robert." Karen handed her a mug of coffee, poured one for herself, and sat opposite her friend. "Is there anything else I can do to help with the investigation?"

"Not that I can think of. These lists will put me light years ahead. Just send me Bill Castor's report from Vegas as soon as you get it." Linda sipped her coffee. "I noticed the moving van leaving. Are you finished here?"

Karen nodded. "I'm flying home in the morning. You'll keep me informed?"

"Of course," Linda said with a broad smile. "What are friends for?"

Eleven

Using the delay in her flight's departure to check in with her office, Karen hurried to the pay phone on the airport concourse.

Liz Walsh answered on the first ring.

"Is there anything that can't wait until I get there?" Karen asked.

Liz paused. "Your mother called."

"Again?"

"That makes twenty times. Not so calm and friendly. I had to hold the phone at arm's length."

Karen groaned. "I'd better call her before she has a stroke. What else?"

"Nothing that won't keep until you arrive. How's it going up there?"

"The FBI is handling the case. Knowing their propensity for fouling things up, I'm less than hopeful."

Liz made a tsking sound. "You're biased. You've been fighting them in court too long—and winning. Do you want me to pick you up?"

"No need, thanks. My car's at the airport. I'll come straight to the office."

Karen hung up and closed her eyes. What had begun as a minor tension headache threatened to develop into a major migraine. She hadn't suffered one of those in years. With the certainty that her head was going to feel a lot worse—and soon—she punched in her mother's number.

"I told you it was a fake," Martha bellowed as soon as she heard Karen's voice.

"Yes, I know."

"Why the hell haven't you called? I've called you at least fifty times. What is it? Can't stand the fact that I was right?"

"I've been very busy—"

"We're all busy. That's no excuse."

Karen spoke through gritted teeth. "Is that all you want to talk about, Mother? You just want to dump on me?"

"No, I told you that tape was a damn lie, and I was right. I also told you Robert was murdered. I'm as sure about that as I was the tape was a phony. What the hell are you going to do about Robert's murder?"

Karen took a deep breath. "The case is in the hands of the FBI."

"Big deal. Those people are the biggest screw-ups the world has ever known. Even you know that. You'll have to do this yourself."

"Do what?"

"Prove that Robert was murdered, you fool."

Karen hesitated for a moment. "Mother, you don't really believe that?"

"Like I didn't believe the tape was a phony? Will you wake up, Karen?"

"The autopsy confirmed suicide."

"Bullshit! Anyone smart enough to make that tape is smart enough to make a murder look like suicide. Can't you see that? All the stupid cops want is to close the case, and unless you keep on their asses, that's what they'll do. You're supposed to be smart, Karen. Right now you're acting like a moron."

"Mother," she said as calmly as she could, "in the first place, there were witnesses to Robert's suicide. Claire was there. So were the gardener and Ursula. No one saw—"

"Exactly!" her mother thundered. "No one saw him do it. They arrived a few seconds *after* the shot was fired. That's precisely my point. Someone could have shot him and disappeared before anyone else arrived on the scene, don't you see?"

"Yes, but—"

"But nothing. I was right about the tape, and I'm right about this. Robert was murdered, and if the stupid police can't find the people responsible, you'll have to."

Head pounding, Karen gave in. "I'll look into it, Mother."

For a moment, Martha Perry was silent. Then, the volume of her voice dropped about thirty decibels. "I want you to say that like you mean it, Karen."

Karen ignored the ridiculous ultimatum. "Mother, as personal representative for Robert's estate, I intend to file a wrongful death suit as soon as the makers of that video are identified. Under Florida law, as one of Robert's survivors, you will be named in the suit, along with Claire, Richard, and Michael. Do you have a problem with that?"

"File a suit? The people who made that tape are criminals, worse than scum. They should go to jail."

"Sending them to jail is the FBI's problem. Whoever had the equipment to make that tape had to have money," Karen explained. "I plan to hit them for damages in the millions."

"Ha!" her mother said. "And you'll charge the es-

tate a fat percentage off the top. You can't hide your
motives from me."

With the benefit of long practice, Karen held her
temper against the below-the-belt insult. "I won't
charge a fee, if that's what you mean. All I want is
justice for Robert."

"File your suit, but you should be spending your
time looking for Robert's murderer. I told you—"

Karen hung up the phone.

Karen surveyed the grounds with a satisfied smile,
then knocked at the door of the gray clapboard Cape
Cod house, set in three wooded acres on the shore
of Lake Tarpon. Carl had chosen exactly the right
place for Claire and the twins to escape the glare of
the public eye. The heavily treed lot, accessible only
through a gated entry, guaranteed privacy.

Ursula answered the door. "Hello, Ms. Karen. I'm
sorry, but Mrs. Jameson is asleep."

"Don't disturb her. I came to see Richard and Michael before they return to school."

"They aren't—" Ursula bit off whatever she had
been about to say. "The boys are out on the dock.
Do you want to come through?"

Karen pointed to an exterior sidewalk. "Does that
lead to the lake?"

"Yes."

"I'll go that way."

Karen followed the wide brick walk to the back of
the house and crossed the lawn to a small dock that
reached out into Lake Tarpon. For a moment she
stood, listening to gentle waves slap the sun-bleached
dock pilings, bathed in golden light by the setting
sun.

Michael and Richard sat on the dock with their

legs hanging over the side, their shoulders slumped, their faces slack with despair. She had hoped the press conference would have lifted their spirits but, if anything, her nephews appeared even more depressed than the day of their father's funeral.

Their greetings were halfhearted, as if speaking was an effort.

"I came to say good-bye," she said.

Puzzlement, the first emotion they had exhibited, showed on their faces. "Are you leaving again already, Aunt Karen?" Michael said. "You just got home."

Fear that her nephews were losing touch with reality made Karen shiver in the warm air. "You're the ones who are leaving. You both have plane reservations for tomorrow morning."

Richard shook his head. "We're not going back to school."

"Not— why?"

"We just can't," Michael said, avoiding her gaze.

"You have to get on with your lives. Your father would want that."

Richard shook his head. "This nightmare's not over."

"But the press conference—"

"Didn't make a hill of beans worth of difference," Richard continued, the lethargy in his voice at odds with the forcefulness of his words. "Once that tape appeared on television, everybody figured Dad was a pervert. The damage is done. The story was on the front page of newspapers, discussed on talk shows, featured in news magazines—everybody's talked of nothing else for days."

Michael nodded in agreement. "I don't know how many people knew who Dad was before this happened, but they sure know who he was now. And they'll always believe he was guilty. No matter what happens, most will continue to believe he was a pervert."

Karen shook her head. "The FBI's working on the case. They have some very good leads—"

"Then they'll soon find out that Dad wasn't exactly Mr. Straight-and-Narrow," Michael said sadly.

"What are you talking about?" Karen demanded.

Michael blushed, then looked at Richard. Richard averted his eyes from Michael's steady gaze.

"We know Dad didn't do the things on that tape," Michael said, "but we're beginning to wonder how well we really knew him. We're finding out all sorts of things—"

"Things like what?" Karen asked with more sharpness than she'd intended.

"One of my classmates was in Washington this summer," Michael said, "staying at the Marriott in Bethesda. Dad was in the next room. With Marie Morley."

"It could have been—"

"Don't try to tell me it was innocent. My classmate had met both Dad and Marie before when I took him on a tour of the city last year. Barry was walking by their suite as a waiter was delivering stuff from room service. He saw Dad at the door, then Marie lying on the bed, dressed in nothing but a bath towel. Dad didn't seem to notice Barry, and Barry made sure of it by keeping his mouth shut."

Karen said nothing.

"You didn't know?" Richard asked, surprised.

Karen shook her head. "Does your mother know?"

"If she does, it never came from us," Michael said, "but I don't think she does."

The three of them stared at the water for a moment.

"There's a big difference between infidelity and pedophilia," Karen said. "If, and it's quite possible you're making a judgment about your father's supposed infidelity without adequate evidence, even *if* it's true he was having an affair with Ms. Morley, that flaw doesn't negate how much he loved you and your mother, or how much he did for others."

They refused to look at her. She tried another approach. "You've lost your father. The circumstances of his death are almost impossible to bear, and I understand that. But your mother is alive, suffering as you are, bewildered, angry, and filled with the same emotions as both of you."

Richard and Michael gazed unblinking across the lake. Feeling as if she were talking to herself, Karen tried harder to get through to them.

"Your pain will never go away completely, that's for sure, but if you allow this tragedy to ruin your lives, you will stick a knife in your mother's heart. She needs and warrants your support, your love, whatever you can provide."

"And what about *us*, Aunt Karen?" Richard looked at her with lackluster eyes. "Who's going to be here for us, now that Dad's gone?"

"I am," she said with conviction, knowing as she spoke, that for now, being there was all she could offer. And it was not enough.

Karen had tucked Andrea in bed and now snuggled beside Carl on the sofa in the family room.

"Tired?" he asked.

"More worried, but tired, too."

"I could tell something was bothering you the minute you walked in the door. Is it Robert?"

She shook her head. "The boys. They're not going back to school. I'm no psychiatrist, but I recognize serious depression when I see it."

"Didn't Claire follow my advice about counseling for them?"

"Claire is in worse shape than her sons. Only Ursula is keeping that household together.

"They all need help," Karen said. "Robert's suicide hit them hard, the accusations on that tape hit them harder, at a time the boys were already grappling with the uncomfortable knowledge of an alleged affair between Robert and his chief-of-staff. No wonder they're reeling."

"Do you want me to talk to Leo Zimmer? He worked wonders with Andrea when Michelle was killed. Maybe he can help the twins, too."

"Could you speak to him tomorrow? From the way they looked tonight, they're going to need all the help they can get, and soon." She relished the warmth of Carl's body next to hers. She had been away too long.

"Something else is on your mind," he said. "You're too quiet."

"I was thinking, when I put Andrea to bed, will I ever disappoint her the way Robert did his sons? The sense of responsibility is staggering, and she seemed so vulnerable, so fragile, lying there asleep. I can't bear the thought of hurting her."

Carl pulled her tighter into the circle of his arm. "I read a treatise on maturity that said one characteristic of a mature individual is to realize one's parents are flawed and to accept that knowledge, to admit it's okay that one's parents aren't perfect."

Giddy with exhaustion, Karen laughed. "Whoever wrote that never met my mother."

"To hell with your mother. I've missed you."

She slid her arms around his neck and lifted her face to his kiss.

Bill Castor, newly arrived in Las Vegas, looked across the battered desk of Detective-Sergeant Vince Paterno. "You work fast."

"This is a fast town," Paterno answered. "Anybody works for a casino has to give us their prints. With Kraven, the porno producer, we just got lucky, though all we have on him is one DUI."

Castor looked through the material in the file Paterno had given him, then closed the folder. "Thanks. I'll take it from here."

"You want company?" Paterno asked. "I'm kind of a fixture on the strip. I know a lot of people. It makes things easier."

Castor thought for a moment. "Why not?"

Fifteen minutes later, accompanied by a hotel security guard, the two men entered the main kitchen of the Golden Eagle Hotel and Casino, a spacious room, all gleaming stainless steel and white tile, filled with steaming water, frying grease, all manners of food, busy white-uniformed cooks, short-skirted waitresses, and a mouth-watering assortment of smells. The security guard pointed to a man leaning over a large vat of what looked like chili. "That's Williams."

Hearing his name, Williams turned and faced Castor and Paterno, a question in his eyes.

"Jeffrey Williams?" Castor asked. The conviction that something wasn't right tickled in the back of his mind. Finding Williams right off the bat had been too easy.

"Yeah, I'm Jeffrey Williams."

Paterno showed his badge. Castor introduced himself. "Is there somewhere we can talk?"

"The employee lounge okay? What's this about?"

"Just routine," Paterno said. "No big deal."

Williams was a big man, about thirty, with tattoos on both arms. Castor recognized one as a Navy insignia. The cook seemed calm, though justifiably curious.

In the lounge, the three men sat in a corner, away from the other employees taking a break. Williams lit a cigarette and blew the smoke toward the ceiling. "So?"

"I want to talk about *American Exposé*," Castor said.

"American what?"

"The TV show."

"Never watch it. What's it got to do with me?"

Castor pulled out a small notebook. "They say you were there last Sunday."

Williams pointed to his chest. "Me? Who says?"

"The people who produce the show."

"That's bullshit."

"You weren't there?"

"I don't even know where the hell they are. What the hell is this?"

"Where were you last Sunday?"

Williams spread his arms. "Where else? Here. Ask the head chef. Wednesday's my day off. I got a wife and two kids to support. I don't take no extra time off. Ever. Ask."

"When's the last time you were in New York?" Paterno asked.

"Six, maybe seven years ago. I was still in the Navy. Since I started workin' here a year ago, I ain't been nowhere. You can ask my wife. Ask anybody. I ain't lying."

"You always been a cook?"

Williams shrugged. "I sold cars for a while, but I found out pretty quick I ain't no salesman. I was lucky to get a job here. What the hell is this all about, anyway? Who was the asshole said I was in New York?"

Paterno turned to Castor. "I'll check with the head chef."

"While you're at it," Castor said, "find out his hours for October second."

Paterno nodded and left. Castor turned back to Williams. "Where're you from originally?"

"Philly. What's this about October second?"

"How'd you get from Philly to here?"

"The wife's from here. She likes it here, and I don't give a shit where I live."

"You know anything about making videos?"

"You mean like at home?"

"Yeah."

"I can't afford one of those things, but I'd like to get one 'cause of the kids. It's nice to watch later when they're older, you know?"

"You ever make videos?"

"I just told you, I can't afford one of those gadgets."

Castor looked at his notes. "You know a woman by the name of Robin Sturgess?"

"Robin? Sure. She used to work here as a waitress. Now she works at the Hilton."

"When's the last time you saw her?"

"Her last day here. That was last week. Friday."

"Why'd she leave?"

"She got a better offer. The Hilton has a better tip

policy than this dump. She's been on the waiting list for a year."

"How about a guy named Jack Kraven?"

"Never heard of him."

"You sure?"

"Positive. Listen—"

They were interrupted by the return of Paterno. "He checks out," the detective said. "Hours are four to midnight. He was here on both days."

Castor stood and extended his hand. "I wish I could tell you about this, but I can't. Just an investigation where someone with obviously the same name as you came up. Thanks for the cooperation."

It was the same with Robin Sturgess. She'd been working the morning shift the day the tape was delivered to *American Exposé*. Even in a Concorde, she couldn't have made it to New York in time.

Then there was Jack Kraven. He was somewhat, as purported, a distributor of pornographic videos, the professional kind, the legal kind—at least, in some states they were legal—and his office was filled with posters extolling their prurient perfection.

Kraven looked more like a minister than a purveyor of porn, with his short hair, smoothly shaven face, lack of ostentatious jewelry, and his attire, from his glistening black oxfords to his light-gray worsted suit to his button-down blue shirt. A small gold lapel pin featured a rendering of Old Glory.

Kraven told him he'd never been involved in making the stuff, just selling it, and he'd *never* sold kiddie porn in his life. As for Williams and Sturgess, the names rang no bells. When shown a picture of the ten-year-old girl, he shook his head. "I told you, I never sell that shit, just straight porn."

"Okay," Castor said, "but look at the picture again. Maybe you watched some of that stuff. No harm done. I'm just trying to locate the kid."

"I can't help you," Kraven insisted. "And if you want to keep this up, I'm gonna call my lawyer."

That left Castor with two remaining tasks. Check out the motel where the mystery couple had claimed the tape had been made and the hotel where Robert Jameson had stayed on his last trip to Vegas. Castor was certain he'd draw blanks.

Three hours later, his suspicions were confirmed. He returned to his motel room, typed up his report, and set out to find a place to fax it to Karen.

Twelve

"Karen," Liz Walsh announced on the intercom the next morning, "you have a call from Linda Holt."

Karen abandoned a pretrial motion she was drafting and picked up the phone. "Did you receive Bill's report I faxed you?"

"Your man is thorough, but I wish he'd had better luck. Tucker is on his way to New York to talk to Toth."

Karen pulled Bill's report in front of her. "The descriptions Toth's people gave of the two who delivered the tape don't match those of the real Sturgess and Williams."

Linda sighed. "According to your PI, both Sturgess and Williams have rock-solid alibis, which means they have to be red herrings. Somebody went to an awful lot of trouble to set them up. The question is why?"

"It could be a backup position," Karen said softly.

Linda was quiet for a moment. "Where are you going with this?"

"Stockman may be a megalomaniac, but he's no fool. If, in fact, he is behind the tape, I doubt he anticipated Robert's death. Nevertheless, a man like Stockman would think ahead, anticipate Murphy's Law, and have an overall contingency plan in place should anything go wrong. By taking circuitous routes in getting the tape to *American Exposé*, Stockman lessened the chance of anyone connecting him to the scheme."

Linda was immediately interested. "Go on."

"Two people identifying themselves as Williams and Sturgess brought the tape to the program. We can't connect the real Williams and Sturgess to Stockman, but I'm sure Toth is telling the truth, that the tape was delivered by two people, a man and a woman. No way Stockman would deliver the tape personally. He needed a shield. Otherwise, using the names of two Las Vegas people makes no sense."

"I agree," Linda said.

"If we can find the two who handled the tape, we still might find a connection to Stockman. But as careful as Stockman seems to have been, I'm less than hopeful."

"I'm way ahead of you. I put their descriptions on the wire."

"Good," Karen said. "Did you lift any prints off the statements they signed?"

"Nothing. Those two knew what they were doing."

"You're sure Toth didn't make all this up?" Karen asked.

"It's possible, but I really doubt it. But I do think Toth knows more than he's saying. And he does work for Stockman, albeit indirectly. That's why I've asked Tucker to run a full background check on Toth to see what shakes out."

Karen smiled. "Good. Have you talked to any of the senators on Marie Morley's list?"

"Seven, so far. None will admit to being blackmailed or pressured in other than the normal Washington fashion."

"And you believe them?"

Linda paused. "I'm not sure. These guys are used to lying with a straight face. But we do have one small break."

"I could use some good news."

"We've found the girl who performed in the original porno tape. Right before I called you, I was on the phone with Gustavson of the Swedish National Police. Let me check my notes."

The rustle of paper carried over the telephone.

"Here," Linda said, "the girl's name is Helga Gliest. She's now eighteen years old. The tape was made in Bonn six years ago. By her father."

"Her father?" Karen said, gasping.

"He was the DeMille. It gets better—or worse, depending on your point of view. Her partner in the original film was her brother."

Karen winced. "My God! Such animals. How did Gustavson find this out?"

"The Berlin cops found the girl working in a legal brothel in the city. The father was busted a few years back for larceny. He's still in prison. The brother's dead, OD'd on heroin two years back. Little Helga just got out of prison two months ago after serving time for assaulting a john."

"Sweet child," Karen said with a grimace of distaste. "How did they find her so fast?"

"Gustavson has an extensive catalog of faces of actors appearing in kiddie porn films. He matched the fax we sent him with one of those photos, then distributed copies to all major European law-enforcement agencies. The Berlin police responded almost immediately. Must be a slow crime week in Germany."

"Incredible."

"Helga's not your most cooperative witness, though. When first approached, she admitted being in the original video, told the locals some of the details, then clammed up. I think she perceives this is more than your ho-hum investigation. She says anything else will cost money."

"What a sweetheart."

Linda sighed. "We can't force extradition. We can't even question her without her say-so—and a suitcase full of money."

"Which would make her testimony useless," Karen added.

"Right. Meanwhile, Gustavson's trying to find a copy of the original tape, since Helga's not helping."

"So what are you going to do?"

"I don't know." Frustration was evident in Linda's voice.

"We need that original tape," Karen said, "but the tape alone is not enough. Without the testimony of witnesses, who's to say the FBI didn't manipulate the Jameson tape? You ever think of that?"

Linda groaned. "You can't be serious."

"Look at this from a skeptic's point of view. The FBI has the equipment. They *could* do it. Even once they have this case locked up tight, the FBI could still be accused of doctoring the evidence. We need credible testimony from at least five or six people to make a case, and even then, there will still be a question in some minds."

Before she could continue, she heard someone speak to Linda in the background.

"Hold on a minute, Karen," Linda said.

Karen returned to her motion. Five minutes later, Linda was back on the line.

"Something strange is going on," Linda said. "I

just spoke with MacLean, who was just contacted by the director, who just got a call from Benjamin Rose."

Karen recognized the name. Benjamin Rose headed a list of influential and respected criminal attorneys. "Did Rose call about this investigation?"

"It appears Mr. Rose represents Walter Stockman."

"*What?*"

"Politics," Linda said, as if the word tasted bad. "It has to be."

"I don't follow you."

"You and I have been working on the assumption that Walter Stockman has been out of the country the last two weeks, fishing in some northern Canadian lake. Well, the vacationing Stockman has just returned and is shocked to learn of the furor surrounding the death of his good friend Robert Jameson."

"Good friend?" Karen's anger skyrocketed. "The bloody hypocrite."

"That's not all. Mr. Rose wants to talk to George MacLean and me about it."

"Now?"

"This you'll love. He wants to talk to us at exactly one-fifty this afternoon—in a conference room equipped with a television set capable of receiving UCN News. Does that sound like show business or what?"

Karen thought for a moment. "How do you suppose Stockman discovered the FBI was checking on him?"

"I don't know."

"How many senators did you say you've talked to?"

"Seven."

"One of them may be another victim. Maybe there are more tapes floating around Washington."

"God, Karen, the thought of it makes me sick to my stomach. Sometimes, I swear, I think it's time to pack it in."

"Not until you crack this case."

At one-fifty that afternoon, Karen sat in the conference room of Hewitt, Sinclair, Smith & Perry-Mondori, her gaze fastened on the television tuned to the United Cable Network, broadcasting from its headquarters in Orlando. She had already placed a new videotape in the VCR.

Bill Castor sat beside her.

After a series of commercials, the face of UCN veteran news anchor John Gobbins appeared. "At the top of the hour, we have a special report concerning the unfortunate death by suicide of Senator Robert Jameson. This special report is presented by the Chairman of the Board of Directors and CEO of United Cable Network, Walter Stockman."

Karen leaned forward in her chair and double-checked that the VCR was recording.

The camera panned to Stockman, seated next to his anchorman.

The communications titan, usually impeccably dressed, looked like a man just waking after a two-week drunken binge. His straw-blond hair was matted, his eyes red and puffy, and a two-week growth of beard covered much of his face. Instead of his typical attire—suit and tie—he wore a white T-shirt under a light blue nautical jacket. The image was startling.

"Thank you, John," Stockman began in an uncertain and raspy voice. "And good afternoon, ladies and gentlemen. I've just now returned from a two-week fishing trip, so please excuse my appearance, but I wanted to make this statement as quickly as possible because it's vitally important."

He fidgeted in his chair, then stared into the camera lens. "I learned as soon as I arrived home of the terrible news concerning the death of Senator Robert Jameson. It's clear that the senator killed himself after viewing a pornographic videotape in which he is depicted as one of the participants.

"The FBI has rightly determined this video was a fabrication, and they are now in the midst of an investigation to discover those responsible for the production of this videotape."

He took a deep breath. "They can stop looking. I am the one responsible."

"Holy shit," Bill muttered.

Karen's adrenaline surged. "That bastard!"

"I want everyone to know I am responsible for this tragedy," Stockman continued, his tone somber, his voice more assured, "especially the family of Senator Jameson."

Karen clasped her hands on the tabletop, squeezing until her knuckles whitened.

"There are no words," Stockman said, "to describe how bad I feel, nor are there any actions I can take to alleviate the horror of what has happened. I can only explain how this terrible thing happened, express my deepest sorrow and regret, and beg forgiveness from God, the Jameson family, and all of you."

He drew another deep, ragged breath. "Senator Jameson was a close personal friend. He was a man with many friends, for Senator Jameson was a man of honor, who consistently kept the interests of the American people in the forefront of his thinking. He was a leader, an innovator, an altruist, and a gentleman. He was also a man with a great sense of humor.''

Sense of humor? Karen frowned. "Where the hell is Stockman going with all this?''

Bill shrugged as Stockman continued.

"There are times when friends, with the best of intentions, can make a mess of things. I made more than a mess. Indirectly, I cost a man his life. Some of us were planning a surprise party for Robert on his fifty-third birthday in about three weeks. This party was to be a stag affair, where friends and associates get together and have some fun, free of the pressures of the day and away from the prying eyes of the media.''

His grin was self-effacing. "Robert liked to laugh. He was also a man who could take a joke—'' He stopped and wiped his eyes with a white handkerchief.

Dumbfounded, Karen couldn't take her eyes off his performance.

"I'm sorry.'' Stockman took another moment to gather himself. "Two months ago, one of our sister companies did a story on the new breed of computers entering the market and the possible misuse of such machines. An example of such unscrupulous utilization is the secret altering of photographs, movies, and videotapes by a process known as digital manipulation. In the process of producing a special documentary on digital manipulation, our technicians, by necessity, developed techniques allowing them to alter existing videotapes.

"When I saw what this new machine was capable of, I was seized by a childish, irresponsible impulse. What if we could take an existing movie, alter it in such a way that Robert Jameson was the star, and show it at his surprise party?''

He shook his head sadly. "As a joke. It was always meant to be a joke."

Bill made a face. "Jesus, I think the guy's going to cry."

"Shush," Karen said.

Stockman again took time to recover. "Before leaving for my vacation, I issued instructions to Marc Krovnik, an employee I've trusted for eight years. I asked him to produce a single copy of this . . . surprise tape, keep it locked up, and give it to me as soon as I returned from Canada. Even though it was meant as a joke, I was aware of the dangers. Unfortunately, I was unaware of the weaknesses of Krovnik's character.

"I've learned that in my absence, Marc Krovnik attempted to use the tape in a mendacious, vicious plan to extort money from my dear friend. As a result of this attempt at extortion, Robert Jameson is dead." Stockman closed his eyes, as if in pain.

"Give me a break"—Bill twisted in his seat—"this guy's acting is over the top."

"Not satisfied with extortion alone," Stockman continued, "Krovnik arranged for another copy of this tape to be sold to the television show *American Exposé*. He used the money gained from that sale to flee the country."

Karen pushed to her feet, balled her hands into fists, her chest heaving, her chin thrust forward. She wanted to put her foot through the television set.

"I've instructed my attorney," Stockman continued, "to contact the FBI and cooperate in every way possible in this investigation. I've also instructed all employees involved in the tape's production to cooperate. But, while others were involved, this tragedy originated with me. I want everyone to know that I accept fully the responsibility for this stupid, unthinking, and careless action.

"To the Jameson family, I express my deepest condolences, my sympathy, and my sincere regrets. I know you can never forgive me, nor will I ever forgive myself."

At that moment, he burst into tears. The camera panned back to anchorman Gobbins, who said, straight faced, "That was a statement from . . ."

Karen, red faced with anger, switched off the television set and turned to Castor.

"Do you believe him?" Bill asked.

She shook her head, too outraged to speak.

"What will you do now?" Bill asked.

She smiled grimly. "The question is, what will *you* do?"

Bill held up his hands. He'd investigated for Karen long enough to predict her instructions. "I know. Find Marc Krovnik."

Karen nodded. "*If* he's still alive."

When Stockman finished, George MacLean turned off the television in the Bureau conference room with a wrench that almost tore off the knob and turned to Benjamin Rose, Stockman's lawyer. Linda Holt said nothing.

"You've got four hours, Rose." MacLean's voice was almost a snarl.

"Excuse me?" the dapper little criminal attorney said.

MacLean pointed his index finger at the man. "I want Stockman here, in this room, within four hours. With his private Lear, that shouldn't be a problem."

Rose shook his head. "I'm afraid that's quite impossible. As you can see, Mr. Stockman is emotionally and physically exhausted. He's under a doctor's care."

"Bullshit—"

"I have a letter here. . . ." Rose opened his alligator-skin attaché case.

MacLean scanned the letter, a notarized doctor's statement attesting to Stockman's severe illness, diagnosed as clinical depression. MacLean recognized the name of the nationally known practitioner and personal physician to the governor of Florida.

"Perhaps in a day or two," Rose said.

"How does Stockman know this Krovnik has left the country?" MacLean asked.

Rose shrugged. "We really didn't have much time to discuss this. As Mr. Stockman said, you are free to talk to anyone involved. I have a list . . ."

MacLean snatched it from the lawyer's hand. "You're a big help, Mr. Rose. Anything else?"

"Only to reaffirm Mr. Stockman's desire to assist you in any way possible. The purpose of his statement is to establish the various levels of responsibility, assess the damages, fix the punishment, and move on."

MacLean glared at the lawyer. "He wants to help? Fine. Depressed or not, you have him here in four hours. I'm depressed. Hell, we're *all* depressed."

"Mr. MacLean—"

"No, you listen. If he's not here, I'll have him arrested."

Rose's face reddened. "As I said to the director—"

"You talked to the director *before* your client announced his responsibility for this so-called joke. Now *I'll* talk to the director. You just get your client here. Four hours. You want to see him dragged in here in handcuffs?"

Rose simply smiled. "You're a fool, MacLean. I say again, talk to your superior before you do something you'll regret."

"You stay here," MacLean said. "I'll do just that."

Linda and Stockman's lawyer waited, without exchanging a word. When MacLean returned ten minutes later, his face was a cold mask, expressing nothing.

"We'll be in touch," was all he said.

Benjamin Rose smiled, bowed dramatically, and left the room.

"The phone is ringing off the hook." Liz stepped into Karen's office. "I've got three people on hold. NBC, Associated Press, and the St. Pete *Times* all called at once. They're asking for a comment from you on Stockman's news conference. I thought you might want to talk to one of them."

. Karen looked at the phone. "Which one is the *Times*?"

"Line three."

"Did the reporter give a name?"

"Dick Ramsey."

Karen picked up the phone and punched a button. "Good afternoon, Dick."

"Any comment on Stockman's statement?"

"Not right now."

"Come on, Karen, you have to give me something. Just a small quote. I'm not asking for the Sermon on the Mount."

Her mind was awhirl. Her initial shock at Stockman's "confession" was buffeted by incredulity, her surprise stoked by outrage. "I'll have a full statement as soon as I've had the opportunity to fully digest Mr. Stockman's remarks. You can say that I'm relieved that those responsible for making that horrible tape have come forward and been identified. It's one small step toward the ultimate goal of clearing my brother's name."

"Can't you give me something more?"

"It'll have to do for now."

"Will you call me once you're ready to make a full statement? Not that you owe me favors, but I have been pretty evenhanded in my stories on you. I'm sure you agree."

"Stockman's announcement came out of left field. Give me a chance to think, will you? As soon as I get a handle on this, I'll talk to you first. Promise."

She hung up the phone to find Liz still waiting. "Is there something else?"

"I watched the special report on the set in the lounge. If Stockman was responsible for making that tape, why would he make his confession in such a public way?"

Karen took a deep breath, held it for a moment, then exhaled. "That's the reaction I'm curious about."

Liz, her expression reflecting her confusion, looked at her.

"You don't see it?" Karen asked.

"Not really."

"Stockman's very, very clever."

"A public confession? That's clever?"

"You bet it is. Even before he's been charged with anything, he's prepared his defense and announced it to the world. Birthday party, my ass."

Karen punched some numbers into the telephone. Linda Holt was unavailable. She slammed down the phone.

"I'd better go see Claire." She leaped to her feet and stormed out of the office.

* * *

Claire was standing by the rear window of the living room, her arms crossed, her gaze resting on the glassy tranquility of Lake Tarpon on a windless day. Karen heard the telephone ringing in a distant room, Ursula answering, then hanging up. The stampede of publicity was starting all over again.

"You saw the broadcast?" Karen asked.

Without turning, Claire uttered a soft, "Yes."

"Stockman's statement is as big a lie as the tape."

"I know. Robert hated surprise parties. None of his real friends would have come, let alone been part of such arrangements. They knew how he felt, knew how he'd walk out the moment it started. His aversion to surprises was one of his few idiosyncrasies, but one he felt strongly about. As soon as I saw that terrible man on television, I knew he was lying."

Smoothing her skirt with shaking hands, she turned from the window. "I called, but Liz said you were already on your way over."

"We'll fight this."

"How?"

"Leave that to me."

Claire offered a wan smile.

"Did Robert ever meet with Stockman?" Karen asked.

"Several times. Stockman was a big contributor to both parties, as well as many individual campaigns. Because his name never appeared on anything, he even managed to chair a fund-raiser for Robert two years ago that raised over a hundred thousand dollars. When Robert found out after the fact, he was livid. He despised the man."

Something flashed in Karen's memory. "But Marie

Morley said Robert had refused to accept money from Stockman. Was she wrong?"

"Robert did refuse to accept money directly. This wasn't Stockman's money. He simply arranged the fund-raiser through intermediaries. Robert needed the money, and he didn't realize at the time it was coming from Stockman's efforts."

"Did Marie know Stockman was involved?"

Claire took a moment to answer. "I don't know. I can't imagine she would have."

Karen let it go. "Did anyone ever discuss a birthday party with you?"

"I arranged all of Robert's birthday parties. Our close friends knew that. He was very fussy about who was invited to our home—but that wasn't general knowledge for obvious reasons. You have to be circumspect in this business."

"But he and Stockman met several times?"

"If you're asking was it possible Stockman was arranging a party, I'd have to say yes. But the moment he started inviting any of Robert's friends, I'm sure Robert would have been told."

Karen nodded. "That's the way I have it figured."

Claire crossed her arms across her breasts as if warding off a chill. "What are you going to do now?"

"First, I'm going to talk with the FBI. They may not be buying Stockman's story either. What happens next depends on their reaction."

Claire sighed and gazed out the window again. "Maybe we should just let it all go."

"You can't really mean that?"

For a moment, Claire didn't answer. Then, very slowly, she shook her head.

"I want to initiate a civil suit aimed at Walter Stockman, his company, and everyone else involved in this," Karen said. "On behalf of you, the twins, and Mother."

Claire pivoted to face her. "A civil suit?"

"A wrongful death suit. Stockman can't be held responsible for Robert's death under criminal statutes, but he can sure as hell be held liable under civil law. I want to bring the suit immediately, before he begins to shift assets, which he is almost certain to do."

"I don't know." Claire wrung her hands. "If we sue, won't that keep this awful story in the press, the public eye, that much longer?"

Claire's reluctance puzzled Karen. "The truth needs to be told, over and over. Besides, Stockman deserves punishment, and hitting him in the pocketbook will be the best punishment in the world."

"But surely, if the FBI can prove Stockman's lying about the tape as a party joke, he'll go to prison."

"Don't count on it. A man of Stockman's influence will not roll over on this. Not for a second. He'll fight to the end, and that can take time. A lot of things can happen between when he's charged and whenever the trial occurs. That's why we need to move fast."

"I'm not sure I want to." Claire moved away from the window, settled gracefully into a brocaded armchair, and lifted her chin in a stubborn way. "I want to get on with my life. Every moment this drags on is agony for me—and particularly for Michael and Richard. Of course, I'm hoping Robert's name will be cleared, but the incessant intrusions, the questions . . . I want them ended."

Her sister-in-law's attitude stunned Karen. "You can't do that. Not yet. You *owe* Robert something, even if he's not here to see it."

"Karen—"

"Hear me out. If the FBI makes their case, it could be years before Stockman faces a jury. *Years*. You'll not escape public interest until that trial is over. As long as you're stuck with this, let's make the best of it and take the offensive. Stockman has the resources to beat the criminal charges, but I doubt he can side-step the civil penalties. You *must* do this, Claire."

The older woman's face, once beautiful and calm, was ravaged by grief and indecision.

Karen pressed her point. "If we sue Stockman for wrongful death, I absolutely affirm he will face a jury. It may take time, but he can't weasel out of it."

Claire was silent for a moment. "Would you handle the suit?"

"Yes. If Mother, Michael, and Richard give me the go-ahead, I'll file tomorrow."

"But—"

"No *buts*, Claire. We move now. I want this bastard crushed. Don't you?"

Again Claire paused. "All right."

"Good girl. I'll get back to you." She started toward the door.

"Karen?"

Karen turned in the foyer and returned to the living room.

Once more, Claire stood with her back to the room, watching the lake. "Any news on the sale of the Virginia house?"

"The broker has shown the house to three prospective buyers, and one's returning tomorrow for another look."

"Good," she said without turning, "the sooner it's off my mind, the better. I can't tell you how grateful I am for your taking care of this."

"I'm happy to help, but I still think selling so quickly is a mistake."

Claire sighed. "It won't be my first."

Not knowing how to reply, Karen left her sister-in-law by the window and let herself out the front door.

Thirteen

Four hours after Stockman's broadcast, Bill Castor showed his ID to the big man sitting behind the paper-strewn desk. "Mind if I take a seat?"

The Reverend Moses Elliot waved a fat hand. "Be my guest."

Once Elliot had been a feared defensive lineman for the Tampa Bay Bucs. Then, after twice testing positive for substance abuse, he'd been banished for a year by the NFL. In a comeback try, he'd torn up a knee, spent two weeks in a hospital and months on crutches.

Claiming to have had a vision while under general anesthesia, he had embraced Christianity with the same fervor he'd once exhibited tackling opposing quarterbacks.

Back on his feet, he'd been ordained a minister and had established a small church in one of Orlando's gamier sections. The church was an abandoned, crumbling warehouse saved from the wrecker's ball by the fast-talking Elliot, who'd managed to convince the aging owner of the building that certain little-known tax advantages accrued to those who worked with minority volunteer organizations. Thus was born the Elliot Drug and Alcohol Rehabilitation Center.

The building still looked like a warehouse with its bare brick walls, but the industrial-style windows gleamed and the concrete floor shone. Flat benches took the place of pews, and the felt-covered altar was fashioned from plywood. More than a church, it was also a day-care center, kindergarten, and a community center where Reverend Elliot did everything from marriage counseling to job training to running four different drug rehab groups—all with minimal government financial assistance. Financial stability had taken years, but donations, once a mere trickle, were now swelling to a steady stream.

Castor pulled a photograph out of his pocket and placed it on the desk. "Know him?"

The reverend nodded.

"Name?"

"Marc Krovnik."

"He was a member here?"

"He *is* a member here."

"When's the last time you saw him?"

Elliot glared at the private investigator for a moment. "He hasn't been to many meetings since the summer. His last one was sometime this past August."

"He seem okay to you then?"

"Sure. Look, I watch TV. I know what this is about."

"Which is?"

"That big shot Stockman is sayin' this tape thing is all Marc's idea. I say that's shine, man. Marc was one of the better ones. He was one of about twenty white folks in all the groups, but it didn't bother him at all. He's educated, real smart, and he's helped a lot of people here, black and white. Didn't matter to him."

Castor smiled. "I think he's been set up, but that's between you and me, okay?"

"Your ID says you're a private dick. Who you workin' for?"

"Senator Jameson's sister. I'm just gathering facts, putting them together with other facts, trying to sort this mess out. Krovnik came here for how long?"

"Five years. Every week without fail. When he wasn't in group, he was helping with the retraining program. He taught about a hundred of our folk how to operate computers. Even taught some how to program. At least fifty of those people are working today, and they owe their jobs to Marc Krovnik."

"Sounds like a great guy."

"He is, man."

Castor unfolded an artist's sketch, one of two Linda Holt had faxed to Karen, and handed it to Elliot. "That look like anyone you know?"

The reverend looked at it for a moment, then laid it on his desk. "No."

"Too bad. Might be one of the people who helped set Marc up."

Elliot picked it up again. "Like how?"

"Two people delivered a package to a New York television production house about a week ago. You're looking at a sketch of one of them. I have another." He took the second sketch and placed it on the desk. "According to Walter Stockman, they had to be working for Marc Krovnik. We don't think so."

Elliot picked up the second sketch. "This one looks familiar."

"Name?"

"Trudy Bellows. And the guy . . . could be Fred Daniels. I'm not sure, mind you. These sketches aren't too good."

"But they could be the ones?"

"It's possible. Both Trudy and Fred were here as part of their probation."

Castor opened his notebook. "You have addresses on them?"

"Not without a warrant."

"I'm sure the FBI will be happy to provide one."

"Think again. This is a church, man."

"Let me put it another way. If Marc Krovnik is being set up, these two may have had something to do with it. And if Marc is as good a guy as you say, you want to help him, don't you?"

The reverend stared at Castor a moment, then started spinning his Rolodex.

The address Elliot had given him was less than twenty blocks from downtown Orlando, but in the worst kind of slum. Abandoned vehicles, stripped of anything remotely valuable, cluttered both sides of the street. On one corner, men, obviously out of work and money, gathered in the parking lot of a convenience store whose sheet glass display windows were covered with iron bars. On another corner, two women beckoned to passing cars, trying to sell the only thing they had left.

Castor brought his car to the curb and stopped. With a cautious survey of the street, he climbed out, locked his car, and activated its burglar alarm. He walked quickly to the ancient motel converted to apartments, approached Number Three, and knocked. No one answered.

He pressed his face against the dirty glass of a window beside the door, but heavy drapery obscured his view. On a hunch, he tried the door, and the knob turned easily in his hand. He pushed the door open.

"Anybody home?"

He had wasted time and energy. The apartment was empty, with no signs of habitation.

Frustrated, he returned to his car and called Karen on his cell phone.

"They're gone. Krovnik and his two sidekicks, Trudy Bellows and Fred Daniels. A friend of Krovnik's ID'd the last two from the sketches of the pair who delivered the tape to *American Exposé*."

"Can you pick up their trail?"

"I'll have to check with the Department of Motor Vehicles to see if they owned cars. And probably every bus, train, and plane out of Orlando for the last month. Maybe rental car agencies, too. Jesus, that could take weeks."

On the other end of the line, Karen was silent for a moment. "Where did Stockman say he'd been the last two weeks?"

"Isolated at his fishing lodge on some lake in northern Canada."

"If you were Stockman and had three people—or bodies—you wanted to hide, what better place?"

Castor smiled. "Finding the exact location of Stockman's lodge should take only a telephone call or two. I'm on my way to the airport as we speak."

"If you find them—alive," Karen said, "talk them into coming back with you. I want to take their depositions *before* the FBI gets hold of them. Tell them I can't represent them—conflict of interest—but I'll find them a damned good defense attorney."

Karen entered the front door with weary steps and dropped her attaché case on the table in the foyer. She had returned to the office after convincing Claire and Richard and Michael to file suit, called her

mother and received her approval to be included in
the suit, dispatched Bill Castor to Canada, and then
put in several long hours catching up on work she'd
neglected since Robert's death.

"Mommy!" Andrea raced down the stairs and
greeted her with a hug that almost knocked her off
her feet. "You're home in time for dinner."

Karen experienced a twinge of guilt. Too often
Rahni fed Andrea alone, and Karen arrived home
only in time to put her daughter to bed. If she went
after Stockman, she'd have even less time to spend
with Andrea and Carl.

And if she didn't, the bastard would probably
walk with little more than a slap on the wrist for his
crimes, a seductive example to others with wealth
and power who aspired to wield their influence and
thwart the democratic process. Her conflicting needs
for time with her family and assuring justice for Robert were tearing her in two.

"How was school?" She returned her daughter's
hug and shoved aside the dilemma that was making
her head ache.

"Cool. We're studying dolphins and whales in science." Andrea skipped ahead of her to the family
room. "And if our grades are good, the teacher will
take us to Sea World next month."

Karen feigned a worried look. "Do you think your
grades will be okay?"

"Oh, Mom," Andrea said with a giggle. "You
know they will. They always are."

Carl turned from the bar as they entered the room
and handed Karen a glass of white wine. "Rahni says
we have time for a drink before dinner."

Karen accepted the glass with a grateful smile,
sank into a comfortable chair, and kicked off her

shoes. "Andrea's class is planning a trip to Sea World."

"Only if we study hard enough," Andrea added.

Carl smiled at their daughter with a warmth that melted Karen's heart. "The park has added some new features since we were there last year. Which reminds me"—he glanced at Karen with a significant lift of his eyebrows—"we're overdue for a family weekend together."

No one spoke of it, but she knew they were all thinking of the visit they'd planned to Robert's to see the fall leaves. They had made the trip to Virginia, but it hadn't been the enjoyable family vacation they'd originally anticipated.

"We'll see." She avoided his gaze. "I'm still behind at work."

Propping her feet on a hassock, she sipped her wine, half listening to the words as Andrea chattered happily about her science project and luxuriating in the sound of her daughter's voice, the sight of Carl's handsome face, and the reassuring warmth of home. Robert's death had been a jolting reminder of how quickly life could change, sweeping away all that one cherished.

Her bittersweet mood lasted through Rahni's delicious curry, after-dinner coffee, and the ritual of Andrea's bedtime. She returned to the family room, where Carl was watching television, a rerun of Stockman's speech, and settled beside him on the sofa.

"What do you think?" she asked when Stockman finished speaking.

Carl shook his head. "As my Italian grandmother would have said, '*Un po di verita rende la menzogna credibile.*' "

With her scant knowledge of Italian, Karen struggled to translate. " 'A little bit of truth makes the whole lie believable?' "

Carl nodded. "Everything's too pat. Too fully explained. Life's not that simple."

"I agree. That tape was *not* simply a stupid joke gone awry. I sense layers upon layers of deception, and it's frustrating not to have the authority or the resources to peel those layers away to expose Stockman for the bastard he is."

"The FBI's investigating."

She clenched her hands into fists. "I feel so powerless. The only information I receive, except from Bill Castor, comes in bits and pieces. Thank God for Linda, or I wouldn't even get that."

"Bringing Stockman down is that important?"

"I'd rather think of it as justice for Robert."

"So you're going ahead with your wrongful death suit?"

Karen hesitated. "The moment I file suit against Stockman, he'll assemble a team of legal luminaries to make the Simpson trials look like minor cases on a small claims docket. I won't go after him unless I intend to win."

Carl smiled. "I sense a *but* in there somewhere."

She nodded. He knew her too well. "I don't want to take that much time away from you and Andrea."

"You'll have a hard time living with yourself if you *don't* go after Stockman."

She looked at him in surprise. "You sound as if you *want* me to sue him."

He grasped her chin and tilted it until their eyes met. "I want you to do what you think is right."

"But you and Andrea—"

"Andrea and I love you, even as totally addicted

to truth, justice, and the American way as you are. We'll be fine."

The ringing of the telephone interrupted their kiss. Carl raised his head and smiled. "It's probably for you. Go ahead. I have to finish writing some reports."

Reluctantly, Karen withdrew from his arms and went to the phone. Linda Holt was on the line.

"You saw Stockman's broadcast?" Linda asked.

"I saw it."

"His attorney must be crazy, letting Stockman make such a confession on national television."

"From what I've learned of Stockman," Karen said, "I doubt he listens to anything his lawyer says. The man's a law unto himself."

"MacLean ordered Stockman's attorney to bring him in for questioning, but Stockman's claiming illness—depression."

Karen grimaced. "What's your take on his statement?"

"I thought he was lying when I first heard it. Now I'm even more convinced."

"Why?"

"Earlier this evening, I reinterviewed Senators Graham Woolsley and Patrick O'Halloran."

"The ones who were helping Robert draft the bill on CEO compensation?"

"Right," Linda said. "Neither of them mentioned Robert's surprise party when I first questioned them, but tonight they both claim Stockman called them the middle of last month and invited them. They didn't tell me before, they said, because they didn't think it was important."

"Are they on the level?"

Linda snorted in disgust. "I've been in this business long enough to recognize lying when I hear it. Stockman got to them. They both claim that because Robert was the driving force behind the bill, it's now a dead issue."

"Aside from gut instinct, do you have any proof?"

"No, but I'm not through with Woolsley and O'Halloran yet. When I asked if they'd had any dealings with Benjamin Rose, Stockman's attorney, they both looked guilty as hell and claimed their conversations with Rose are privileged."

"Claire doubts there *was* a party planned, that if any of Robert's close friends had known about it, they would have warned him. He hated surprises."

"Stockman may be in for a few surprises of his own. MacLean's ready to chew him up and spit him out."

"Good," Karen said. "A more aggressive FBI investigation can't hurt. Right after the Stockman telecast, Bill Castor left to locate Marc Krovnik."

"Krovnik. Now there's a man I'd like to talk to. Our agents are looking for him, too."

"If Bill finds him, I'll let you know."

At nine the next morning, Karen walked into Brander Hewitt's office, the most sumptuous of four corner offices on the top floor of the stainless-steel-and-glass, five-story building on Highway 19 near Countryside Mall. With over six hundred square feet of space, the office faced north and west, both directions visible through walls of plate glass. Another wall boasted a large Jackson Pollack print, and the fourth held a multitude of diplomas, certificates, and awards given the firm for its philanthropic efforts. Brander, as venerable head of the partnership, believed that law firms should be part of the community, and he often put his money where his mouth was. Karen hoped he was feeling philanthropic today.

The senior partner greeted her with a warm smile and motioned for her to have a seat. "Coffee?"

"No, thanks." Her stomach was already churning. Any added acid would eat through the walls. "I want to talk with you about a suit I intend to file."

Brander's raised eyebrows spoke volumes. The majority of Karen's work with the firm had been criminal defense. She hadn't filed a civil suit in over three years.

"The plaintiff?" Brander asked.

"The estate of Robert Jameson."

"You're going after Stockman."

"If he'd done this to your family, wouldn't you?"

"In a heartbeat."

Encouraged, Karen pressed ahead. "I'll ask for both compensatory and punitive damages."

"On what grounds?"

"Having that tape produced was both wanton and reckless. Even without the blackmail threat, the tape, if released, could have destroyed Robert's career. Point in fact, it drove him to suicide."

"It's a straightforward charge"—Brander steepled his well-manicured hands on his desk— "so I take it you didn't come to me for advice."

"I may need your counsel before this is over. I *have* to win this case, for my brother's memory and for his family. It's going to take months of preparation, and the trial itself could last almost as long."

"Any other major cases on your calendar now?"

She shook her head. "But time is only part of the issue."

He sat silently, waiting for her to continue.

She took a deep breath and plunged on. "I can't accept a fee for this. And if I don't get paid, neither does the firm."

She waited for his reaction, but he gave none.

"If you want me to resign—"

"Don't be ridiculous. You're the best rainmaker we have. Take whatever time you need. And as many associates."

"But the cost—"

"Don't worry about the cost." He smiled. "At the risk of sounding crass, the publicity alone will be worth millions to the firm." His expression sobered. "And that same limelight will put an inordinate amount of pressure on you."

Karen stood. "I work best under pressure."

"The full resources of the firm are at your disposal." He rose from his chair, and his grin returned. "Walter Stockman never should have messed with Karen Perry-Mondori's family. When you get through with the media mogul, he won't know what hit him."

Karen thanked him with a hug, returned to her office, and buzzed Liz on the intercom. "Bring your notebook."

Liz hurried in, flipped open her stenographer's pad, and poised her pencil above the page. "A letter?"

"A civil suit."

Liz nodded, waiting.

"Against Walter Stockman for the wrongful death of Senator Robert Jameson."

Liz almost dropped her pencil.

"Ready?" Karen asked.

At Liz's nod, she dictated the complaint.

Liz scribbled furiously. "Got it."

"Now the allegations," Karen said with grim satisfaction. "Walter Stockman did with wanton and reckless disregard order the production of a computer-manipulated videotape falsely portraying the late Senator Robert Jameson committing the felonious act of sexual intercourse with a minor. Stockman was conscious of this order and had knowledge of circumstances and conditions that this videotape would naturally and probably result in injury to Robert Jameson, and . . ."

Liz kept pace with Karen's rapid dictation.

"How soon can you have that typed and ready?" Karen asked when she'd finished.

"Within the hour."

"Good. Call the courier. I want this filed today with the circuit court here in Pinellas. And schedule a process server."

"You want the papers served on Stockman personally?"

"No telling where he'll be. The FBI wants him in Washington for questioning. Have them served to Stockman's residence and to his corporate offices in Orlando."

Liz started to leave, then stopped at the door. "Don't you feel a bit like David facing Goliath?"

"Yeah," Karen said, grinning, "except this David has a hell of a stone in her slingshot."

"Stone?"

"Stockman's personal confession, broadcast nationwide to millions of witnesses. Due to the man's unspeakable arrogance, he's practically handed me a liable verdict on a platter."

Bill Castor consulted the map clipped to the jiggling instrument panel of the noisy de Havilland DHC-2 Beaver. Frank Walsingham, the pilot, had told him he'd purchased the aircraft from the Royal Cana-

dian Mounted Police after its thirty-three years of
service with them. It was showing signs of age.

From the map, Castor recognized the outline three
thousand feet below as that of the southern end of
Knife Lake, as Walsingham cut his throttle back
twenty percent. Once the airspeed slowed to one
hundred knots, he gave the flaps fifteen percent and
dropped the nose. The aircraft began its slow descent
to the snow-covered frozen lake.

Three minutes later, flaps fully extended, a slight
flare-out at sixty knots, and the skis kissed the snow,
throwing up a rooster tail of white powder. Walsingham immediately shoved the throttle forward to
full and jerked the plane back into the sky. He circled
at less than a hundred feet while he examined the
spot where the plane had touched the snow-covered ice.

"No evidence of cracking," he explained to Castor,
"which means the ice is strong enough to support the
plane. At this time of year, one can never be sure."

Walsingham brought the plane around and landed
again, this time chopping the throttle at touchdown.
The plane quickly shuddered to a crawl. The pilot
taxied toward a large cabin some five hundred yards
away, where a thin candle of smoke rose from the
chimney.

"Looks like somebody's here," Castor said.

"Could be anybody," Walsingham said. "In this
isolated area, cabins, often fifty or more miles apart,
are rarely locked. There's little point in safety mea-
sures. Experienced owners try not to leave anything
behind worth stealing. Often roving bands of Indians,
laying or checking traps, use a cabin as a place to
rest or warm up. They usually leave the cabins just as
they found them, although occasionally, they don't."

Walsingham seemed pleased someone was using Stockman's cabin. "If these Indians are regular trappers, they'll have the answers to most of your questions."

The pilot killed the Beaver's engine, opened the door, and climbed to the ground. Castor followed.

"Usually, at this time of year," Walsingham said, "the howling north winds would take your breath away, but there's no wind today."

Castor nodded. The temperature was about fifteen degrees above zero, but the absence of wind made it feel like a spring day. With less than six inches of snow on the ground, they'd left the snowshoes on board.

He felt the snow crunch beneath his heavy boots as they made their way toward the cabin. The door of the cabin opened, and a white man stood in the doorway, a rifle poised at his shoulder and pointed straight at them.

Slowly, Castor and Walsingham raised their hands.

Fourteen

George MacLean looked down at a few errant coffee grounds floating in the remains of his coffee, considered a refill, then discarded the idea. He'd already consumed six cups, and his nerves were starting to protest. He placed the china cup and saucer on a small table next to his green leather chair and waited.

United States Attorney Raymond Logan, tall and portly with a florid complexion and deeply hooded eyes, finished reading the blue-covered report MacLean had prepared, sighed, then gently placed the report on his desk. He leaned back in his chair, clasped his hands over his ample stomach, and stared at the ceiling. "Once we've talked to Stockman, I'll be in a better position to make a judgment."

MacLean looked at his watch. Stockman and Rose were due in his office in a half hour. "Stockman's not about to change his story. He had Rose contact the director before he went public. That's some clout, Ray."

Logan's eyebrows shot up. "That's not in your report."

MacLean gave him a sour look. "Get serious."

"So what did the director have to say about this case?"

"He wants to wait until we have more."

Logan smiled. "Well?"

"I think you're both wrong. This can fester like a boil if we don't get the facts out immediately. Waiting allows falsehoods to take root and grow. Eventually, no matter what the evidence, no one will listen to the truth."

"And what exactly *is* the truth?"

MacLean hesitated. "Stockman made the tape all right, but his story is a crock. I'm convinced he was trying to pressure Jameson and other senators to back off on a piece of legislation Stockman didn't like. This isn't just hardball lobbying, it's criminal behavior. This tale of a so-called surprise party is pure baloney, made up solely to cover his ass."

"What makes you so sure?"

MacLean pointed to the report. "It's right there in Part Three. The two senators Holt talked to last night have stated they were in on the party plans, excluding knowledge of the phony tape. But when Holt spoke to them the first time, *before* Stockman's announcement, they knew of no such plans. Both claim their failure to mention it during the first interviews was simple oversight, but both men were supporting Jameson's planned legislation, which seems to be stalled at the moment. A little too convenient, wouldn't you say?"

Logan shook his head. "You're reading things that aren't there. There's no evidence they're lying."

"Stockman must be blackmailing them as well."

Logan shook his head again. "You have no evidence."

"If I'm to get the evidence we need, I have to shake some trees. Charging Stockman under the RICO statutes leaves the senators facing a conspiracy rap. It's just the kind of leverage I need."

Logan frowned. "No way, George. The minute we charge Stockman with a felony, we're committed to follow through. I'm not ready for that yet. You want to use charges as a sledgehammer. Rose won't stand for it. Neither will the grand jury. They'll never indict on what you have at the moment, and you know it. If I charge Stockman on anything, it will have to be based on his statement, and, at this time, it looks very much like a simple misdemeanor. Until you prove probable cause and clear intent, I can't turn you loose."

"Probable cause? The man admitted he did it on national television!"

"I mean probable cause for malicious intent, conspiracy, and the RICO deal. You know that."

"That's for a jury to decide," MacLean said.

"The hell it is."

MacLean stood up, fighting his building anger.

"I'm with you on one thing, though," Logan said.

"Yeah? What's that?"

"I don't think Stockman's story will change. Why should it?"

MacLean held his tongue. He simply glared.

Logan glared back. "I'll do this much. I'll talk to a judge about getting you a warrant to check the telephone records of Stockman, his company, Krovnik, and the others. You can also look at bank records. But that's as far as I'll go right now."

MacLean suppressed a smile. Long ago, he'd learned how to deal with Raymond Logan. Ask for the moon, then settle for less. Logan was an expert at compromise.

So was MacLean. "I appreciate it."

Logan tapped the report on his desk. "Interesting

guy, this Krovnik who made the tape. Have you checked out the material Holt got from Kendall?''

"The security guy? Yes, we've checked it out. Krovnik worked for the CIA as an electronics specialist until he was canned for drug abuse. He was considered a bright guy, but he developed a taste for cocaine. He hooked on with Stockman five years ago, right after he was sacked by the CIA. That's one of the reasons I think this was a setup."

Logan smiled. "You're getting paranoid, aren't you. Maybe you should start smoking again."

"Maybe. Look . . . Stockman was in Las Vegas on October second when Jameson was there, and Krovnik was with him. Doesn't it strike you as odd that the people who delivered the tape were supposed to have been from Vegas?"

"Krovnik could have cooked that up without Stockman's knowledge. Don't forget, the tape was delivered while Stockman was out of the country. So far, there's nothing to indicate Stockman is lying. All you have is suspicion.

"Bellows and Daniels were in a rehab program with Krovnik. And Krovnik, being a computer expert, hacked his way into some database in Vegas, looking for people as covers for Bellows and Daniels. Both have criminal records, so he either conned them or paid them to deliver the tape to *American Exposé*. Nothing ties Bellows or Daniels to Stockman."

"Maybe you're right, but I still say the people to pressure are Senators O'Halloran and Woolsley. If they were blackmailed by Stockman, we've got our case."

"Forget it." Logan shook his head. "You don't really listen very well."

* * *

Karen slogged through the avalanche of accumulated paperwork on her desk. This afternoon, once they had received notification of her suit, Stockman and his attorney had twenty days to respond. If she worked more overtime, she could have her desk cleared by then.

Her intercom buzzed.

"Linda Holt on one," Liz announced, and Karen picked up the phone.

"Thought I'd bring you up to speed on the latest," Linda said.

"Glad you called. I have some news of my own. But you first."

"Stockman came in with Rose earlier today to give his official statement to George MacLean," Linda said.

"And?"

"It was essentially the same thing he said on television."

Karen frowned. "You should have polygraphed him."

"U.S. Attorney Raymond Logan suggested it, and Stockman agreed, until Rose reminded him that as part of his physician's treatment, Stockman's taking Inderal."

"Why am I not surprised?" Karen said. Inderal was one of several drugs that negated polygraph test results.

"We're in the process of seizing Stockman's and Krovnik's bank and phone records. Unless we find something there, Logan is reluctant to charge that Stockman's committed *any* crime."

"That's what I was afraid of." Karen told her about the civil suit she'd filed against Stockman. "He may not serve time, but I intend to wring millions out of him in punitive damages.''

''Don't think we've given up on the criminal case. A world-wide alert is out for Krovnik, Bellows, and Daniels. Their statements could provide the proof we need.''

''In the meantime,'' Karen said, ''Stockman is using millions of dollars worth of air time, showing himself as a caring, loving man now devastated by angst—a victim himself of nothing more insidious than a temporary lapse in judgment.''

''Won't do him any good if we find the proof we need to charge him.''

''Oh no?'' Karen said, ironically. ''With the breadth of UCN's viewership, he's preconditioning prospective jurors.''

''Contrary to what Stockman thinks,'' Linda said with a laugh, ''not everybody watches UCN.''

''Who the hell are you?'' the man in the cabin doorway demanded. Castor recognized Fred Daniels from the FBI sketch.

''Frank Walsingham. I'm a bush pilot.''

''And him?''

''Bill Castor.''

''What do you want?''

Bill lowered his hands. ''I'm here to check out a cabin I might want to rent, a place belonging to Walter Stockman. That you?''

''He's back in the States. Why don't you turn around and get the hell out of here?''

''That's fine with me,'' Walsingham turned and started toward the plane. Bill held his ground.

''Hold it!'' a voice cried from within the cabin.

Walsingham stopped in his tracks.

"Take off your parkas," the voice ordered, "and if you have any weapons, drop 'em."

The men slowly did as instructed.

"All right," the voice commanded, "walk this way . . . real slow."

Castor, heart pounding, did as instructed. Soon he and Walsingham were inside the cabin, staring into the eyes of two men and a woman. Marc Krovnik and Trudy Bellows, looking leaner and meaner than their sketches, joined Daniels, who continued to train a high-powered rifle at the new arrivals.

"So, what's your interest in Stockman?" Krovnik asked.

"I'm just checking his cabin," Castor said. "Look, why don't we discuss the situation?"

"What situation?" Trudy asked.

Bill shrugged. "I don't know who you are or what you're doing here, but at the moment, you're not in serious trouble. You take this further, and you will be."

As he talked, he studied their eyes. With two decades of experience under his belt, Castor was a keen judge of character. But his skill wasn't just from experience. He had a natural gift. Some special training had enhanced his ability to distinguish those dangerously violent from those not. In his line of work, he dealt with some of the wildest, craziest, most violent men and women found anywhere, and he'd done it well. He prided himself on his ability to make quick judgments on potential danger.

These three looked nonviolent. In fact, if anything, they looked confused and more than a little afraid. He reasoned the best course of action was to remain calm, appear nonthreatening, and see what developed.

He chose his words carefully. "Why don't you tell me what you're doing here?"

"Why don't you shut the fuck up?" Daniels answered.

"Okay, if that's what you want, but time is ticking away. I have to report to the RCMP office in Winnipeg pretty soon. They knew we were headed here, and if they come up here and find us dead or injured, they'll hunt you down. They're real good at that, believe me."

"And you," Walsingham told them, "you're a hundred miles from the nearest village."

With a relaxed smile, Castor leaned against the back of a chair. "Maybe we can solve this problem, okay?"

He kept it up, a steady stream of chatter, for almost half an hour. He smiled as he talked, made jokes, asked innocuous questions, and acted as if all was right with the world. It wasn't. A rifle was always pointed in his direction, even while his three captors held whispered discussions among themselves, then addressed him and Walsingham with emotions ranging from simple curiosity to outright hostility.

Walsingham kept quiet, letting Castor call the shots.

Still, the private investigator held to his judgment that these were nonviolent people and, while wary, he experienced far less fear than in other situations. Now, after another of those whispered discussions, Krovnik sat down in a chair facing Castor and the pilot. "If we agree to surrender, what happens?"

"I can't say for sure," Castor said. "I'm not going to bullshit you. But I can see you're not killers. Whatever you're facing, it can't be too bad."

"We're not killers."

"I didn't think so. What was it? Bank robbery?"

For the first time, Krovnik laughed. "Nothing that mundane. You know Walter Stockman owns this cabin, right?"

Castor nodded. "He's a big man back in the States."

"Very big," Krovnik agreed. "I work for him. I did a job for him. Something illegal. Not murder, nothing like that, but I know what I did was illegal. So does he. The thing is, he's a big man, and I'm nothing. I don't know what the charge will be, but I know I'll be the one taking the fall. My friends, too."

Bill pursed his lips for a moment. "Look, why don't we start by getting rid of the rifle? I think better when I'm not worried about a bullet coming my way."

After some hesitation, Krovnik turned to Daniels and motioned for him to put the rifle down. Bill sighed with relief. "Thanks."

"Don't make me regret doing that."

"I won't. Why don't we start by you telling me your names." Castor stuck out his hand.

"Marc Krovnik," the leader said, shaking Castor's hand. In turn, Daniels and Trudy Bellows introduced themselves.

"Much better," Bill said. "Okay, what do you mean, you don't know what the charge will be?"

"Just what I said," Krovnik replied. "You know about the Stockman case?"

"A little."

"Like what?"

Bill rubbed his chin and pretended to ponder the question. "Well, this Stockman fellow made some sort of fake pornographic video involving a U.S. senator. There was something about extortion, if I remember."

"You musta heard about this deal?"

"Like I said, I did. The senator killed himself after seeing the tape. Stockman claims it was a gag, and that one of his employees was responsible for the extortion. You must be the missing employee, right?"

"That's me. But the tape was no gag. It was Stockman's idea to use it as extortion from the start."

Bill nodded. "I get the picture. What you're really worried about is whether the cops will believe you or your boss, right?"

"Exactly."

"Stockman set you up?"

"I didn't think so at the time. I'm still not sure. But the idea is growing on me."

"Care to explain that?"

Krovnik took a deep breath. "I figure there's got to be a way for me to make a deal with the FBI."

"I'm sure there is. Look, I want to level with you. I'm a private investigator, working for Karen Perry-Mondori, the late senator's sister. She's an attorney who'd like nothing better than to fry Stockman's bacon for the death of her brother. If she tells the FBI that you cooperated with us, it'll carry some serious weight."

"What about the fact you've been our prisoner?"

"Nobody has to know that. Fact is, you did put the gun down. If you were going to harm me, it would have happened already. Come on, let's talk about this setup."

Krovnik relaxed visibly, and his friends slid into chairs on either side of him.

"It happened like this," Krovnik began.

*   *   *

The afternoon after her conversation with Linda Holt, Karen was concluding the paperwork on a plea bargain for John Farrow, the drug dealer whose trial had ended in a mistrial the day Robert had died.

Liz buzzed her on the intercom. "Bill Castor's on the phone."

Karen picked up the receiver. "Bill, any luck?"

"I'm en route now with Krovnik, Bellows, and Daniels. We'll arrive at your office in two hours."

"You found them!"

"Right where you said, Stockman's cabin at Knife Lake in Manitoba. Stockman, obviously, never figured we'd look there."

"What did you find out from Krovnik?"

"Not much."

"Will he talk?"

"I think so. He's bright, like everybody says. He wants to make a deal with the FBI before he talks to them. He told me enough to make things interesting."

"Like?"

"He says he can prove sending the blackmail tape to your brother and the copy to *American Exposé* was Stockman's idea. That's where you come in."

"Me?"

"Call Linda Holt in Washington and ask her to have communications set up a low-wave transceiver and tune it to three hundred and forty cycles."

"You mean megahertz."

"No. Krovnik says this is very low wave."

"Low wave? It's subterranean. And who is Linda going to talk to?"

"This is the good part," he said. "Krovnik and Stockman are going to have a conversation at midnight, and the FBI get to listen in."

Karen's jaw dropped. "Stockman and Krovnik have been in contact all this time?"

"You got it." She could almost picture his boyish grin. "I left my car at the Orlando airport, so can somebody pick us up at TIA?"

Karen scribbled his arrival time. "Not just somebody. Deland Jackson has agreed to represent Krovnik and company if we ever found them. I'll have him meet you with a limo. He can confer with his clients on the way here."

"And I'll book them return flights to Washington before we leave the airport," he said.

"Great work," Karen said. "I knew I could count on you."

Fifteen

They were a sorry-looking lot. Krovnik and Daniels sported a week's growth of beard, and the fatigues they all wore were stained and filthy. Trudy Bellows looked the worst. Her long black hair was matted, partially covering her unattractive face. They all smelled in need of a bath.

They sat at the table in the conference room, looked at one another, then at Karen. They seemed relieved to be back in civilization.

Marc Krovnik looked Slavic, with a bony face and wide mouth. His scruffy brown hair was pulled back in a ponytail and tied with a rubber band. He was desperately thin, and his gauntness gave added sharpness to his features and accented his deep-set eyes. For a moment, Karen thought of photos she'd seen of Holocaust victims.

Deland Jackson, white-haired and distinguished in his Armani suit, looked out of place alongside his clients. A sixth person was also present, a court stenographer, her fingers poised above the keys.

Karen made short work of the preliminaries and got right down to business. After Bellows and Daniels left the room, she began with Krovnik.

"Who is your employer?"

"Walter Stockman, president and CEO of United Cable Network."

"And how did you come to be hired by Mr. Stockman?"

"He looked me up after I was fired from my computer job at the CIA."

"Why were you fired?"

Krovnik looked to Jackson, who inclined his head.

"For substance abuse," Krovnik said, "but I'm clean now. Until recently, I attended regular group sessions with the Reverend Moses Elliot. He'll vouch for me."

Karen nodded. "When you worked for UCN, where did you live?"

"In a small apartment on the other side of Orlando, in Altamonte Springs."

"And what was the nature of your work for Mr. Stockman?"

"I developed in-house computer programs for graphics."

"Is that all?"

"I also developed computerized switching equipment for UCN's satellite uplinks."

"Anything else?"

"A compression system for videotaped movies."

"What's that?"

"It allows a ninety-minute movie to be shown in eighty. Nothing of the original is lost. It's used by the network to eliminate cutting classic movies to fit a certain time slot—"

"Did you ever digitally manipulate preexisting film?"

"Yes."

Karen despised Krovnik for what he'd done, but she despised Stockman more. If Krovnik could give her what she needed to nail Stockman's hide to the door, she'd at least be civil to the man. She kept her voice level. "Were you involved in the production of a videotape which depicts Senator Robert Jameson having sexual intercourse with a minor?"

Krovnik looked uncomfortable. "Yes."

"Will you tell us the circumstances surrounding the production of that video."

"On September twenty-ninth, Stockman brought me a pornographic video and several videotapes of Senator Jameson's speeches. He instructed me to remove the European actor from the film and replace him with a digitally manipulated image of Senator Jameson."

"In his televised statement, Mr. Stockman said the video was made as a joke—"

"That's bullshit!" Krovnik started to say more, until he saw Jackson shake his head.

"Did you agree to make the tape?"

"Yeah. What choice did I have? He said if I didn't, I would face certain arrest on drug-trafficking charges."

"Were you involved in drug trafficking?"

"No, but Stockman would have no trouble cooking up evidence and witnesses to set me up."

"Did Mr. Stockman say why he wanted you to produce this video?"

Krovnik checked for Jackson's approval before he answered. "Stockman planned to use the tape for extortion, for blackmail."

"How do you know that?"

"Stockman said so when he viewed the finished tape. He laughed and rubbed his hands together. 'This will put the squeeze on Robert Jameson,' he said."

"Did Mr. Stockman ever specify what that squeeze would be?"

"No. I figured it was money, judging by the message he asked me to insert on the video."

"What message was that?"

"For Jameson to pay a million bucks to stop the tape from being made public."

"Were you paid to produce this tape?"

Krovnik snorted. "Are you kidding? Stockman's as cheap as they come. Said it was part of my regular job, covered in my weekly salary."

"How much salary did Mr. Stockman pay you?"

"Fifty-five thousand dollars a year."

"Did Mr. Stockman give you any other instructions concerning this video of Senator Jameson?"

"He asked me to find two people, a man and a woman, to deliver a copy of the tape to *American Exposé* studios in New York."

"Did you do as he asked?"

"Yeah, I asked Trudy Bellows and Frank Daniels from my rehab group."

"Did they agree?"

"Yes."

"So they worked for you?"

"Yeah, they never met Stockman until we all three joined him at Knife Lake."

"Bellows and Daniels identified themselves to the television producers at *American Exposé* as two employees of the Golden Eagle Casino in Las Vegas. Do you know anything about those false identities?"

Krovnik nodded. "On October second, I accompanied Walter Stockman to an electronics convention in Vegas. He asked me to hack into the casino's computer system. I bribed an employee for his password, gained access, and lifted the personnel records of two employees. Trudy and Frank used the info as their covers."

Karen glanced down the list of questions she had hurriedly assembled while waiting for Castor and the trio to arrive. If Krovnik, Bellows, and Daniels were to make the evening plane to D.C. as she'd promised Linda, she'd have to move faster.

"Where have you been living the last few weeks, Mr. Krovnik?"

"At Walter Stockman's fishing lodge on Knife Lake, outside Winnipeg in Manitoba, Canada."

"And why were you living there?"

"Mr. Stockman ordered me to join him there after he learned of Senator Jameson's suicide."

"What date was that?"

"October twenty-fifth, the same day the senator shot himself."

"How did you communicate with Mr. Stockman?"

"There's a radio transceiver in the cabin, and one at Stockman's studio."

"Did Mr. Stockman say why your coming to Canada was necessary?"

"Yeah. He hadn't figured Jameson would kill himself or that any of this would come out. He wanted Trudy, Frank, and me to take the rap for the extortion and disappear. When I learned the senator had killed himself—"

His attorney placed his hand on Krovnik's arm. "Just answer the questions."

Krovnik shook off his hand. "No, man, I want this on the record. After the senator's death, I radioed Stockman and told him Jameson was dead. Said I wanted to cancel plans for Trudy and Frank to deliver the tapes to *American Exposé.*"

"What was Stockman's response?" Karen asked.

"He threatened to have me arrested for drug charges if we didn't carry out his plan."

"How long did you plan to stay at Mr. Stockman's lodge?"

"Stockman said that after things settled down, he'd give us money and arrange for us to go to South America."

"For how long?"

"He said he'd give us enough money to live there comfortably the rest of our lives."

"And you were willing to do that?

"What choice did we have? If we came back to the States and Stockman set the feds on us, it would be just our word against his. And Stockman has powerful friends. We didn't want to risk it."

"Why did you decide to leave Knife Lake today and return to the States?"

"When this private eye, Bill Castor, showed up and said he was looking for us—or our bodies, it made me think. There we were in the middle of nowhere, and nobody except Stockman knew we were there. Made me nervous."

"Nervous. Why?"

"Stockman's a pragmatist. Does whatever it takes to get the job done and keep his nose clean. If that meant having the three of us whacked and buried in the Canadian wilderness, I don't think the guy would hesitate. I'd rather take my chances with the FBI."

Karen thanked Krovnik for his testimony. An hour later, she had deposed Bellows and Daniels as well. They both corroborated Krovnik's testimony and each other's. When the depositions were over, Deland Jackson stood and shook Karen's hand. "I'll be accompanying my clients to Washington to turn themselves in to the FBI. I'll ask for immunity in return for their testimony."

"Do you think they'll get it?" Karen asked.

Jackson flashed a restrained smile. "Will the FBI give up three small fish to snag a shark? What do you think, Counselor?"

"I believe things will go their way as long as Krovnik plays the ace up his sleeve."

"I don't follow you."

"At midnight, he can reel in Walter Stockman for them—on a radio antenna."

At eleven-thirty P.M., Deland Jackson sat with Marc Krovnik in an FBI conference room across the table from George MacLean and Linda Holt. A stenographic machine operator was also present.

"Before we proceed," MacLean said, "I want to advise you of your rights once more—"

"Mr. Krovnik is aware of his rights," Jackson said. "I want full immunity for all three of my clients. If you guarantee them immunity from prosecution, they'll tell you everything. Otherwise, they have nothing to say."

MacLean leaned forward. "We can't guarantee immunity until we know what you've got."

"Enough to expose Walter Stockman," Jackson said.

"Maybe you do, maybe you don't," MacLean countered. "Your word alone isn't good enough. You'll have to give me something."

Jackson nodded to Krovnik.

Krovnik looked at his watch. "Stockman will be trying to contact me in less than thirty minutes. That conversation should convince you."

"But," Jackson said quickly, "my client won't talk to him until he has your guarantee."

"I can't do that," MacLean said.

Jackson lifted distinguished white eyebrows. "Why not?"

"Because a man died. Stockman may have been the instigator of this, but your clients were certainly involved. According to Ms. Perry-Mondori, they knew what they were doing."

Krovnik made a face. "Let's not bullshit each other. You give cold-blooded murderers immunity when they turn on somebody more important. We didn't kill anybody. What you've got here is Stockman buying politicians, plain and simple. The ones he can't buy, he finds other ways to make them do things his way. That's what this is all about."

"So you say," MacLean said tersely.

"Senator Jameson killed himself," Krovnik said. "If I keep quiet, I may end up with jail time or I may not. If I talk, you can lock Stockman up. Do you really want to piss away an opportunity like this?"

MacLean spread his hands on the table. "You do the radio thing, and if I think that little bit of evidence is strong enough, I'll take your request to my superiors."

"Not good enough," Jackson said, checking his watch. "The meter is running."

"Mr. Krovnik," Linda said, "you're well aware of the situation you're in, and it's not to your liking. You made the decision to cooperate when you allowed Bill Castor to fly you back to Florida and then agreed to turn yourself in to the Bureau. Why not stick with your decision? You know what you really want."

"What's that?"

"An end to this mess. From everything I've heard, you're a pretty decent guy. We're not after your hide. We just want to know what went on, so we can assess blame properly and put this thing to rest."

Krovnik, obviously exhausted, rubbed his eyes, then glanced at Jackson.

"It's your call," Jackson said.

Krovnik nodded.

MacLean stood up. "We have the radio setup ready. Let's go to the communications room and see what happens."

At midnight, Krovnik pressed the button at the base of the microphone stand and leaned forward. "This is Tony. You read me? Over."

The only answer was a rush of dead air. Krovnik repeated the message, using the code name Stockman had given him. Then a voice boomed over the speaker mounted in the console. "Go ahead, Tony."

MacLean squeezed Krovnik's arm. "That's him?"

"That's him."

"Okay, go."

"Tony here. What's new?"

"Nothing," was the answer. "Just keep sitting tight."

"It's cold as hell up here. We've been talking it over. I don't think we can take much more of this weather. We want to come out now."

"No way. You sit tight. In two weeks, this will all be over. There's plenty of food and water. Lots of wood for the fire. Read some books."

"I've been reading until my eyes are about to fall out. I'm serious. We want out now. We talked about it and we're all agreed."

There was a pause. "You listen to me. Everything

is going according to plan. Don't screw it up now. The minute's up. That's all we can afford to take. Sit tight. This is the biggest break of your life and you know it."

Krovnik looked at MacLean. "You got enough?"

"Okay, sign off. Tell him you'll call him again tomorrow."

"We'll give it some thought," Krovnik said into the mike. "I'll call you tomorrow. Over."

There was a click, then nothing but the quiet rush. Jackson turned to MacLean. "Well?"

"I'll let you know as soon as we've done a stress analysis of the tape. If that was Stockman, your clients have their immunity."

Krovnik's bony face broke into a wide grin.

It was after two in the morning when Karen undressed for bed after waiting up for Linda's call. Strangely, her earlier weariness was gone, and she rode an adrenaline high. Through hard work and some luck, the evidence against Walter Stockman was building to its inevitable conclusion. According to Linda, FBI agents were on their way to arrest him for extortion, conspiracy, and eight other charges. Other agents were in the process of getting warrants for the arrest of Senators O'Halloran and Woolsley.

Linda had said nothing would be given to the press until ten the next morning, at which time she and George MacLean would participate in a news conference that was bound to be the lead item in every television news program in the country.

Karen climbed into bed and slid against Carl, molding herself to his back as he slept on his side. She fell asleep, smiling, wondering how UCN would handle the story.

Sixteen

A week after the FBI arrested Stockman and Senators Woolsley and O'Halloran, Karen met Linda Holt for lunch at a restaurant on the Tampa Causeway that overlooked Tampa Bay and the Howard Franklin Bridge.

They ordered no wine or drinks, just small salads. The waiter hovered, and the room buzzed with conversation. A few evidently identified the women from their appearances on news broadcasts. Some nodded in recognition and smiled knowingly, as if to express their good wishes. Karen, used to the local spotlight, didn't mind, but Linda seemed to find the lack of anonymity unsettling.

Aware of potential eavesdroppers, Karen kept her voice low. "Funny, the anger is still there, but now I think that Stockman will receive more than a slap on the wrist. The entire Justice Department took off the gloves on this one."

"Where do you stand with your suit?"

"Stockman's been served, and I intend to hit him as hard as I can. Where do the federal charges stand?"

"We go to the grand jury next week," Linda said. "I can't discuss the details, but I think you'll be pleased with the outcome."

"All things are possible when the pressure comes from the real power, right?"

"That's the sad reality." Linda picked at her salad as if she'd lost her appetite. "Six bills are being pushed through various Congressional committees at the speed of light, all of them a direct result of this case."

"Knee-jerk legislation?"

Linda nodded. "Bills to license and regulate video-production equipment, fund the regulatory agencies involved, appropriate additional funds for research, and a couple of others that'll probably make you cry."

Karen paused with her fork in midair. "Cry?"

"One bill makes it a federal crime—a felony at that—to publish, display, reproduce, or otherwise allow to be seen outside a court of law any photograph, video, or film, of any member of the Administration, Congress, or member of the Supreme Court engaged in any felonious act. The penalty is five years in federal prison."

Karen didn't cry. She laughed, long and hard. They both did, so much that people at surrounding tables began to stare.

Karen wiped her eyes and shook her head. "Wait until the Supreme Court gets their hands on that one. Talk about a conflict of interest."

"Can you believe it?" The humor appeared to restore Linda's appetite, and she dug into her salad.

"Politicians," Karen said, "are mighty resourceful when it comes to protecting themselves. You think that bill will get out of committee?"

Linda laughed again. "Who knows? No matter. Once the story comes out, the fur will fly. Maybe public outrage will be strong enough to make a difference."

"Don't count on it." Karen scowled so strongly the waiter hurried over to inquire about her meal. She waved him away.

"You don't think the public cares?" Linda asked.

"The public has known about Washington, either factually or instinctively, for decades. They've been told often enough what goes on, but they shrug or wring their hands and moan, 'What can I do?' They *could* do a lot, but they're too damn lazy. They'd rather sit back and let someone else do the work. In the long run, nothing will change."

"My friend, the optimist," Linda said with a wry smile. "You haven't changed a bit since law school."

"I call things as I see them."

"Well, I think you're wrong. Stockman's trial will be a show, I assure you. Not only Stockman, but the entire influence-peddling environment will be on trial. Remember the Keating Five?"

"A perfect illustration of my point," Karen said.

Linda smiled again. "That's why I brought it up. Their defense was: 'Hey, I didn't do anything the rest of you haven't done.' Stockman showed us the ultimate. If he couldn't buy what he wanted, he found more insidious ways to achieve his goals. There's no limit to what he would have done—has done. We can't have the government held hostage to special interests any longer, and Stockman's trial will focus on that. Wait and see."

"I hope you're right."

Linda glanced around the room, then leaned forward. "I'll tell you one secret, but I want your word this goes no farther."

"You have it."

"Those stag parties Stockman used to throw—he made videos. We found them all. Stuff you wouldn't believe, made in the days before digital manipulation was possible. He had an extensive collection, which he used to blackmail politicians, regulators, all kinds of bureaucrats—even his own lawyer."

Karen almost choked on a piece of lettuce. "You're kidding?"

"Walter Stockman is a very resourceful man. We've never encountered anyone this totally ruthless."

"Are you going to release those tapes?" Karen asked, knowing they'd provide a dynamite exhibit for her civil suit.

"I doubt it. In the first place, all videos are now suspect. In the second place, releasing this information would only add to the general public's discontent with government. We have to rebuild faith, not destroy it."

"Are you sure those tapes *are* legitimate?"

Linda laughed and signaled the waiter for the check. "See how quickly things change?"

Outside, in the sun-drenched parking lot, Linda turned to her. "Claire and the boys, how are they?"

Karen pulled her dark glasses from her purse and slipped them on. "Better, since Stockman's arrest. All three were so deeply depressed, I encouraged them to seek help. Claire dismissed the idea outright. The boys made one visit to Dr. Zimmer, but refused to return or take the antidepressants he prescribed. A grand jury indictment of Stockman might be just the medicine they all need to pull them out of their slump."

"No one should have to endure what they've been through. Once Stockman's been punished, maybe they can get on with their lives."

"I hope so." Karen hugged her friend before they

went to their separate cars. Inside the oven of her Beemer, Karen started the engine and switched the air-conditioning on high.

Once Stockman had been punished, maybe she could get on with her life, too.

On Christmas Eve, the mercury reached a record high, even for Florida. The soft, white noise of air-conditioning filled the background and gently rippled the branches of the Christmas tree as Rahni served coffee in the living room.

Karen observed her nephews and sister-in-law with concern. Robert's death had quelled everyone's holiday mood this year. Except Andrea's. The child had reluctantly climbed the stairs after dinner. The warning that "Santa" wouldn't come until after she was asleep had finally encouraged her to subdue her exuberance and go to bed.

Although Stockman had been indicted by the grand jury, as Linda had predicted, the criminal trial wasn't scheduled to begin until next fall, six months after the start of his civil trial. Karen sighed at the realization that her family's ordeal stretched far into the foreseeable future.

"Do you have special plans for tomorrow?" Carl asked Claire.

Claire shook her head. "It doesn't seem like Christmas without Robert. We haven't put up a tree or bought presents. . . ."

Her eyes misted with tears and her voice trailed off. Michael stirred his coffee like a sleepwalker, and Richard slumped in his chair. Over Rahni's traditional dinner of roast turkey with oyster stuffing, Karen had attempted to raise their spirits with happy memories of past holidays, but the three Jamesons had responded monosyllabically and merely pushed the delicious food around their plates with their forks. Now the silence in the living room had grown so oppressive that Karen jumped up with relief when the doorbell rang.

She opened the door to Linda Holt standing on her porch. "Merry Christmas! Come in."

"I came as quickly as I could—" Linda began as Karen ushered her into the living room.

"Good to see you again," Carl greeted her and introduced Claire, Richard, and Michael.

"Sit down," Karen invited. "Want some coffee?"

Linda remained unmoving in the arched doorway, her brown eyes wide, her hair tousled, face pale. "I had to let you know how sorry I am."

At Linda's condolences, Claire seemed to pull herself together. "Thank you. My sons and I appreciate all you've done to bring Walter Stockman to justice."

Linda's mouth worked silently. She thrust her fingers through her hair and stared at them, like a nocturnal animal frightened by the light.

"What is it?" Karen asked with alarm.

Linda found her voice. "You haven't heard?"

The desperation in the agent's tone jostled the twins from their lethargy. They focused on Linda, waiting.

"Heard what?" Karen prodded.

Linda shook her head. "I still can't believe it."

"Tell us!" Karen snapped. A cold foreboding spread through her bones.

"Tonight's news," Linda said. "My god, I came to apologize because I was sure you'd heard."

At Karen's glare, she continued hurriedly. "U.S. Attorney Raymond Logan accepted a deal proposed by Benjamin Rose, Stockman's attorney."

"A deal?" Michael said with a sputter. "That bastard's in no position to deal."

"If you have enough wealth and power," Richard said wearily, "you can do whatever you want."

"Stockman," Linda said, "has agreed to plead guilty to a single charge of criminal mischief."

"What?" Karen cried in disbelief.

"He won't serve any time," Linda said. "He was ordered to pay a fine of $50,000, provide five hundred hours of community service, and was placed on probation for three years."

Karen's legs buckled, and she sank onto the sofa next to Claire.

"Probation and $50,000?" Michael shook his head. "My father's life was worth more than that."

"You're right," Linda agreed, "much more. Stockman must have something on someone higher up." She turned to Karen with pleading in her eyes. "It was out of my hands. I never imagined—"

"Neither did I," Karen said, "but I should have. Stockman's too slick to let the federal charges stick."

"I'm sorry to be the bearer of bad news. If I could have done something, I would have. By the time I heard of it, it was a done deal." She turned to go.

Karen followed her to the door. "I appreciate your coming by. And all the work you did on this case. But Stockman's not home free yet. He has to go through me first."

Linda nodded. "Give him hell, Karen. For all of us."

When Karen returned to the living room, Linda's final "Merry Christmas" echoed with bitter irony in her ears.

The weather remained unseasonably warm for late December. Karen took off the week after Christmas to spend with Andrea and Carl, hoping to make up for the dismal events that had ruined their usual family celebration.

Damn Walter Stockman.

She had doubted he could do worse after Robert's suicide, but the man continued to wreak havoc on all of them. Her brother was dead because of Stockman, senators had been blackmailed, and all the man had received was a tap on the wrist.

To add to the tragedy, Claire had suffered a transient ischemic attack, often a precursor to a stroke, after the news. The episode of confusion and disorientation had lasted less than an hour, but had frightened Richard and Michael, who, as they rushed her to the emergency room, feared they were losing their only remaining parent. The doctor had run several tests, placed her on aspirin therapy, and sent her home.

Both Michael and Richard had become even more depressed at the news of Stockman's plea bargain and the effect it had on their mother's health. Even Bonnie Graham, Richard's girlfriend from college, who'd visited over the holidays, had been unable to shake him from his gloom and had finally returned home to New York early in defeat. Only with Ursula's cajoling and bullying would either of the twins eat. Both refused to leave the house.

"You're thinking about Claire and the boys, aren't you?" Carl slipped into the lounge chair beside her on the patio, while Andrea and Tiffany, who lived three houses away, splashed in the pool.

"You're a mind reader." Karen leaned across the gap between their chairs for a kiss.

"Not your mind, the death grip you have on the

arms of your chair. You've been tighter than a coiled spring since Christmas Eve."

"I'm worried."

"Claire's going to be fine—"

"Not so much about Claire. At least she's under a doctor's care. It's Richard and Michael. They seemed to be rallying when they believed Stockman would be tried and punished. Now they're slipping deeper into depression every day."

"I could ask Leo to make a house call."

"He tried before, bless him, with no luck. I had something a bit more drastic in mind."

"Good God." Carl's eyes widened with disbelief. "You're not going to Baker Act them?"

Karen shook her head. "I wouldn't force hospitalization on them. At least, only as a last resort. I'm going to ask them to assist me in preparing for the civil trial."

Carl's tanned forehead creased in thought. "Your suit is the last chance to punish Stockman. You'll need the best help you can get."

"The twins are extremely bright. Richard's completed over a year of law school, and Michael's a quick learner. They lost interest in school when Robert died. Now they need a purpose in their lives. Helping guarantee that Stockman pays through the nose for their father's death *might* be enough incentive to drag them out of their beds."

Carl nodded. "It's worth a try. But what am I going to do about you?"

"Me?"

He reached over and kneaded her shoulder. "You're still tied in knots."

Karen grinned. "I know the perfect cure."

She called to Rahni to watch the girls, then pulled Carl into the house and upstairs to the bedroom.

Two weeks later, Michael and Richard Jameson met with Karen in her office. Both young men were thin and somewhat pale, but their eyes were alight with interest.

"You have another job for us?" Richard asked.

"Have a seat"—she motioned to the chairs in front of her desk—"and take a look at this."

They sat, and Karen handed them copies of a deposition taken from Jack "Skid" Pascoe, Stockman's Canadian pilot, by one of the firm's attorneys Brander had assigned to help with the Stockman suit.

The twins read, and their faces reddened with anger.

"This Pascoe"—Michael shook the paper at her—"claims, *under oath*, that Stockman wasn't at the cabin when he flew Krovnik, Bellows, and Daniels up there."

"He's perjured himself," Richard said with a nod of satisfaction.

"Not if we can't prove it," she said. "It's his word and Stockman's against the three Stockman accused of initiating the blackmail. Whom do you think the jury will believe?"

Richard's dark eyes flared with anger. "Why would Pascoe lie? *He* hasn't committed any crime."

"You tell me," Karen countered, "why would he lie?"

"Because Stockman's paid him to keep his mouth shut," Michael said, "that bastard."

Richard nodded. "And probably threatened him with bodily harm if he doesn't."

"My thoughts, exactly." Their anger was encouraging. Any emotion was better than the horrible numbness that had enveloped them before she'd convinced them to aid her in trial preparations. "That's where you two come in."

"Just say the word," Michael said.

She handed them each a plane ticket.

"You're sending us to Winnipeg?" Richard asked.

"Better take your woollies, because it's the dead of winter and you'll be there a while. I want you to dig out every scrap of information you can find about Skid Pascoe. Especially financial details."

"If we can throw doubt on his testimony," Richard said with a smile, "the jury will believe Krovnik and company instead of Stockman."

"That's a big *if*," Karen said, "and it all depends on what you can find."

"We won't let you down, Aunt Karen," Michael said.

Karen nodded with satisfaction. "Just be careful."

Liz knocked at the door, and at Karen's nod, entered and handed her a blue folder. "This just arrived."

Karen flipped open the document and groaned. "I expected something like this. Benjamin Rose has filed a motion to suppress the FBI tape of Stockman and Krovnik's radio conversation."

"Is that bad?" Michael asked.

"Our biggest ace in the hole is Stockman's televised confession," Karen admitted. "But if we intend to focus attention on Stockman's underhanded manipulation of the political process, we need more. Without that tape or evidence of Pascoe's perjury, proving Stockman's devious practices just got a whole lot harder."

Seventeen

Several days after dispatching Richard and Michael to Winnipeg, Karen shifted in the heavy, overstuffed chair in front of Judge Georgia Porter's antique mahogany desk in the judge's courthouse office. She recalled that the tiny judge had inherited her massive office furniture from her father, Andrew Hayward Porter, the last in a long line of Southern gentlemanly judges who had served the county over the past century.

Georgia Porter, a woman about Karen's height with a starched backbone and a demeanor to match, leaned back in her chair and surveyed her visitors over wire-framed bifocals.

Karen had breathed a prayer of gratitude when she'd learned Porter would be presiding over the civil trial. For once, Karen wouldn't have to fight a judge's chauvinism as well as battle for her client. An ardent feminist and strict constitutionalist, Porter didn't suffer fools gladly and quickly reprimanded any attorney who attempted to rely on charm rather than points of law.

"You're serious about this motion?" Porter directed her question with an astonished glance at Benjamin Rose, seated beside Karen in front of the desk.

Rose's fatuous grin faded. "Of course, I'm serious,

Your Honor. I wouldn't presume to waste your valuable time."

"Hmmmm." Porter returned to studying the motion, leaving Rose to stew silently.

Suppressing a smile, Karen shrugged at Rose, a small man, less than five-foot-six in height with a compact, muscled body. With his silver hair, pleasant face, impeccably tailored silk suit, and probing blue eyes that appeared capable of penetrating steel doors, he usually presented an intimidating persona, a presence that could fill an ample room. With her noncommittal "hmmmm," Georgia Porter had effectively deflated his ego and reduced him to the status of guilty schoolboy.

Karen grimaced, remembering Rose's impressive appearance on *Larry King Live* just two nights ago. She didn't kid herself. Rose made a formidable adversary. In spite of the evidence on her side and his brief putdown by Judge Porter, his considerable skill could sway any jury—unless she outmaneuvered him.

While Judge Porter perused the motion, Karen scratched a few notes on her pad. She intended to open a few eyes, not only to the machinations of Walter Stockman, but to the posturing of his attorney as well. She nodded coolly when Rose glanced toward her with a tight smile, then turned her attention to Georgia Porter, who appeared ready to render her opinion.

After the meeting in Porter's office, Karen joined Brander and Len Spirsky, the young partner who had assisted her in the Uccello trial, in a corner of the restaurant nearest the courthouse, crowded now with lawyers during lunch recess.

Len glanced around, nodded, and smiled to several colleagues before turning back to the table. "Know what the general public would call a bomb detonated here?"

"A good start?" Brander said dryly.

Any other day, Karen would have smiled, but she was still analyzing the arguments Rose had presented to Judge Porter in defense of his motion.

"It looks like the gloves are off," she announced.

Brander appeared surprised. "Don't tell me Georgia granted Rose's motion to suppress the tape of Stockman's radio conversation?"

"Not a chance. Had the communication been over the telephone instead of radio—or the motion been decided by a less stalwart judge—Rose might have pushed it through. Judge Porter was apparently unimpressed by Rose's reputation. She pointed out that participants in a radio broadcast have no expectations of privacy. She's allowing us to present the tape."

"That's a relief," Len said.

"But we face another problem," Karen said. "You've both appeared before Porter. What's her biggest hot button?"

Len took a second to think, but Brander knew immediately.

"First Amendment rights," the senior partner said.

Karen nodded. "Considering Rose's comments on *Larry King Live* night before last, I believe he intends to use a First Amendment defense."

Brander waved to catch a waiter's attention and set aside his menu. "A smart move, in light of Georgia's predilection toward fanatical protection of freedom of speech."

Len shook his head. "But Rose's defense ignores the issue of *mens rea*, Stockman's intent."

"His intent won't be an issue," Karen said, "if Krovnik, Bellows, and Daniels aren't credible. Remember, they all have arrest records. If Rose can make a jury believe they're lying to cover their own crimes, Stockman could come out of this smelling like—"

"A Rose?" Len suggested.

"Rose'll smell pretty sweet if he can discredit our witnesses," Karen said. "He already has a sworn statement from Pascoe that Stockman was alone at his fishing cabin when he flew him in and out, and that Krovnik and Co. arrived only *after* Stockman left."

Brander tapped his index finger against his lips. "And if Rose cites First Amendment protection precedents, like those from the *Jenny Jones'* talk show trial, to justify Stockman's production of the tape, Stockman's practically home free."

"Obviously Pascoe's lying," Len said. "You haven't heard from your nephews?"

Karen shook her head. "That's not necessarily bad. If they had reached a dead end in gathering information on Pascoe, they would have flown back immediately. They're worried about their mother and don't want to be away too long. I have Bill Castor searching for Pascoe."

"How is Claire?" Brander asked and rubbernecked around the restaurant as a newly arrived group crowded through the entrance.

"She's hated this civil suit from the start," Karen said, "because of the media spotlight it puts on her, her sons—and also on Robert's memory. The intense pretrial coverage has only increased her discomfort."

Brander nodded toward the closed door of the private dining room where he'd watched Benjamin Rose and two of his associates disappear seconds earlier. "You want to know where Pascoe is, those are the folks to ask."

The white wicker sofa creaked as Karen settled in the cheerful sun room of her sister-in-law's Cobb's Landing house Sunday afternoon. "Carl rushed to the hospital to perform an emergency surgery, and Andrea's gone to the new Disney movie with a friend. With the twins away, I thought you'd like some company."

Claire, coiffed and elegant in a Liberty cotton shirtwaist dress, sat in a chair across from the large-screen, muted television. A half-empty glass sat on the table beside her chair, and smoke curled from a lighted cigarette in a porcelain ashtray. She had obviously decided to ignore her doctor's warnings against cigarettes and alcohol. To a casual observer, she might have appeared fresh and relaxed, but Karen noted the listlessness in her sister-in-law's voice and the dullness in her eyes.

"I saw Benjamin Rose on *Larry King Live* last week," Claire said, after offering Karen a drink that she declined. "He sounds very optimistic about winning this suit. I couldn't bear that. If you drop the suit now, I'll gladly pay any expenses you've incurred."

A passing cloud allowed sunlight to flood the room and illuminate the finely etched lines of fatigue around Claire's eyes and mouth. Robert's death and the ensuing scandal had taken their toll on his beautiful widow.

"It's Rose's job to sound confident." Karen said

reassuringly. "Believe me, I wouldn't press this suit if I didn't believe we could win."

Claire leaned back in her chair and closed her eyes. "What's the point? We don't need the money—"

"Money's *never* been our objective, except as a means to punish Stockman." Karen reached across the table and grasped her sister-in-law's hand. "I know how difficult this is for you, but you have to remember, we're doing this for Robert."

Claire opened her eyes, and her expression was bleak. "I'm not sure Robert would want any of this, especially us torturing ourselves for his sake."

"Robert would have wanted us to make certain men like Stockman are punished when they operate outside the law—" A movement on the television screen caught Karen's eye. "Speak of the devil, there's Stockman now. Where's the remote?"

With a languid wave of her fingers, Claire indicated the tabletop beside her. Karen grabbed the control and punched the volume button.

"I'm Patrick Weiland, your host," the pompous, balding moderator was saying. "Welcome to UCN's *Sunday Afternoon*, where each week we present an indepth interview with the people who shape our lives."

"You can say that again," Karen muttered.

"Today's guests are Walter Stockman, CEO of United Cable Network, and renowned attorney Benjamin Rose."

The camera panned to Rose and Stockman, who sat across from Weiland on the pseudo-living-room set. The media mogul looked much different from the day of his infamous television confession. Dressed in a dark blue suit of Italian silk, an almost incandescent white silk shirt, and a blue tie embroidered with red

UCN logos, he was the epitome of the conservative businessman. His carefully groomed blond hair was combed to one side above clear and focused penetrating blue eyes. His lips were fixed in that familiar sneer, the result of a much-publicized skiing accident ten years ago that had severed some facial muscles. Plastic surgery had removed the scars, but not the smirk.

Benjamin Rose's smirk, while not permanent, was more a reflection of attitude—and more maddening.

"What are they up to now?" Claire said.

Karen sank into her chair to watch. "They're trying the civil suit in the court of public opinion, doing damage control before the fact."

"Is that legal?"

"As long as no gag order's been issued."

"Can you tell our viewers," Weiland continued, "about the civil suit brought against you by Senator Robert Jameson's family? What purpose does such a suit serve?"

"Good question," Rose said with a smooth, eager smile. "Mr. Stockman has already admitted on national television his responsibility for the production of the videotape that precipitated Senator Jameson's suicide. And he has expressed his sincere regret and remorse."

Weiland nodded. "Then you think the senator's family is out for revenge?"

"How dare he!" Claire gasped.

"It's money, pure and simple," Stockman said easily, without apparent malice. "Everything boils down to it sooner or later. I have some of the deepest pockets in the world, and the senator's family is using the tragic occasion of his death to attempt to line their own."

"The senator's sister, Karen Perry-Mondori," Rose added, "the attorney who filed the suit, is also endeavoring to blacken my client's name by insinuating he intended to cause harm to Senator Jameson."

Weiland leaned back in his chair with a superior smile and chuckled. "But don't her charges have merit? After all, didn't you, Mr. Stockman, plead guilty a few weeks ago to extortion, conspiracy, and eight other charges? Aren't you doing public service now as a result of that plea?"

Stockman leaned forward, and the camera moved in for a close-up of his earnest, boyish expression. "I appreciate this opportunity to explain that plea to the American people. From the beginning, the Jameson family, unable to accept the foibles and weaknesses of the senator that were so well known to his friends, have looked for a scapegoat in this tragedy."

"But if you were a scapegoat," the host asked, "why did you plead guilty to the government's charges?"

Stockman looked to Rose, who nodded his approval to answer the question.

"I could have fought the charges. I certainly had the resources to do so."

"Why didn't you?" Weiland asked.

"Above all," Stockman said in a voice dripping with sincerity and with his right hand over his heart, "I am a patriot. I didn't want my country shouldering the expense and embarrassment such a pointless exercise would have cost them."

Karen's jaw dropped at the man's blatant pandering. Claire snorted and downed the remainder of her drink.

Stockman continued. "I am also a compassionate

man. I wanted to save the senator's family further suffering and embarrassment."

"Embarrassment?" Weiland asked, like a shark sniffing blood. "What kind of embarrassment?"

"In spite of their obvious vendetta against me, I had no desire to destroy their memories of the senator as a man both virtuous and beyond reproof."

"You mentioned weaknesses and foibles earlier," Weiland said with an oily smile. "Surely, we *all* have them."

Somewhere in another room of the house, a telephone rang. Claire, her attention riveted on the set, didn't move.

"For the sake of this country and its future," Stockman said sanctimoniously, "I hope we all don't have foibles to the extent the senator did."

Weiland looked alarmed. "Could you explain that, please?"

Stockman looked to Rose, who shook his head.

"Senator Jameson," Stockman stared, unblinking, into the camera, "was a ladies' man. Let's leave it at that."

Anger suffused Claire's pale complexion. "That's slander! How can he say that?"

"Because Robert's dead. The laws of slander don't apply." Karen wondered if Stockman knew about Robert's affair with Marie Morley. If he did, she was grateful he hadn't mentioned it. Claire was agitated enough.

Ursula stepped into the room. "Telephone, Mrs. Jameson."

The housekeeper handed Claire the portable, and Karen muted the sound on the television as the program faded to a commercial message.

Claire listened for a few minutes. "Yes, I'll have Ursula pick you up at the airport."

She turned off the phone. "Richard and Michael will be home tonight. Please, can't we withdraw this suit and put a stop to these terrible rumors?" She pointed to the television, where a car commercial had replaced Walter Stockman's pious profile.

Concern for Claire vied with Karen's obligation to her brother's memory and prodded her in conflicting directions. She'd have to protect her sister-in-law as much as she could while punishing the man responsible for Robert's death. "If the suit goes forward, it should be over in a matter of weeks. Once a verdict is reached, the media will move on to their next sensation *du jour*, and you'll have peace again."

"I suppose," Claire intoned listlessly, unconvinced.

"If we back out now, we give credence to everything Stockman just said, without a chance for rebuttal."

Claire brushed a strand of blond hair off her forehead with a haggard movement. "You're right, of course. My problem will be surviving the next few weeks."

Richard and Michael appeared at Karen's office before nine the next morning, each toting a briefcase filled with documents. Karen led them down the hall to the conference room and waited while they unloaded their findings.

Michael's handsome young face was lit with the enthusiasm and vitality Karen remembered from before Robert's death.

"We have Stockman by the short hairs now," he said with a satisfied chuckle.

"Only if you've found solid evidence of Pascoe's

perjury." She settled into a chair across from her nephews. "What have you got?"

Richard slid a document across to her. *"Mrs. Pascoe's statement."*

Karen hefted the heavy sheaf of papers. "Give me a summary."

"We found Mrs. Pascoe and her four kids," Richard said, "living close to the poverty level in a run-down suburb of Winnipeg."

"Evidently," Michael added, "when Pascoe took off, he left her with only enough money for a few weeks' expenses—and he hasn't sent her anything to live on since. If Pascoe knows what's good for him, he won't show his face in Winnipeg again. His wife'll draw and quarter him."

"She wasn't reluctant to talk to you?" Karen asked.

"Reluctant?" Michael gave a sharp laugh. "She was eager. Said anything we could do to throw the worthless bastard behind bars was all right by her."

"So what have you got on him, besides desertion of his family?"

"Let me fill in the background first," Richard said. "Until the week you filed the civil suit against Stockman, the Pascoes were in dire financial straits. The mortgage on their house and the loan on his amphibious plane were both on the verge of foreclosure for nonpayment. Their only income came from Pascoe's infrequent charters."

Michael leaned forward, dark eyes glowing behind wire-rimmed glasses, and took up the story. "Three days after your suit was filed, an associate from Rose's law firm appears in Winnipeg and takes Pascoe's statement. Within days, Pascoe and his plane disappear. Neither has been seen since."

"Anything to suggest foul play?" Karen asked.

"It was foul, all right," Richard said, "but not what you think. Right before Pascoe flew the coop, he shows up at his bank, pays off his house mortgage *and* the loan on his plane and opens a four-thousand-dollar checking account for Mrs. Pascoe."

Karen's pulse began to race. "Please, don't tell me he won the Canadian lottery or inherited a fortune from a rich aunt."

Michael shook his head. "He paid his debts in cash. U.S. dollars. Told the loan officer at the bank he'd made the money in the U.S. stock market. The loan officer's statement is among these papers."

"We checked," Richard said, "and found no records of any stock transactions bearing Pascoe's name. We tried tracking Pascoe's windfall and reached a dead end. His wife has no idea where the money came from. She thinks it peculiar the cash appeared within days after Rose's associate visited. Her husband told her he told the lawyer 'what they wanted to hear.' That's in her statement."

"These," Michael waved his hand over the papers covering the conference table, "are Pascoe's financial records, going back almost a decade. During that period, the man and his family lived hand to mouth, barely surviving. They were on the verge of going under financially, until four days after Pascoe gives his fraudulent deposition. Why would a man let his family go hungry if he actually had thousands invested in the stock market?"

"Great work," Karen said. "This could give the jury reason to doubt Pascoe's statement."

"What's our next assignment?" Richard's eagerness was unmistakable.

"Give me time to sift through these documents," she said. "Meanwhile, spend some time with your mother. The recent publicity's been rough on her. And Richard, why don't you give Bonnie Graham a call? Ursula said she phoned the house several times while you were gone.''

When her nephews left, Karen picked up Mrs. Pascoe's statement and began to read. The woman's words cast serious doubt on the veracity of Pascoe's claim, but Karen hadn't had the heart to tell Richard and Michael that the statement alone wasn't enough. She could pin responsibility for Robert's death on Stockman, but to prove the videotape was more than just a poorly conceived party prank, she needed the testimony of Pascoe himself.

And nobody knew where Pascoe was.

Eighteen

Karen stepped into her office, closed the door, and turned the lock. It was going to be one of those days.

Andrea had awakened with a sore throat and low-grade fever and cried for her mother to stay home with her. Karen had shed a few tears herself before she'd placated Andrea enough to leave for work. She was already a half hour behind schedule when a three-car pileup on Highway 19 had turned her twenty-minute commute into an hour's crawl. To top off her frustrating morning, she'd snagged her panty hose on her attaché case as she climbed out of her car.

She rummaged in the bottom left drawer of her desk where she kept a spare pair, stripped off the ruined garment, and had struggled halfway into the new when her intercom buzzed.

"Benjamin Rose is here," Liz announced.

"Here?" Hobbled by half-donned panty hose, she crossed to her desk with mincing steps and glanced quickly at her calendar. Rose didn't have an appointment.

"He says it's urgent, that he must see you right away."

Rose's appearance was the perfect touch to a disastrous morning. "Wait five minutes. Then show him in."

She yanked the panty hose to her waist, smoothed her skirt, and settled in her chair to compose herself. While this morning had been a nightmare, the previous week had brought nothing but triumph, from her nephews' information on Pascoe's finances to Bill Castor's locating Pascoe in Mexico and convincing him and his family to go into hiding until the trial.

Voir dire began in a few days, and soon she would have Stockman right where she wanted, hanging out all his dirty linen for the world to see. In spite of Rose's legal expertise, Stockman didn't stand a chance.

Her mood darkened as she realized that was probably exactly why Rose wanted to see her. With a resigned sigh, she crossed the office and unlocked the door. "Good morning, Mr. Rose. Care for coffee?"

Stockman's attorney entered without his usual swagger, refused coffee, and waited until she was seated behind her desk before sinking stiff-backed into the chair in front of it. "I won't take much of your time this morning. I have an offer from my client."

Karen managed not to gloat. "I thought you might."

Rose withdrew a folder from his briefcase. "We're ready to settle."

Over my dead body. "Terms?"

"Fifteen million and an agreement by both parties not to reveal the terms of the settlement."

"Fifteen million! You're joking? Stockman could take that out of petty cash."

Rose didn't bat an eyelash. "That amount will more than compensate Mrs. Jameson, her sons, and your mother for any loss of income they've suffered from the senator's untimely death."

Karen stood, placed her palms flat on her desk, and leaned toward Rose. Wrath inched its way up her throat and seared her words. "What about the agony and the humiliation they've suffered? Their emotional pain? Your insulting offer doesn't begin to address any of that."

Rose lowered his gaze, snapped his case shut, and stood. "That's our final offer. Once voir dire begins, it's off the table."

With a curt nod, he pivoted on his heel and marched out of her office like a soldier on dress parade. He'd said his offer was final, but she knew better. This time, above his patronizing smirk, she had read the fear in his eyes. She grabbed the settlement agreement, longing to hurl it after him, but procedures had to be followed.

She dropped the papers on her desk and punched her intercom. "Liz, get my mother on the phone. And hold my other calls."

Andrea snuggled beneath the covers and considered her mother with intelligent eyes. "Am I going to bed early so you can argue with Gramma?"

Karen smiled, inwardly saddened that the deplorable state of her relationship with her own mother was so obvious to her daughter. "You're going to bed because you haven't been well, and you've already stayed up thirty minutes past your bedtime."

"Why is Gramma always so angry?"

Karen hesitated, weighing whether Andrea's inquiry was a legitimate concern or a stalling tactic. She had always opted for honesty where Andrea was concerned, never dodging the hard questions because they made *her* uncomfortable.

"Your grandmother is unhappy because her life hasn't turned out the way she wanted. Rather than accepting the blame herself and becoming even more unhappy, she lashes out at others."

"That's not very nice," Andrea replied with the untempered honesty of childhood.

"No, it isn't, not for the people around her, and not for her, either."

"Are you unhappy, Mommy?"

"I miss your Uncle Robert, and I'm sorry Grandmother Perry is a pain to everyone"—she brushed the hair off Andrea's face and tucked the light blanket around her—"but, unlike your grandmother, I have you and Daddy, so I'm *very* happy, sweetheart."

Andrea lifted her arms for a hug. "Me, too, Mommy."

Karen kissed her daughter and hurried downstairs. She would be a lot happier when this evening was behind her.

In the living room, Rahni was serving coffee to her mother, the twins, and Carl. Claire was nursing a large scotch-on-the-rocks. Martha Perry glanced up as Karen entered.

"Well, it's about time. I suppose now you'll tell us why you dragged me here at a moment's notice. What was so damned important it couldn't wait until next week when I come up for the trial?"

Karen accepted a cup of coffee from Rahni, who quietly withdrew, leaving the family alone.

"Is something up?" Richard asked. "I thought since Pascoe was found, we'd covered all the bases."

Karen settled on the sofa beside Carl and studied the remnants of her extended family. Richard and

Michael appeared to have shaken off most of their depression. Earlier, at dinner, they had talked of returning to school for the summer session, after the trial. Richard had resumed a long-distance romance with Bonnie, and Michael had volunteered to help out at the Clearwater Free Clinic two days a week until the trial started.

Claire, however, seemed to deteriorate with each passing day. Drinking and smoking more and more, according to Ursula, she projected the same fragile beauty she always had, but, unlike before Robert's death, frailty had replaced the inner strength that had previously had the Washington press corps referring to her as a steel magnolia. As Karen watched, Claire stubbed out one cigarette and lit another.

Martha Perry was Karen's only relative whom the tragic events of Robert's death hadn't changed. As brittle, prickly, and acid-tongued as ever, her mother's unfailing cantankerousness could still be relied on.

"Before I discuss why I asked you all here tonight," Karen began, "let me recap how the suit against Stockman stands at the moment."

"Really," Martha protested, "it's getting late, and I have to drive back to my hotel."

Karen bit back a sharp reply. Her mother had been invited to stay in their guest room, but had adamantly insisted on being on her own. "This won't take long. We have a very strong case. First, we have Stockman's televised confession that he requested and paid for the production of the videotape that precipitated Robert's suicide. We also have the FBI tape of Stockman's radio conversation with Krovnik, whom Stockman hid in the Canadian wilderness, along with Daniels and Bellows, whom he paid to deliver a copy of the tape to *American Exposé*."

"What's the point?" her mother interrupted. "As long as you prove the son of a bitch made that disgusting tape, isn't he liable for Robert's death?"

"The point, Gramma Perry," Richard said, "is to reveal Stockman for what he is, a ruthless blackmailer who uses his financial power and media empire illegally to influence the affairs of this country."

"Why bother? Isn't that what muckraking journalists are for?"

"We bother," Michael said with patience and surprising gentleness, "because it's what our father would have wanted."

Karen nodded. "This will be a high profile trial with every aspect covered by the media. Judge Porter has approved plans to broadcast it live on the *Court TV* Cable Network. No longer will Walter Stockman be able to masquerade as a concerned citizen and patriot. Once his true colors are revealed, every congressman and senator in Washington will give him a wide berth, afraid of being tainted by association with a man whose self-interests are widely known."

Martha raised her eyebrows at Karen. "You'll be in the national spotlight, too. How much of this is for Robert and how much for the advancement of your career?"

With the steadying pressure of Carl's hand on her shoulder, Karen took a deep breath and silently counted to ten. If the family meeting degenerated into a brawl, nothing would be accomplished.

"That's not fair," Richard intervened. "Aunt Karen isn't accepting a cent for the time she's spending on this case. It's costing her a lot."

"Money has never been the objective for any of

us," Karen said. "We want to prove Stockman is a malicious blackmailer who will stop at nothing to attain his goals. If we expose him, we take away his power. It's as simple as that."

Michael ground a fist into his palm. "And for a guy like Stockman, losing his power is worse than losing his life. He'll pay the ultimate price for what he did to Dad."

"Before we go any farther," Karen cautioned, "you have to realize there's no guarantee of a favorable verdict."

"There you go," Martha said with a sneer, "covering your ass, as always."

Beside her, Carl tensed, and Karen patted his knee in a signal not to come to her defense. Her mother's taunts hurt, but they weren't unexpected and had, at least, lost the sting of surprise.

As if oblivious to the tension swirling around her, Claire drained her glass and drifted to the bar to refill it.

"There's always the possibility Stockman will prevail," Karen continued. "Benjamin Rose is a formidable attorney. Jury selection could work against us. Despite the tapes and Pascoe's testimony, Rose may be able to discredit Krovnik, Daniels, and Bellows."

"You don't really think we'll lose?" Richard asked.

Karen shook her head. "The facts—and the odds—are in our favor. But anyone who's watched television or read a newspaper for the past few years knows the fickleness of the American judicial system. I'd be shirking my responsibility as your attorney if I didn't impress on you that there is a chance, however slight, that we could lose."

Michael frowned thoughtfully. "Where are you going with all this, Aunt Karen?"

"Benjamin Rose brought a settlement offer to my office this morning."

"Settlement?" Richard whooped, jumped from his chair and pumped his fist in the air. "We've got them on the ropes now, or he wouldn't have offered. They're running scared."

"Maybe," Karen said. "Or maybe they figure the exposure will be too damning, even if they win."

"What did they offer?" Michael asked.

"Fifteen million, with neither side revealing the terms of the agreement."

"Fifteen million?" Michael gaped. "That's an insult to Dad's memory."

"I agree," Richard said. "Tell Stockman he can stick his settlement where the sun doesn't shine."

Her nephews had responded as she expected. She turned to her mother. "I'll need a consensus from the four of you. What do you think, Mother?"

Martha placed her cup and saucer on the coffee table with a force that made them rattle. "I think this entire suit is a waste of time."

"What?" Michael and Richard said in one voice.

"That's what I said. A waste."

"But Gramma"—Richard's face reflected his confusion—"don't you want Stockman punished for what he did to Dad?"

"Walter Stockman is the lowest form of slime," Martha replied, "and he temporarily besmirched your father's honor. But while the rest of you are sticking your heads in the political sands of this case, your father's murderer is running free."

"Murderer?" Michael said. "Dad committed suicide. You're not making sense."

"Aren't I?" Martha rose to her feet. "I've known from the beginning your father didn't kill himself. I don't care what the police and FBI said. They've covered up crimes before, and they're covering up this one. Meanwhile, the person responsible for Robert's death is laughing at us all.''

Karen struggled for patience. "Are you saying you want to accept the settlement, Mother?"

Martha swung her hands as if brushing away flies. "I'm saying that as long as we're dilly-dallying over this meaningless suit, we're not searching for the real reason behind Robert's death, the person who pulled the trigger. I told you months ago, Karen, that you should channel your energies in that direction, but no—''

A gurgling sound from Claire cut Martha off.

"Mother!" Richard and Michael rushed to Claire.

Carl beat them to her, checked her quickly and turned to Karen. "Call 911. We need an ambulance. She's having a stroke."

Nineteen

Wishing she could do something—anything—to help, Karen watched Michael and Richard pace the waiting room while Claire underwent emergency surgery, a risky procedure that Carl had warned might end her life as readily as save it.

Across the small room, Martha Perry curled on a vinyl-covered sofa, snored loudly in the silence. The institutional clock on the wall above her marked 3:23 A.M. The family had first waited through batteries of tests, and now the operation stretched endlessly into the small hours of the morning.

At the soft tread of footsteps in the hall, Karen lifted her head. Carl, carrying a grease-stained box and paper bag, entered the waiting room. "I found a Dunkin' Donuts open. At least we can have a decent cup of coffee."

With the same easy grace and air of confidence that had drawn Karen to him when they first met, he distributed coffee and doughnuts. While many orthopedic surgeons had risen to success in spite of their abominable bedside manners, Carl always seemed to know exactly the right things to say and do, especially in times of anxiety and crisis. Even her mother, who'd awakened at his return, had given him an unprecedented smile of gratitude when he handed her a cup of coffee with two sugars, the way she liked it.

Karen sipped the hot brew, a welcome change from the swill the vending machine down the hall had dispensed, and cursed Walter Stockman silently. If Claire died on the operating table, her sister-in-law would be one more addition to Stockman's list of victims.

"Good news, everybody." Brad Dayton, the young fresh-cheeked neurosurgeon, a smile barely hiding his weariness, entered the room. Still dressed in scrubs with his mask dangling around his neck, he'd apparently come straight from the operating room.

"How is she?" Michael asked.

"She came through the surgery fine," Brad said. "The next twenty-four hours will be touch and go, but if she can hold her own, the outlook is good."

"Thank God." Michael collapsed onto a sofa, and Richard dropped beside him and threw his arm around his brother's shoulders.

Brad sank into a chair opposite them. His encouraging smile dissolved into an expression of somber concern. "I don't want to alarm you, but I believe in telling my patients and their families the facts. Your mother has suffered a major stroke. There's a very real probability she'll have another. And next time, she might not survive."

Karen watched the color drain from her nephews' faces, and her heart ached. Only months ago, they'd lost their father under horrible circumstances. Now they faced losing their mother, too.

"Life's not fair," she whispered to Carl beside her and reached for the comfort of his hand.

Brad continued addressing Michael and Richard. "Your mother's refusal to follow my orders about cigarettes and alcohol undoubtedly precipitated this episode. If she expects to survive, she must abstain from both."

"We'll see to it," Michael promised.

Brad nodded. "Your father's death was a terrible blow to her. From now on, you must do *everything* to free her life of stress and turmoil. I can't emphasize enough how important that is."

At his words, Karen leaned back in her chair, engulfed by a terrible sense of inevitability. As soon as Brad left, Richard and Michael turned to her and confirmed her premonition.

"As much as I want Stockman to pay"—Richard shook his head sadly—"I can't risk losing Mother."

Michael's face was a picture of agony. "Richard's right. If we go through with the suit, the pressure of the trial and the subsequent publicity might kill her."

The desire to make Stockman accountable for her brother's death and the suffering he'd caused Robert's family almost suffocated Karen. With an inward struggle, she focused on her duty. She was an attorney, and Richard and Michael Jameson were her clients. Her personal feelings had no place in this decision. Only professional opinions mattered now. "Are you instructing me to accept Rose's offer?"

Her nephews exchanged glances, then nodded.

"Take the fifteen million," Richard said. "It isn't enough to pay for what he did—"

"Fifteen million was only an opener. I can push for more."

Richard shook his head. "Take the offer and end it, for Mother's sake."

Karen looked to Martha, who'd been following their conversation with uncharacteristic silence. "What about you, Mother? Are you prepared to settle?"

"The boys are right. under the circumstances, going ahead with the suit could be fatal for Claire. Take the money."

"You're sure?"

"Now you can put the time you'd have wasted on that civil-suit circus into finding Robert's killer." The fire returned to her eyes and the acid to her voice. "Put that Bill Castor onto it. He's a smart investigator. I'll pay for his time out of my part of the settlement."

Karen grimaced at her mother's one-track mind, believing Martha's fervor came more from a desire to save herself the embarrassment of having a son who killed himself than any true passion for justice.

Karen returned her attention to her nephews. "I'll contact Rose tomorrow with your decision."

After cooling his heels for twenty minutes in an outer office, Benjamin Rose strode into Walter Stockman's private domain at the headquarters of United Cable Network in Orlando. The floor-to-ceiling windows framed a magnificent view of the towers of Cinderella's Castle in the sunset.

"Hope you brought good news," Stockman said with a scowl.

"They settled. For fifteen mil."

"Strings?"

"Only two. Neither party can disclose the amount, and you agree not to malign Robert Jameson or his family."

Stockman's face darkened. "Whose idea was that?"

"Perry-Mondori's. She doesn't like the allegations you've made about her brother in your media interviews. She insists you leave his memory and his family alone."

"The little bitch." Stockman grew quiet.

Rose had worked with the media mogul long enough to recognize his stillness as an ominous sign. Never one to lose control, Stockman hid his seething temper beneath a facade of calm and rationality. The calmer he grew, the angrier he was. This was the calmest Rose had ever seen him.

"Let it go," Rose counseled. "You've won. You dodged the federal charges and now you've avoided the civil suit."

"No one crosses me"—Stockman's voice was icy—"and gets away with it. Even if they're dead. I'm not through with Robert Jameson or his family—"

"What are you trying to do, instigate another suit by Ms. Perry-Mondori? The woman's a brilliant attorney. Overstep the boundaries of this agreement a fraction of an inch, and she'll haul you into court so fast, you won't stop spinning for a week."

Stockman picked up a sterling silver letter opener and pointed it at him. "I don't pay you to tell me what to do, Benjamin. I pay you to keep others from stopping me."

"You've been lucky so far—"

"I've been smart." Stockman began cleaning his fingernails with the letter opener. "I had the government in my pocket until Jameson and his prying sister gave me grief. Well"—his smile grew colder, and Rose resisted the inclination to shiver—"I believe in the Golden Rule. That family has been a thorn in my side. I intend to return the favor. Understand?"

Rose left the office understanding Stockman's ruthlessness too well. The CEO of UCN had reached the pinnacle of power through threats and intimidation. He made certain that any who stood in his way were fully cognizant of the consequences of such actions.

It didn't matter that Robert Jameson was dead and that his family would now turn to getting on with their lives. Stockman would make them an example to others reluctant to bend to his will.

Rose thanked his lucky stars he wasn't in any way connected to the family Stockman intended to destroy.

Karen and Carl sat on a shaded bench at Sea World, eating ice cream cones and watching Andrea feed dolphins in a small pool. But Karen's thoughts were centered several miles away at the headquarters of United Cable Network on International Drive where Walter Stockman continued to wield the power of his media empire.

Three weeks ago, she had carried out her nephews' wishes, flabbergasting Benjamin Rose temporarily with her acceptance of his fifteen million dollar settlement. He had quickly resumed his supercilious sneer.

"Tell your client," she'd instructed him, "that if it hadn't been for the tragedy of Mrs. Jameson's illness, I'd have turned him inside out and backwards in civil court. Just like with the federal government, he got off lightly this time. But one of these days, his deeds will catch up with him."

Rose had raised an imperious eyebrow. "Is that a threat, Counselor?"

Anger and frustration made her throw caution to the wind. "Take it however you wish. But warn him, if he wants to live long and prosper, not to mess with my family again."

She'd regretted her intemperate outburst immediately, and ever since, like a tongue seeks out a sore tooth, her thoughts had returned to Stockman and his callous manipulation of the lives of others. With the civil suit settled, she had no way to touch him, to force him to accountability for what he'd done. That fact rankled, destroying her sleep at night, and ambushing her during the day when her concentration should have been on other matters.

In addition, she was worried about Richard and Michael. Concern for their mother and their inability to bring Stockman to justice had precipitated a return of their depression. They had refused to leave their mother to return to school and slipped back into the habits of barely eating or speaking and spending most of their time sleeping or sitting like zombies before the television set. Richard had even refused to speak to Bonnie on the phone or to return her calls. When Karen returned home, if her nephews wouldn't go to Leo Zimmer's office, she'd convince him to make another house call.

"Lighten up." Carl drew his finger across her frowning lips and interrupted her musings. "You're on vacation, not death row."

Karen looked into Carl's dark eyes and forced a smile. "Sorry."

"You can't get Stockman out of your mind, can you?"

She shook her head. Carl always read her like a book. "It's been three weeks since the papers were signed, but the settlement was so . . . anticlimactic. Like training long months for a title bout and having your opponent forfeit only seconds before the opening bell. I'm all pumped up with no one to slug it out with."

"You were planning to beat the crap out of him," Carl said with a grin.

"I could have. In spite of what I said to Richard and Michael about the vagaries of the jury system, I had a damned good case, a *winnable* case."

She rose, tossed her unfinished cone into a Shamu-shaped trash receptacle, and returned to her seat. Over at the feeding pool, Andrea lifted her head and waved. Karen waved back and blew her daughter a kiss.

"You've been more preoccupied than ever today," Carl said. "What's happened?"

"I talked with Liz at the office this morning, while you were in the shower. She gave me a message from Marie Morley, and I returned her call."

"Robert's chief of staff? What did she want?"

"Marie was upset, said she wanted to contact me before she did anything drastic."

Carl finished his cone and wiped his fingers on a paper napkin. "What's Marie contemplating?"

Karen took a deep breath. "Last night on one of UCN's talk shows, a couple of the panelists spent the hour blackening Robert's name."

"Was Stockman one of them?"

"He's too smart for that. I wrote conditions into the settlement to guard against his using his network as a bully pulpit to retaliate against Robert and his family."

"The show was broadcast by his network. Can't you sue him?"

She shook her head. "Stockman has other people doing his dirty work, so we can't touch him without violating their First Amendment rights. Last night the panel focused on Robert and his ongoing affair with Marie."

"Then Marie should sue them."

"That's why she called me."

"To represent her?"

"I told her no."

Carl said nothing. Karen watched Andrea laughing

with the other children as they petted the sleek gray dolphins. A cool breeze off the nearby lake dispersed the broiling heat from the landscaped plaza and ruffled hanging baskets of bougainvillea above their heads. If only her anger with Stockman could be dispersed as easily.

She thought of Richard's and Michael's depression. At the house on Cobb's Landing, when they could rouse themselves from their inertia, they took turns with their Grandmother Taylor and Ursula, caring for Claire, who was confined to a hospital bed with her left side partially paralyzed. With the help of a therapist, her speech was slowly returning, but her doctor doubted she would ever walk unassisted again.

"I'm surprised you didn't accept Marie as a client," Carl said. "It's not like you to turn down a fight. Of course, I know how much the last six months has taken out of you."

"My refusal had nothing to do with fatigue. Marie and I discussed the situation and decided another lawsuit would only provide more fodder for the media cannons. If the perpetrators of these rumors don't get a rise out of Marie, public attention will soon turn elsewhere."

Carl leaned against her and nibbled her ear. "You're not only beautiful, you're smart, too. Let's go back to the condo, check Andrea into the day camp, and—"

Laughing, Karen pulled away. "You'll have a full-scale rebellion on your hands if you try. You promised Andrea she'd see the polar bears this afternoon, remember?"

Carl stood, pulled her to her feet, and placed his

arm around her shoulder. "Then let's go. How long can it take to view polar bears?"

A week later, Karen wondered if her advice to Marie Morley had been so wise after all. Stockman had orchestrated a persistent and pervasive campaign against Robert Jameson's memory. Whether his purpose was revenge for Karen's exposing his nefarious plots and activities or a strategy to impress upon other members of Congress the folly of crossing him or a combination of both, the attacks against the late Senator Robert Jameson on Stockman's network and in the newspapers he owned were relentless and vicious.

Stockman had investigators who located women alleged to have had affairs with Robert. These pitiful, weeping females grabbed their fifteen minutes of fame on UCN's talk shows, accusing Robert of everything from kinky sex to rape. Added into the mix of pathetic women were others who claimed Robert Jameson had somehow offended them during his lifetime, from a disgruntled landscaper to a parking attendant who maintained the senator had consistently refused to tip him. Claire, her sons, and Karen were also targeted for abuse, portrayed as money-grubbing opportunists who perverted the legal system to rob patriotic Walter Stockman of his hard-earned millions.

One spring afternoon, on her regular Sunday visit to the house at Cobb's Landing, Karen found herself sequestered in the den with Richard and Michael.

"You have to do something, Aunt Karen." Richard shoved his fingers through his hair in frustration. "The other networks are picking up on this character assassination. They're making Dad look like a combi-

nation of Don Juan, Adolf Hitler, and Hannibal
Lechter."

"Can't we file another suit?" Michael asked.
"Mother wouldn't have to know. We've managed to
shield her from the news so far. We record all her
favorite shows—she has only a playback monitor in
her room—and screen her telephone calls. Seeing this
filth on TV or hearing it from a friend would kill her.
We're even censoring her newspapers and magazines."

Karen sank into a leather armchair and faced her
nephews. Their appearance, worse than after their
father died, frightened her. Pale and gaunt with dull,
dark eyes sunken in their tortured faces, they bore
the brunt not only of the attacks on their family but
also of shielding their mother from them. At twenty-
three, they were no longer boys, but neither had they
developed the experience or resilience of adulthood.

Their entire lives, lived in the spotlight of public
attention as sons of a famous politician, had been
sheltered in all ways. Never wanting for anything,
neither material goods, their parents' approval and
affection, nor the adulation of their friends, they'd
had little experience with the cruel truths of life.
Until now. Since their father's death, they'd been battered by savage reality. Their anger at Stockman,
which had roused them from their lethargy, was the
only positive aspect of the current situation.

"I've already explained that libel and slander laws
no longer apply, because your father's dead," she
said gently.

Richard looked ready to smash something. "Then
we go after Stockman. He's broken the settlement
agreement. This smear campaign started on his
network."

Filled with an unfamiliar sense of impotence,

Karen shook her head. "We have no proof that Stockman's behind this."

"*Find* proof!" Michael yelled.

"If we found proof and took Stockman to court," Karen said patiently, identifying with his frustration, "a trial would only increase the media feeding frenzy. We have to let the hubbub die a natural death. Given the brief lifespan of most scandals, this should be over in a few weeks."

"And if the allegations kill our mother in the meantime?" Richard asked.

"You're doing all the right things to protect her," Karen said.

"But what if something slips by us?" Michael asked, "and she discovers what's going on?"

Richard stopped pacing and slammed his fist against the doorjamb. "All my life, I wanted to be a lawyer, like my father, like you. But what good's the law if it can't protect innocent people from slime like Stockman?"

Karen said nothing. She didn't know the answer.

"Boys, your mother's asking for you." Ursula had entered the room so quietly, no one had realized she was there.

Karen's nephews headed toward their mother's room, but the housekeeper didn't move. She waited, hands folded in her skirt, until they were out of earshot before speaking again. "I'm worried about them."

Karen sighed. "So am I. They've had to put their lives on hold through all of this."

Ursula shook her head. "It's more than that. A sickness is eating away at them."

"Are you saying they're ill?"

"They're ill, all right. Here—" the housekeeper touched her forehead, then her heart— "and here."

"I know they've been depressed, but . . ." Alarmed, Karen waved the housekeeper into a chair. "You'd better tell me what you mean."

Ursula perched on the edge of her seat and confronted Karen with anxious eyes. "I watched those two grow up, happy, carefree little boys, always laughing and smiling. Now I can't remember the last time I saw either of them smile."

"There hasn't been much to smile about around here lately."

"That's just it," Ursula insisted. "Most folks, when times are hard, make jokes to ease the pain, but Richard and Michael are withdrawing deeper and deeper into themselves. Talking to you today is the most words they've spoken in a month. Mostly they just sit and stare off into space. They don't eat, they don't talk, they don't smile." Tears welled in her eyes. "It's like they're dead inside."

"I thought they were pulling out of their depression."

"They rally when you're around. You're their champion, their only hope of protecting their father's memory and saving their mother from more pain."

Guilt washed over Karen like a tidal surge. If her nephews were counting on *her* to turn their lives around, the situation was even more hopeless than she'd feared.

"You'll do something, won't you?" Ursula begged.

"Of course," Karen assured her. "I love those boys, and I hate to see them suffer."

She was grateful Ursula didn't ask how she planned to help her nephews, because she didn't have a clue.

*   *   *

"Tonight," the Channel 8 news anchor announced, "Walter Stockman, CEO of United Cable Network, spoke to the National Association of Broadcasters at their annual convention at the Sheraton on Sand Key—"

Karen clicked off the late news with the remote as Walter Stockman's smirking face filled the screen. Six months ago today Robert had killed himself. She had no desire to watch Stockman grinning in triumph.

In spite of her promise to Ursula weeks ago, Karen hadn't been able to help her nephews cope with the problems they faced. They had refused another visit to Leo Zimmer, the psychiatrist, and Leo had told her, short of involuntary hospitalization, there was nothing she could do, unless her nephews took the first steps. She closed her eyes, dreading the possibility of admitting Richard and Michael for psychiatric care under the provisions of the Baker Act. If they continued to deteriorate and refused to visit Leo, she might eventually have no other choice. Her feeling of helplessness deepened her fatigue.

"Ready for bed?" she asked Carl, who was engrossed in Nelson de Mille's latest novel.

"As soon as I finish this—" The ringing of the telephone interrupted him, and he pushed to his feet and crossed to the desk to answer. "That's probably Mrs. Campbell. I cure her aches, and she turns on me. She's been a pain in the butt ever since she came out of post-op yesterday."

He picked up the receiver, then handed it to Karen. "It's for you."

"Not Claire?" Karen jumped in alarm. Ever since her sister-in-law's first stroke, the family had been on edge, expecting another.

Carl shook his head. "It's Charlie Simms."

With relief, Karen hurried to the phone. Charlie Simms was a Pinellas County Sheriff's detective who'd worked with her on a case a few years ago. He probably had a prisoner requesting an attorney.

"Karen," he said when she greeted him, "calling you will put my ass in a sling if word gets out, but you need to get down to the jail, ASAP."

"A new client?"

"Two." Charlie's deep sigh transmitted clearly over the line. "Richard and Michael Jameson."

"What are they doing there?"

"They murdered Walter Stockman."

Twenty

Less than an hour after Charlie Simms's call, Karen arrived at the Pinellas County Jail, presented her identification card, and asked to see Richard and Michael Jameson.

"Can't. They're in interviews with the detectives," the desk sergeant told her.

She drew herself to her full height and leaned across the desk. "I'm their attorney, and if they're being interviewed without benefit of counsel, there'll be hell to pay. I demand to see them *now*."

"Have a seat." The sergeant picked up a phone. "This'll only take a minute."

Three minutes later, Detective Dan Frazer passed through the electronic gates of the sally port. "What's the problem, sergeant?"

The sergeant nodded toward Karen who surged to her feet and approached Frazer, a detective she'd butted heads with before over his propensity to bend any rules to obtain the results he wanted.

"I'm representing Richard and Michael Jameson, and I demand to see my clients."

Frazer blinked in surprise. "How'd you know they were here?"

She ignored his question. She wouldn't repay Charlie Simms's kindness by disclosing her source of information. "You questioned them without an attorney present. You know the law, Frazer, even if you do ignore it."

"I know the law, for sure, counselor. That's why I had your clients sign a waiver *before* we questioned them."

Shock drove the air from Karen's lungs. "They waived their right to an attorney?"

Frazer's grin was smug. "Right before they confessed to killing Walter Stockman."

"Confessed?"

"Signed, sealed, and delivered. This is going to be—what's the old cliché?—an open-and-shut case if I ever saw one. I have an eyewitness *and* signed confessions, and Walter Stockman ain't even cold yet. I'll be looking at a promotion for this one."

Karen recovered her composure. "I want to see my clients."

"If you insist." Frazer, magnanimous in victory, shrugged, and called to the sergeant, "Bring the Jamesons to the interview room."

With eyes blazing, Karen confronted the detective, "If I find you've violated their rights—"

"Don't count on a plea bargain on this one," Frazer interrupted with an arrogant smile. "This case has high-profile written all over it. With the state attorney planning to run for governor next year, he'll want the media attention of a major trial. Sorry, counselor, but looks like your boys are going to *fry*."

With a mock salute, he turned toward the exit, chuckling as he left. Awash in shock, fury, and concern for her nephews, Karen took a deep breath, stepped through the sally port, and followed the guard to a small room with a metal table and stools bolted to the floor.

She'd visited these rooms countless times before, but never in expectation of interviewing her own kin. Long minutes dragged by before the door was yanked open and Michael and Richard stumbled into the room.

Dressed in the bright orange coveralls of county inmates, their expressions slack and dull, she hardly recognized Richard and Michael. At the guard's instruction, they sat at the table across from her and waited until the guard had left and closed the door behind him.

"Go home, Aunt Karen," Richard said with a terrible weariness that wrung her heart. "There's nothing you can do here."

Between the harsh glare of fluorescent lights and the brilliant hue of their clothing, Richard and Michael appeared washed out and sallow. Even worse was the lifelessness in their eyes.

"Is it true?" she asked. "Did you sign a confession?"

"I shot him." Richard looked away. "He can't ever hurt Mother, or Dad's reputation again."

Realizing that their actions could very well mean the death of their mother, Karen bit back an angry reply. They clearly weren't thinking rationally, not when they shot Stockman and certainly not now. Whatever their reason for killing Stockman, Richard and Michael, as sons of an attorney and nephews of a nationally known criminal defense lawyer had always known the first thing to do if arrested was to request legal counsel. That they hadn't indicated the depth of their turmoil.

"Did you ask to call me, or any lawyer?"

"What was the point?" Michael said. He folded his arms on the Formica tabletop and lowered his head to them. "There's nothing you can do."

"Don't you believe that for a minute." She wished she felt as positive as she sounded. "But first, tell me everything that happened, while your memories are still fresh."

Richard shrugged. "If that's what you want."

What she wanted was to shake him until he showed some emotion. Instead, she pulled a pad from her attaché case. "Who's going to start?"

Richard sat silently, staring at the wall behind her head. His demeanor was depressed, not sullen.

Michael finally spoke, his voice tentative and hoarse. "We tried for weeks to contact Stockman. We drove to his office in Orlando several times, but he refused to see us. His secretary wouldn't even let us make an appointment."

"He wouldn't take our calls. I wrote him letters," Richard added, "but they were returned unopened."

"What did you hope to accomplish by seeing him?" she asked.

"To make him realize what he was doing to Mother," Michael said, "to appeal to his humanity and beg him to stop. We were even going to offer to return our share of the settlement money if he'd just end the smear campaign against Dad."

"Nothing worked," Richard said. "We couldn't get through to him—not face-to-face, not even on the phone—much less make him listen to reason."

Karen took a deep breath. "Is that when you decided to kill him?"

"We didn't mean to kill him," Michael said with an earnestness that couldn't be faked. "We only wanted to *talk* to him."

"Last week," Richard said, "I saw on TV that Stockman would be speaking at the convention on Sand Key."

Michael nodded. "He always travels in that stretch limo of his. We figured if we could run it off the road and corner him, he'd *have* to listen to us."

"So we made a plan." Richard leaned toward her. "I bought one of those portable flashing blue lights like the unmarked cop cars use—"

"And I bought a gun—"

"A gun?"

"Once we'd pulled him over and he realized we weren't the cops," Michael said, "all Stockman had to do was give the word to his chauffeur, and they'd just pull away. We needed the gun to make the driver stay put while we talked to Stockman."

"We went to the Sheraton early," Richard said, "and waited for Stockman to arrive. Then we parked our car where we could see the limo when it left. A little after nine o'clock, it drove away, and we followed it through Clearwater, onto the Courtney Campbell Causeway. I stuck the blue light on the roof of our car and turned it on. Stockman's driver pulled over immediately."

"We got out and approached the car," Michael said. "When the chauffeur rolled down his window, Richard pulled the gun and told him to get out of the car. The driver climbed out, but Stockman refused, so I grabbed the keys from the ignition and unlocked the back door. Stockman was using the limo's phone when I pulled him out."

Karen took notes furiously and struggled to maintain objectivity. "What happened then?"

"I told Stockman we didn't want to hurt him," Michael said, "we just wanted him to promise to stop maligning our father, for our mother's sake." His voice broke. "I told him he was killing our mother."

"He laughed at us," Richard continued, shaking

his head in disbelief, "and said he wasn't finished with Dad or with any of us yet, that he'd teach us to mess with Walter Stockman. I tried to explain what his propaganda was doing to Mother, but he laughed harder and said he didn't care what happened to—" he hesitated over the words—"to our mother."

"I'm glad he's dead," Michael said quietly.

"How did he die?" Karen asked.

"When he kept laughing," Richard said, "I blanked out, like, everything went black. When I came to, Michael was shaking me—and Stockman was lying on the ground—dead."

"You shot him?"

"I didn't mean to." Tears coursed down Richard's cheeks. "I'm not a murderer. I must have gone berserk. I emptied the gun, all nine shots."

The more she heard, the more Karen's hopes for saving her nephews plummeted. According to what they'd told her, the state attorney had an ironclad case of murder in the first degree. She hid her pessimism. "Then what?"

"We heard the sirens," Michael said. "What else could we do? We waited for the police, and they brought us here."

"Why didn't you call me?" Karen said.

"Because not even you can help us now. It's done." Richard raised his head and looked at her with pain-filled eyes. "I didn't mean to kill him, but, like Michael, I'm glad he's dead."

At nine o'clock that morning, although she'd had no sleep the night before, Karen entered the conference room where the partners had gathered at her request. Brander Hewitt, the only remaining found-

ing partner, sat at the head of the conference table.
Darren Smith, who'd joined the firm shortly after its
creation, a bland-looking man with black, thick-
rimmed glasses that gave him an owlish look, sat at
Brander's right.

Across from Darren sat Len Spirsky, the firm's
newest partner, and Sharon Chin. Karen stood at the
foot of the table opposite Brander. "Thank you all
for coming on such short notice. If you've heard this
morning's news, you know why I've called you
together."

"It's true, then?" Brander asked.

Karen nodded and, fighting fatigue and despair,
dropped into her chair. "My nephews, Richard and
Michael Jameson, have been arrested for the murder
of Walter Stockman."

"Did they do it?" Len asked with his usual
bluntness.

"Yes, and what's worse, they signed a confession
before I could speak with them.

"The state attorney's office is claiming premedita-
tion because Richard and Michael had the gun in
their possession and ran the car off the road. Richard,
who did the shooting, is being charged with first degree murder, and Michael is being charged with felony murder as accomplice." Referring to her notes
taken at the jail, Karen gave the partners the details
of her nephews' crime. "So you see," she said when
she'd finished her recapitulation, "I have my work
cut out for me."

Brander looked pensive. "Detective Frazer's right
about one thing. This trial could be a political spring-
board for the state attorney. You could short-circuit
his plans with a plea bargain, of course."

"No plea bargain," Karen said. "We're going to trial."

Sharon's jaw dropped. "But they've signed a confession."

"Unless you can prove they signed under duress," Len suggested with a hopeful expression.

Karen shook her head. "I won't have to. We'll plead not guilty by reason of temporary insanity. I intend to argue that from the moment of my brother's death, my nephews have been mentally impaired—"

"Depressed, surely," Sharon said, playing devil's advocate, "but not to the point of being unable to distinguish between right and wrong."

"I'll argue that coming face-to-face with the man responsible for their father's death and experiencing Stockman's taunts and threats firsthand pushed them over the edge into temporary insanity."

Concern etched Brander's kindly face. "It's a long shot, Karen. Not guilty by reason of temporary insanity is a tough verdict to persuade any jury to agree to. It's been abused too often."

Karen faced him down the length of the table. "My brother is dead because of Stockman. My sister-in-law is at death's door. Richard and Michael are all I have left. Even if they escape the death penalty and go to prison, in the mental and emotional state they're in, their lives are effectively over. I have to try."

Brander nodded. "I understand."

"You'll need a second chair," Len said. "I'll be glad to assist—"

"Thank you, Len," Brander interrupted, "but that won't be necessary. It's been too long since I darkened the courthouse door. I'll be assisting Karen on this case."

Karen swallowed hard and blinked back tears. "Thank you, Brander."

"Now," Brander rubbed his hands in anticipation, "we need to get to work, all of us, if Karen's going to win this. Sharon, have every available clerk researching temporary insanity precedents."

"I'll contact our jury consultants," Darren said, "tell them what we're up against and have them begin preparing profiles and questions for voir dire. And I'll consult our file of expert witnesses for a psychiatrist."

"I have a friend in the state attorney's office," Len said with an uncharacteristic blush. "I'll see what I can ferret out of her about the prosecution's strategy."

"Any cases I can take off your desk to clear it for this one?" Sharon asked.

"I don't know how to thank you all—" Karen began.

"Yes, you do," Brander insisted forcefully. "Win this case. Not only will we have the satisfaction of seeing your nephews freed, but you'll knock Stephen Randall, that pompous blowhard of a state attorney, on his fat ass where he belongs."

With laughter at the shock of refined Brander's comment, the partners adjourned to their assigned tasks.

Twenty-one

Len Spirsky waved his arm over the document files stacked a foot deep on the conference table. "You always say preparation is the most important factor in any case. You've certainly lived up to your motto."

Karen had refused to waive Florida's speedy trial statute that guaranteed her nephews a trial within 175 days of their arrest. Her move denied the prosecution more time to build their case and lessened the time Richard and Michael had to spend behind bars. Now she surveyed the results of five months of study, interviews, and depositions with a sinking heart. "Preparation won't make the difference in this trial."

"You're worried about jury selection."

She slid into a chair. "The verdict will hinge on the jury's composition—and the prosecution knows that as well as we do. They'll fight like tigers to keep anyone sympathetic to Richard and Michael off the jury."

"But we have Leo Zimmer's testimony. And that hotshot psychiatrist you're flying in from L.A." Len's efforts to reassure touched her. "And the chauffeur's statement—that could work to our benefit."

Karen stretched to ease the tension in her shoulders. Every bone in her body ached from weariness.

Since the night Stockman had died, preparation for her nephews' defense had consumed every waking hour and much of her dreams, and sometimes she worried that she'd forgotten what Carl and Andrea looked like. After all this time, while Richard and Michael languished in their cells awaiting trial, she shuddered at the knowledge that the outcome of her labor hinged on the willingness of twelve people to believe Richard had been temporarily insane when he pulled the trigger and killed Stockman.

She thumbed through the files until she found the one she needed, a compilation of the jury consultant's recommendations. "With voir dire starting tomorrow, we should have a good idea in a few days which way this case is headed."

"If anyone can save them," Len said, "it's you."

She flashed him a warm smile, at odds with the icy knot in her stomach. Her nephews had made the same statement, numerous times.

She shoved her fears to the back of her mind and slammed a mental door on them. Failure wasn't an option. Richard and Michael were her flesh and blood, Robert's sons, and if she never won another case in her life, she had to win this one.

The new Pinellas County Criminal Justice Center had been completed over two years earlier, but this trial was a first for Karen in the large courtroom set aside for high-profile trials and ceremonial purposes. Like the twenty-one smaller courtrooms, this one had been designed to provide greater security for the judge, with a bullet-proof bench equipped with remote controls for lighting, audio and visual aids, and surveillance cameras monitored in the security office, staffed by personnel from the sheriff's department.

The high-tech building had been planned for maximum security during court proceedings. Secured elevators and hallways were designed to separate incarcerated defendants from judges, attorneys, jurors, witnesses, and the public. Richard and Michael had been brought to the courthouse from the jail by way of a second-floor bridge and then taken up to the courtroom by a special elevator. Until the trial began, they were kept in a holding cell located off a secure corridor, where jailed defendants could wait or confer with their attorneys.

Karen scanned her notes as she waited for the judge to appear and ignored the whispering crowd behind her. The defense hadn't begun presenting its case, but she had already suffered two strokes of bad luck.

The first had been the appointment of Colonel Roderick Harding to preside over her nephews' trial. A former Navy SEAL who had attended law school after bad knees forced him out of the armed services, Harding was a no-nonsense, hard-hearted man with little sympathy for a defendant's circumstances. Moral fiber, according to Harding, was the key to law and order, and people either had it, or they didn't. How life treated them was irrelevant, as long as that inner compass kept them on the straight and narrow. Mental illness, he'd been rumored to profess, was a sign of weakness and lack of character and should be no excuse for criminal behavior. If Karen could have proved those rumors, she would have asked to have him removed.

The second strike against Richard and Michael had come during jury selection. Following the jury consultants' advice and her own instincts, Karen had interrogated each potential juror in an effort to lay bare any biases that might work for or against her nephews. At the top of her list of choices were men who believed defense of their families was a sacred duty. Such jurors would be inclined to vote not guilty, whether they believed her nephews temporarily insane or not. Also at the top of the list were women with a sympathetic understanding of emotional stress. When ten jurors had been selected, out of five men, Karen believed only two fit her criteria for sympathy to Richard and Michael's case. Of the other three, one appeared vaguely hostile, while the remaining two showed no prejudice one way or another.

Of the five women selected, all seemed willing to admit that severe emotional stress could drive a person to extreme behavior he might never display under normal circumstances. Whether the women would accept that her nephews had been pushed to that brink remained to be seen.

Karen had used all her peremptory challenges trying to assure sympathetic jurors. As she interviewed the juror who would make number eleven if selected, she wished she'd saved a challenge. The woman, in her fifties, wriggled in her chair and smoothed polyester slacks over plump thighs.

"Have you ever known anyone with a mental illness?" Karen asked.

A grim expression replaced the pleasant smile on the woman's lined face. "My late husband suffered from depression."

"So you understand how a person's actions can be affected by such an illness?"

The woman grimaced. "In my husband's case, he was a lazy no-good. Sometimes he faked depression to get out of doing what he didn't want to do."

"You believe people fake their illnesses?"

The woman nodded emphatically. "Who's to say, after all, what's really going on inside somebody else's head? Anybody can act crazy and get away with anything."

"Thank you." Karen had returned to her seat, ignoring the broad grins from the prosecutor's team. They couldn't have obtained a better juror for their side if they'd handpicked her.

Now, waiting for the judge to begin the trial, Karen glanced at Juror Number Eleven sitting in the jury box and scowling at no one in particular. The woman's frown lasted throughout Karen's opening statement.

A day later, Juror Number Eleven was still scowling as State Attorney Stephen Randall called Brad Brown, Stockman's chauffeur, to the stand. Brown, a stocky man in his mid-thirties with a buzz haircut, the physique of a body builder, and a deep tan, looked more like a beach lifeguard than a driver. His inexpensive suit stretched taut over bulging muscles, and a tic in his left cheek proclaimed his nervousness.

With an unctuous grin, the prosecutor attempted to put Brown at ease. "You were employed by Walter Stockman?"

"Yes."

"In what capacity?"

"Driver and bodyguard."

"How long had you worked for Mr. Stockman prior to his death?"

"Four months."

"Tell us, Mr. Brown, the events of the early evening that preceded Walter Stockman's murder."

"I was driving Mr. Stockman back to Orlando from Clearwater. We were crossing the causeway toward Tampa, when I saw a flashing light behind me. I pulled off onto the access road and stopped."

"Was there other traffic on the access road?"

"No."

"Aren't you trained in tactical defensive driving?"

"Yes, sir."

"Why would you stop on a deserted access road and place your passenger in potential danger?"

Brown shifted uneasily in the witness chair. "When I saw the flashing light, I realized I was speeding. I hoped if I cooperated, I'd get a warning instead of a ticket."

"Why were you afraid of getting a ticket?"

"In the four months that I'd worked for Mr. Stockman, I'd received three citations for speeding. I was afraid Mr. Stockman would fire me if I got another."

"What happened after you stopped?"

"Two men in civilian clothes approached my window. When I rolled it down, they stuck a gun in my face and ordered me out of the car."

"Did you know these two men?"

"I'd never seen them before, but I'd know them if I saw them again."

"Are they in this courtroom?"

Brown pointed to the defense table. "Those two."

"Let the record show," Randall said, "that the witness has indicated the defendants, Richard and Michael Jameson." He turned his back to Brown. "What was Mr. Stockman doing when the Jamesons approached the limo?"

"He had been reading some files. As soon as he saw them pull the gun, he dialed 911 on the car phone."

"Did Mr. Stockman then exit the car?"

"Not at first."

"When did he leave the car?"

"When one of the defendants—I can't tell which,

'cause they look alike—took the keys from the ignition and unlocked the back door. The one with the gun told him to get out."

"And after Mr. Stockman did as he was asked, what did the defendants do?"

"The one with the gun shot him."

"Before the shots were fired, did Mr. Stockman make any move toward the two, threaten them physically in any way?"

"No, sir."

"Was Mr. Stockman armed?"

"No, sir."

"As Stockman's bodyguard and chauffeur, were you armed?"

"Yes."

"Why didn't you draw your gun?"

"When I got out of the car, the man without the gun frisked me, found my weapon, and tossed it in the bay."

"So at no time did you or Stockman make a threatening move toward the Jamesons?"

"Objection," Karen said. "Asked and answered."

Judge Harding glared at her, but sustained the objection.

"How many times did the gunman shoot Mr. Stockman?" the prosecutor continued.

"I lost count, but it was at least six. He emptied the clip in the automatic."

"Did the man with the gunman make any move to stop him from shooting?"

"Not that I saw. It all happened so fast, and I was pretty freaked out when the bullets started flying."

"Thank you, Mr. Brown." With a self-satisfied smirk, Randall took his seat.

"Your witness, Ms. Perry-Mondori," Judge Harding said.

Karen stood, straightened her jacket, and approached the stand. "Mr. Brown, you said that one of the defendants ordered Mr. Stockman to get out of the car. Is that all the defendant said before he fired the gun?"

Brown's gaze flicked toward the prosecutor. "He said they only wanted to talk to Mr. Stockman."

"And that was all he said?"

"He said if Mr. Stockman would just hear what they had to say, there wouldn't be any trouble."

"And *that* was all either Richard or Michael Jameson said?"

"The other one, the one without the gun, said they didn't want to harm anybody, that they just wanted Stockman to stop hurting their mother."

"And that's when Richard Jameson shot your boss?"

"No." Brown shifted in his chair and ran his finger beneath the too-tight collar of his shirt.

"What happened next?"

"The guys, uh, the defendants begged Mr. Stockman to stop the people telling lies on his station and in his newspapers."

"Lies? Did the Jamesons specify what kind of lies?"

"They said Stockman was spreading lies about their parents."

"What was Mr. Stockman's response to their request?"

"He laughed."

"Did he say anything?"

"Yes."

"What did Mr. Stockman say?"

"He called their mother names."

"Can you remember his exact words?"

"Yes."

"What were they?"

Brown looked to the prosecutor's table again.

"You will answer the question," the judge instructed.

Brown swallowed hard. "Stockman said he didn't give a rat's ass about their whore of a mother. That every Jameson could burn in hell for all he cared."

"Did Mr. Stockman say anything after that?"

"He laughed and said he'd see every member of Robert Jameson's family totally destroyed, just as they'd tried to ruin him."

"Mr. Stockman verbally threatened the defendants?"

"Yes."

"And their mother?"

"Yes."

"He didn't appear afraid of the Jamesons?"

Brown shook his head. "The two of them seemed more frightened than Mr. Stockman."

"So Richard Jameson fired at Stockman only when he threatened to destroy every member of the Jameson family?"

Brown nodded.

"Answer aloud please, for the record."

"Yes."

"After the shots were fired, what did Richard and Michael Jameson do?"

"Do?"

"Did they try to escape?"

"They sat down on the side of the road until the cops arrived."

"And they said nothing?"

"No."

"So they sat, silently waiting for the police?"

"Not silently."

"They were making noise?"

"They were crying."

"Crying?"

"Yeah, they had their arms around each other, and they were bawling like babies."

"Did they strike you then as a couple of cold-blooded murderers?"

"Objection," Randall shouted, "calls for a conclusion."

"Withdrawn. No further questions."

After the luncheon recess, prosecutor Stephen Randall called Wanda Cavell, Walter Stockman's executive assistant to the stand. An attractive auburn-haired woman in a hunter green suit, Ms. Cavell moved and spoke with an efficiency that indicated why Stockman had hired her.

For an hour and a half, the prosecutor walked Ms. Cavell through her telephone and visitor logs of the weeks prior to Stockman's death, documenting for the record every call or visit made by Richard and Michael Jameson in their attempts to contact Stockman.

Karen assumed his strategy was to establish a pattern of harassment, even stalking of Walter Stockman by the twins. She could only hope in his meticulous fervor Randall was boring the jury to death. When he finished his questions, Karen approached the witness. The jury watched, their eyes glazed from the ninety-minute recitation of dates and times.

"Ms. Cavell," Karen said, "in your numerous conversations—both on the telephone and in person—with Richard and Michael Jameson, did either man ever threaten to harm Walter Stockman?"

The woman flicked her glance toward Stephen

Randall at the prosecutor's table, as if looking for instruction. "Not exactly."

"Not exactly? What *exactly* was the substance of the Jamesons' discussions with you?"

"They asked to speak with Walter Stockman."

"On"—Karen consulted her notes—"forty-three occasions, twenty-nine telephone calls and fourteen personal visits to the office, as you have just testified, these young men simply asked to speak with Mr. Stockman?"

"Yes."

"They said *nothing* else?"

Ms. Cavell studied her well-manicured fingers, clasped in her lap. "They said their business with Mr. Stockman was a matter of life and death."

"Life and death? Did you ask the nature of this life-and-death matter?"

"Yes."

"And what did the Jamesons reply?"

"They said that Mr. Stockman was killing their mother."

"Let me be certain I have this correctly. On forty-three occasions, Richard and Michael contacted Walter Stockman, either by telephone or in person at his office, and asked to see Mr. Stockman because they said he was killing their mother. Is that right?"

"Yes."

"Did either Richard or Michael Jameson at any time threaten Mr. Stockman in any way?"

"No."

"Would you categorize their attitudes as hostile?"

"Objection," Randall said. "Calls for a conclusion on the part of the witness."

"I'm attempting to establish state of mind, Your Honor," Karen said.

The judge nodded. "I'll allow it. Ms. Cavell, you will answer the question."

The witness licked dry lips. "No, they didn't seem hostile."

"How did they seem?"

"Pleading. Desperate."

"On the forty-three occasions that the Jamesons pleaded to speak with Walter Stockman, was he out of the office?"

Ms. Cavell dropped her gaze to her lap again. "No."

"How often would you estimate that Walter Stockman was out of the office when the Jamesons attempted to contact him?"

The witness muttered an answer.

"Could you speak louder, please?" Karen asked.

Ms. Cavell took a deep breath. "Less than half those times."

"So on more than twenty occasions when the Jamesons tried to contact him, Walter Stockman could have taken their calls or seen them in his office?"

"Sometimes Mr. Stockman had someone else in his office or was in a meeting or on another line."

"So how many times was he available and simply chose not to speak with the Jamesons?"

"At least a dozen times."

"I want to be sure I understand you correctly. Forty-three times Richard and Michael Jameson asked to speak with Walter Stockman about a matter of life and death, out of concern for their mother, and at no time would Walter Stockman take their calls or agree to see them?"

"That's right." Ms. Cavell had the grace to look embarrassed.

"To your knowledge, did he ever attempt to return their calls or make contact with the Jamesons?"

"No."

"Did Mr. Stockman ever issue you instructions about putting through their calls or setting an appointment for the Jamesons to see him?"

"Yes." Her voice was barely above a whisper.

"What were Walter Stockman's instructions regarding Richard and Michael Jameson?"

"They were never to be allowed into his office or to speak with him by phone."

"Never?"

"That's right."

"Did Mr. Stockman say why he refused to see or speak with these two young men?" From the corner of her eye, Karen caught Randall's almost imperceptible flinch at her question.

Wanda Carvell's face knotted in distress, but she said nothing. Judge Harding leaned toward her. "You're under oath, Ms. Cavell. You must answer the question."

The witness nodded. "Mr. Stockman said the Jamesons were a wart on mankind's ass and should be excised."

"Did he show no sympathy for their concern for their mother?"

Ms. Cavell took a deep breath. "He said the sooner the old bitch died, the sooner her whelps would leave him alone."

"Thank you, Ms. Cavell. You've been very helpful."

Karen returned to her seat and scanned the jury box. Several female jurors wore shocked expressions. Good, she thought. She'd just reduced the sympathy factor for Walter Stockman. That reduction wouldn't guarantee a not guilty verdict, but it was a start. She allowed herself a small smile. Randall's attempt to establish a pattern of harassment by the twins had just blown up in his face.

She wasn't smiling, however, after Randall called his next witness, Dr. Aaron Formann, head of the department of psychiatry at the University of South Florida. An attractive man in his late thirties, Formann smiled at the jury as he took the stand. With dark eyes, dark, neatly trimmed beard, and thick wavy hair, the handsome doctor had the immediate attention of every female on the jury.

After establishing Formann's credentials, Randall cut straight to the chase. "Dr. Formann, have you examined Richard and Michael Jameson?"

"Yes."

"When?"

"I was called in by the state attorney's office and first saw the Jamesons the day after they were arrested for murder."

"After that examination of Richard and Michael Jameson, what was your professional diagnosis?"

"Both young men were suffering from severe clinical depression."

"Would you please tell the court what symptoms the defendants presented that caused you to reach that conclusion."

"Both were lethargic, uninterested in what was happening to them. They had both lost weight, according to prison records, in the few short days they'd been incarcerated."

"Prison is a depressing place, Dr. Formann. Is it possible their surroundings precipitated their depression?"

"It's possible. Not having examined the Jamesons

before their imprisonment, I have no basis for comparison of their prior mental state."

"Suppose, as the defense maintains, that the defendants *were* severely depressed prior to their encounter with Walter Stockman, would that depression have negated their ability to discern right from wrong?"

"Absolute not. While depression can be an extremely debilitating condition, it does not impair a person's cognitive function to the degree of rendering them unable to tell the difference between right and wrong."

"So, in your professional opinion, when Richard and Michael Jameson stopped Walter Stockman's car and Richard Jameson fired nine bullets into Walter Stockman, the defendants knew what they were doing—they knew that killing Stockman was wrong?"

"Yes, in my opinion."

"Thank you." Randall waited an instant for Formann's statement to register with the jury. Then, with a leering grin at Karen, he returned to his seat.

Karen rose and approached the witness with a smile. "Dr. Formann, I see from your *vita* that you are affiliated with the American Academy of Psychiatry and Law, is that correct?"

"Yes, I am."

"And are you familiar with their ethical guidelines concerning striving for objectivity in testifying?"

"Yes."

"Good. Keeping in mind those guidelines, can you assert with one hundred percent confidence that Richard Jameson knew what he was doing when he shot Walter Stockman?"

Formann's genial smile faded. "No, not one hundred percent, but—"

"Thank you, Dr. Formann. That's all."

Randall leaped to his feet. "Redirect, Your Honor?"

"Proceed," Judge Harding said.

"Dr. Formann," Randall said, "with what percent of confidence *can* you assert that Richard Jameson knew the difference between right and wrong when he pulled the trigger and killed Walter Stockman?"

The psychiatrist, apparently unprepared for this line of questioning, wrinkled his brow in thought.

The judge shifted toward the witness stand with impatience. "Answer the question, please."

"Seventy percent," Formann said quietly.

Randall's confident smile vanished. "No more questions."

Twenty-two

In the predawn darkness, Karen rubbed sleep from her eyes and padded downstairs to the kitchen. Carl, already dressed for work, sat at the table in the breakfast nook, finishing his coffee and reading the *Times*.

He lifted his gaze from the paper and gave her a smile. "You're up early."

After all their years of marriage, his smile still generated a flutter in her heart. She poured a cup of coffee and joined him at the table. "The prosecution rested yesterday. Now it's up to me."

He slid the metro section of the paper toward her and pointed to a color photo on the front page. "You're getting some good press, at least."

She picked up the paper and studied the artist's rendition of her at the defense table with an arm around Richard and Michael on either side of her. "I make a point of letting the jury observe my affection for the boys. I want them to see Richard and Michael as real people who someone cares about, not impersonal monsters who took a man's life."

He placed his hand over hers and squeezed gently with his long slender fingers, so deft in surgery. "What are their chances?"

Reveling in the comfort of his touch, she shook her

head. "The prosecution's hurt us, especially with their expert witnesses. The jury appears to have bought their psychiatrists' opinion that, while the twins were seriously depressed at no time did they lose the capacity to distinguish between right and wrong."

"Will your psychiatrist from Los Angeles change their minds?"

"He might, if he comes across as compellingly on the stand as he has in my discussions with him."

"You've done an excellent job of pointing out what a slimeball Stockman was, how mercilessly he hounded the Jamesons. Surely that will count for something?"

She shrugged. "Before releasing the jury to deliberate, Judge Harding will lecture them forcefully on the point of law. Stockman's character aside, their verdict should hinge on whether Richard truly didn't know the difference between right and wrong when he pumped nine bullets into Stockman. Basically, it will boil down to which expert witness the jury believes."

"Too bad," Carl said with a teasing twinkle in his dark eyes. "If the outcome was determined by which side had the most brilliant and attractive attorney, you'd be home free."

She tried to smile at his banter, but her face crumpled with concern. "I've never been so personally involved in a trial before, and this one has me scared stiff. Richard and Michael could be sentenced to death—and it would be my fault."

Carl leaned across the table and cradled her face in his hands. "They have the best attorney on God's earth. No one could have fought harder for those boys than you have. Don't let a crisis in confidence

throw you off your stride. It's exactly what that bastard Stockman would want."

She covered his hands with her own and managed
a smile. "Thank you, Dr. Mondori. You've proven
your orthopedic skill by stiffening my backbone
when I need it most."

"You couldn't wimp out if you tried. It goes
against your genetic programming."

A few hours later, Karen prayed she could live up
to Carl's confidence in her as Judge Roderick Harding banged his gavel to bring the court to order.
"Ms. Perry-Mondori, you may call your first witness."

At the defense table, Karen pushed herself to her
feet. "Cameron Erskine."

A tall man, over six feet in his conservative Brooks
Brothers suit, with a shock of salt-and-pepper hair,
took the witness stand and peered at Karen through
round, gold-rimmed glasses.

"Mr. Erskine, what is your profession?"

"Communications."

"Are you currently employed?"

"Since last spring I've worked in programming at
CNN."

"And before that?"

"I was vice president in charge of programming
for the United Cable Network."

"What were the circumstances surrounding your
departure from UCN?"

"I resigned in protest over certain programming
decisions mandated by Walter Stockman, the CEO."

"What decisions did you object to?"

"Last March, Mr. Stockman called me into his office and presented me with an outline of guests and
topics for our prime-time talk shows. He told me I

was to implement his instructions immediately, but that the programming must be perceived as being initiated by me, with no connection to him whatsoever."

"UCN was his network. Why didn't he want to be connected with the programming?"

"It would violate the settlement terms of a civil suit filed by the Jameson family."

"What terms?"

"That Stockman cease and desist from any discussion of any member of the Jameson family or the events leading to and including the civil suit."

"Was his implementation of specific programming unusual?"

"Highly exceptional."

"In what way?"

"First, Mr. Stockman rarely used such a hands-on approach. Most programming grew out of brainstorming sessions with the staff, and while the CEO participated, he never dictated. He usually respected the opinions and professionalism of the people who worked for him."

"How did this programming requested specifically by Mr. Stockman relate to the Jameson family?"

Erskine's thin lips pursed in a moue of disgust. "He had targeted the Jameson family as the subject of his prime-time talk shows."

"Since Senator Jameson's suicide, the family had been in the news. Wasn't his request reasonable in that light?"

"The Jamesons were old news. No one was interested in them anymore."

"You resigned from a lucrative and powerful position with one of the nation's top networks over old news?"

Erskine smiled. "No, I resigned as a matter of conscience."

"Please explain."

"Stockman gave me a list of guests and speakers and ordered me to book them for the shows. He said not to bother to check their backgrounds or stories, that he'd already taken care of that."

Karen frowned. "He was obviously saving you work. Why would you protest?"

"Because in checking later on my own, in direct opposition to Stockman's orders, I found many of these guests were fraudulent."

"Fraudulent?"

"They were actors Stockman hired to make scurrilous and specious claims against the late senator, Robert Jameson—and even his wife."

Karen turned to Judge Harding. "I have several videotaped examples from the archives of UCN that I wish to enter into evidence and would like the jury to view."

"Objection!" Randall surged to his feet and waved his arm toward Erskine. "This entire testimony is irrelevant."

"The campaign by Walter Stockman to discredit Senator Jameson and his wife is central to the state of mind of the defendants," Karen argued.

Judge Harding nodded. "Objection overruled. We'll take a brief recess while the bailiff sets up the video equipment."

Fifteen minutes later, the trial resumed. Karen pushed the Play button on the VCR and the tear-ravaged face of a young woman appeared on the screen. The date stamp indicated April 12th of the previous spring. Marcia Allyn, host of *Hot Talk*, a

UCN weekly gossip show, was speaking to a tearful woman.

"Tell us about your experiences with the late Senator Robert Jameson, Miss Freely."

The guest shuddered and dabbed her eyes with a tissue. "I thought he was so handsome—at first. When we met at the Washington fund-raiser, he asked me to meet him in his hotel room afterwards for a drink. I said yes."

Marcia, a skinny blonde with bouffant hair, leaned over and patted the woman's knee. "I know this is hard for you, but please go on."

"When I went to the senator's room, he was wearing only a robe when he opened the door. I tried to leave, but he grabbed me and pulled me into the room."

Marcia shook her head in sympathy. "Why didn't you scream for help?"

"I did, but he slugged me in the face and threatened to kill me if I made another sound."

"What happened then?"

"He raped me," Miss Freely said, between body-wracking sobs.

Marcia grimaced. "I know reliving this is traumatic, but could you tell us exactly what happened?"

Miss Freely wiped her eyes and nodded. "He ripped off my clothes—"

Karen punched the Stop button and turned to Erskine. "Is Miss Freely an example of one of the fraudulent guests?"

"Miss Freely is actually Venita Burke, a New York actress who was appearing in the off-Broadway production *Up Yours* the night of the alleged encounter."

"Objection," Randall said. "Hearsay."

"Your Honor," Karen said, "I have here an affidavit from the theater manager who swears that Miss Burke was onstage in New York the night of the alleged attack in Washington. I also have an affidavit from the limo driver and a certified copy of his log that he drove Robert Jameson to his home in Virginia immediately following the fund-raiser. Both the manager and driver are willing to appear, if necessary."

"Objection denied. Continue, Ms. Perry-Mondori."

Karen removed the tape from the VCR and inserted another. A half hour and five tapes later, she turned to the judge. "Your Honor, I have fifteen other examples with affidavits to their fraudulent nature that I would like to submit as evidence, if the prosecutor will so stipulate."

Judge Harding looked to Stephen Randall.

"So stipulated," Randall agreed wearily.

Karen turned to Erskine. "When you discovered these fraudulent guests, is that when you resigned?"

"Yes, I wanted no part of an orchestrated attack on the memory of Senator Jameson, and I certainly wanted no part in causing more grief to a family who had suffered enough."

"Thank you, Mr. Erskine. No further questions."

Stephen Randall rose slowly, buttoned his Armani jacket, and approached the witness. "If I've counted correctly, you've documented twenty-one untruthful reports against Senator Jameson and his wife on UCN's programs during the weeks before Mr. Stockman's death. Is that right?"

"Yes."

Randall leaned toward Erskine with a sad smile. "Tell me, if those reports had been broadcast about *your* father, Mr. Erskine, wouldn't you have wanted to blow Walter Stockman to hell and back?"

"Objection!" Karen shouted.

"Withdrawn." Randall flashed her an oily grin as he returned to his seat.

After the lunch recess, Karen called her next witness. "Ursula Olsen."

Eyes wide with fright and hands shaking visibly, Ursula was sworn in and took the witness stand.

"Ms. Olsen, what is your occupation?"

"I am housekeeper for the Jameson family."

"How long have you served in that capacity?"

"Almost seventeen years."

"Do you live in the family home?"

"Yes."

"So you have had ample opportunity to observe Michael and Richard Jameson?"

Ursula glanced toward the witness table, and her face softened with affection. "I have watched them grow up from little boys."

"How would you characterize their behavior before their father's death?"

"They were fine young men. Good students. Never any trouble. And happy. Always happy. They laughed and joked, teased their mother, and filled the house with their friends."

"How would you characterize their behavior after their father's death?"

Ursula's expression saddened. "Their hearts were broken, as if someone had stolen all the joy and laughter from their lives."

"Richard and Michael were enrolled in law and medical school then, so you didn't have much time to observe them?"

"After their father died, they did not return to school."

"They lived at home?"

"If you want to call it living."

"Explain, please."

"They rarely left the house. They spent much time sleeping, some days not bothering to dress. They refused to eat, not even when I prepared their favorite brownies or chicken pot pies. They showed no interest in anything."

"At any time, did they show signs of snapping out of their depression?"

"Yes, at one time."

"When was that?"

"Several months after their father's death, they began to assist in preparations to sue Walter Stockman. They even traveled to Winnipeg, Canada, to do investigative work. I was so relieved, thinking now they would be all right."

"Did their depression return?"

"Yes."

"When?"

"After their mother's stroke, when untrue stories about their parents began to appear on the television and in the newspapers."

"Did the Jamesons see a doctor about their depression?"

"Only once, when Dr. Leo Zimmer came to the house shortly after their father's death. Later, they refused to see him again."

"Why?"

Stephen Randall sprang to his feet. "Objection. Hearsay."

"It goes to the defendants' state of mind, Your Honor," Karen said.

"Objection denied. Continue, Ms. Perry-Mondori."

"Why did Richard and Michael Jameson refuse to see a doctor about their depression?"

"They insisted the only thing that would make them feel better would be for Walter Stockman to stop the damaging stories about their parents on his network and in his newspapers."

"To your knowledge, did they contact Mr. Stockman?"

"They tried. It was the only activity they showed any interest in."

"Did they succeed?"

"Mr. Stockman refused to speak with them, not even on the telephone."

"How did his refusal affect them?"

"Objection." Randall was on his feet again. "The woman isn't a trained observer."

"Your Honor," Karen said, "on the basis of her long service with the family, Ms. Olsen is more qualified to note changes in the behavior of these young men than anyone except their mother."

"Objection denied. Answer the question, Ms. Olsen."

"Each time Mr. Stockman refused to see them, they became more depressed, more withdrawn. I believe the only thing that kept them going was their concern for their mother."

"Think carefully before answering, Ms. Olsen. Did either Richard or Michael Jameson voice threats against Walter Stockman in your presence?"

"Threats?"

"Did they threaten to kill him?"

"No, never. They are not that kind of people. They would never hurt anyone."

"Thank you, Ms. Olsen. You've been very helpful." Karen returned to her seat.

Randall approached the housekeeper. "Do you love these boys, Ms. Olsen?"

Tears welled in Ursula's eyes. "Like they were my own sons."

"And you'd do anything for them?"

"Of course."

"Including lying about their behavior?"

"Objection." Karen glared at Randall.

"Withdrawn."

As Randall returned to his seat and Ursula left the courtroom, Karen studied the jury. Several faces were set in frowns, but whether they were reacting to Randall's underhanded question or to Ursula, she couldn't tell.

Ignoring Randall simpering across the aisle, she called Leo Zimmer to the stand, who confirmed Richard's and Michael's depression prior to the murder. After Leo, Carl described the symptoms of depression he had observed in his nephews. Stephen Randall remained ominously quiet as the two doctors testified, asking only one question of each during his cross-examination.

"Dr. Mondori, did you ever witness either of the defendants so seriously impaired by depression that he was unable to distinguish between right and wrong?" Randall posed the same query to Carl that he had to Leo.

"No, but—"

"Thank you. No further questions."

The following morning, Karen realized Richard and Michael's fate hung on the testimony of her expert witness. "The defense now calls Dr. Ralph Josephs."

An expectant hush settled over the courtroom as

Josephs made his way toward the witness stand. A slender, attractive man in his early fifties with thick, wavy gray hair, the psychiatrist was dressed in khaki slacks, a pale blue dress shirt open at the throat, and a Harris tweed jacket with leather patches at the elbows. With his casual looks and attitude more like a bestselling author's than the stereotypical shrink's, he took his oath and settled at ease in the witness chair.

Karen noted several of the jurors leaning forward in their seats, their interest quickened by the genial man with the twinkling eyes. So far, so good.

"Dr. Josephs, what is your profession?"

"I am a practicing psychiatrist in Brentwood, California."

"You have an office there?"

"At 53 Beverly Drive in Los Angeles."

"How long have you practiced at that location?"

"From 1975 to the present."

"And before 1975?"

"I was chief of the UCLA/Valley VA Medical Center in Los Angeles."

"Will you give the court, please, your professional qualifications."

"I received my undergraduate degree and my medical degree from Georgetown University in Washington, D.C.," he answered in a pleasant voice, thick with his native New York accent.

"Where did you receive your medical training?"

"I served a mixed medical internship at St. Mary's Hospital and Medical Center in San Francisco, and my residency at UCLA Neuropsychiatric Institute in Los Angeles, where I was chief resident of the evaluation and treatment unit."

With a careful eye on the jury's reactions, Karen led Dr. Josephs through a description of his credentials, from professional organizations and teaching assignments to publications and current research. When a few members of the jury began to fidget in their chairs, she stopped, even though she could have continued another fifteen minutes establishing the doctor's impressive qualifications. She wanted to keep the jury interested and friendly, not antagonize them with a surplus of data.

"Now, Dr. Josephs, would you explain to the jury the meaning of the legal term, *mens rea?*"

"*Mens rea* refers to a person's state of mind, in the legal sense, specifically his state of mind at the time a crime is committed."

"And how does *mens rea* apply in this case?"

"The state" —he looked to Stephen Randall and smiled— "must prove beyond a reasonable doubt that the defendant committed the criminal act, i.e. killing Walter Stockman, with the requisite intent."

"Objection," Randall griped. "The man's a psychiatrist, not a lawyer."

"This witness is more than qualified to comment on the defendants' state of mind, Your Honor," Karen said. "I'm merely laying a foundation for those comments."

Harding, who appeared inclined to sustain the objection, grimaced. "Be quick about it, then, counselor."

Karen turned back to her witness. "Why is *mens rea* considered such an important factor, especially in a capital case such as this one?"

"A person's state of mind when committing a crime is extremely important for deciding retribution. For example, a person who sets out to murder someone is more blameworthy than someone who kills accidentally."

"So if a person is insane, for example, at the time he pulls the trigger, he is not culpable for his crime?"

"If insanity can be proved."

"Dr. Josephs, what is the precise, legal definition of insanity?"

The psychiatrist lifted his mouth in a slow smile, and his friendly eyes twinkled. "There is no generally accepted, precise definition of legal insanity."

Karen faked astonishment. "If no definition exists, how are these twelve people supposed to decide whether Richard Jameson was sane when he shot Walter Stockman?"

Josephs gazed at the jury with sympathy. "Many states adhere to the American Law Institute insanity defense standard, or a version of it."

"Would you describe that standard for the jury, please?"

"The ALI test provides that a person is not responsible for criminal conduct if at the time of such conduct as a result of mental disease or defect he lacks substantial capacity either to appreciate the wrongfulness of his act or to conform his act to the requirements of law."

"Have you examined Richard and Michael Jameson?"

"I have."

"Previous testimony has shown that they were clinically depressed at the time of the shooting. Would that depression have destroyed Richard Jameson's capacity to appreciate the wrongfulness of shooting Mr. Stockman?"

"Not the depression alone, but the depression could have paved the way for a more severe impairment that would have rendered him incapable of awareness."

"Would you explain, please—and in laymen's terms?"

"The sudden violent death of their father and the ensuing events precipitated severe depression as well as extreme anxiety over their mother's well-being in both Richard and Michael Jameson. When they developed their plan to confront Walter Stockman, desperation and fear of failure compounded their fragile mental states."

"Are you saying that their mental states were so fragile at the time they accosted Stockman they'd lost their capacity to distinguish right from wrong?"

"No, not at that point."

"At what point, then?"

"Walter Stockman did not take their pleas seriously. His threat to continue his harassment of their mother was the trigger mechanism that pushed Richard Jameson beyond the bounds of sanity, so that in those seconds when he fired the gun, he not only did not know the wrongfulness of his act, he was totally unaware of acting at all."

"Dr. Josephs, for Richard Jameson's conviction of this crime, he must have had not only a criminal state of mind, *mens rea*, but also he must have committed the murder, an *actus rea*. That means his physical movement had to be conscious and of his own volition. Are you suggesting that his shooting of Walter Stockman was neither conscious or volitional?"

"In my professional opinion, Walter Stockman's threats against their mother triggered a temporary insanity in Richard Jameson, rendering his shooting of Walter Stockman both an unconscious and involuntary act."

"Thank you, doctor. No further questions."

The prosecutor stepped to the stand. "Can you

state with one hundred percent confidence that Richard Jameson was temporarily insane at the time he shot Walter Stockman."

"I can state with ninety-five percent confidence that Richard Jameson was temporarily insane when he pulled the trigger."

Deflated, Randall returned to his chair.

Karen suppressed a smile. She had anticipated Randall's question and prepared Josephs for it.

Twenty-three

Karen listened to Stephen Randall give his closing argument. For months, she had devoted her time and energy to preparing for this trial, to the detriment of Carl, Andrea, and her other cases. She had utilized every scrap of skill, all her knowledge and experience to defend her nephews.

As she listened to the prosecutor's summation, Karen feared for Richard and Michael's lives. If Randall convinced the jury that the young men had acted out of malice, not temporary insanity, her nephews were doomed.

Randall stood rigidly in front of the jury box, his face exhibiting the wear of months of preparation and weeks of trial, a sensational trial conducted under the harsh scrutiny of the media. This was the prosecution's last chance to persuade these twelve jurors to see things his way, and he clearly intended to make the most of it.

"First," he said softly, "I want to commend you for the attention you've paid to the witnesses in this very difficult case. You've taken your responsibilities seriously, and no one could ask for more.

"I ask you to continue as you have, to consider the facts of this case. I ask you to apply the same diligence you've displayed throughout this trial to matters of law, without regard for whatever sympathy you might feel for those charged with the crime of murder. You *must* follow the law. Failure to follow the law invites anarchy, and with anarchy comes the destruction of society.

"These two men failed to follow the law. In fact, they took it into their own hands, meting out their own justice for wrongs done to their father. Instead of seeking justice through the courts, they acted as judge, jury, and executioners, ambushing and cutting down Walter Stockman in cold blood, riddling his body with *nine* bullets."

Randall talked for thirty minutes, his voice never rising, reminding the jurors of the various testimony, especially of the prosecution's expert witness on the twins' mental state, and the exhibits. He placed grisly photographs of Stockman's bullet-torn body on an easel so that the jurors had to either look at the graphic photos or close their eyes as he spoke. Finally, he appealed again to their sense of justice. When he finished, he thanked them for their attention, returned to his table, folded his hands, and closed his eyes.

Many thought he was praying.

The judge turned to Karen. "Proceed, Ms. Perry-Mondori."

Karen walked slowly to a position in front of the jury box, shoved her hands in the pockets of her jacket, turned and faced Richard and Michael at the defense table for a moment, then hung her head. She struggled, fighting to control her emotions. Her face radiated pain.

She turned back to face the jurors. "The prosecutor is quite right. The facts in this case are irrefutable. On a dark April night, the defendants did in fact lie in wait for Walter Stockman, did in fact stop his car on the Courtney Campbell Causeway between Clearwater and Tampa, and did in fact shoot him to death with an automatic pistol purchased just a week before."

She gripped the jury-box railing with both hands. "The prosecutor is quite right when he says that you must follow the law. He is also right when he says that if we abandon the rule of law, we fall as a society. But before you retire to deliberate, His Honor will tell you that our system of law allows you to consider the state of mind of the defendants when they committed this act. And it is this *mens rea*, this state of mind, that is at the heart of this case."

She turned and pointed to her nephews. "Here we have two young men whose lives have been ripped to shreds. Before the death of his father, Michael Jameson was studying to be a doctor, to fulfill a lifelong dream of bringing healing and health to others. His brother, Richard, was working hard to become a lawyer, dedicated to justice. Both of these fine young men were near the top of their respective classes, their tranquil and happy lives in order, poised to become productive, contributing members of society. They had never experienced adversity, obstacles, misfortune—nothing to prepare them, to temper them for the horror that was to come."

She pivoted back to the jurors, making eye contact with each of the seven women and five men. "And then they received the news that their father had committed suicide, news that would devastate any young man. But days later, they suffered another, even more destructive blow. The entire world was told that their father, a man they revered and adored, had been a sexual pervert, a pedophile, the kind of human being people relegate to the bottom rung of the societal ladder."

She caught the eye of Juror Number Eleven and forced herself not to react. The woman's gaze was filled with hostility.

"Richard and Michael knew instinctively that this claim was an impossibility, that the father they had respected and loved was no pervert, but the evidence shown to the world seemed irrefutable. And that evidence was readily accepted by a gullible public."

She released her grip on the rail and took two steps backward. "And then, thanks to the efforts of FBI lab technicians, the evidence depicting the sexual perversion of Senator Robert Jameson was proven to be a complete fabrication. Yet there were those in the media who kept insisting the FBI lied, that the *FBI* were the fabricators, simply returning a favor, trying to cleanse the sullied image of a fallen supporter."

She took a deep breath and tried to read the expression of Juror Number Four, a surly man who sat tight-lipped without any sign of compassion. "While still reeling from all of this and caught in the throes of deep depression, Richard and Michael Jameson learned that their father's suicide was the result of a deception perpetrated under the guise of a party joke by Walter Stockman. Further investigation reveals that the tape was no joke, but a blackmail attempt by Stockman to manipulate the outcome of legislation in the halls of Congress.

"While trying to cope, these young men were relentlessly pursued by members of the media looking for some fresh slant on this tragedy. At the same time, they watched an army of lawyers fighting to prevent Walter Stockman from ever having to answer for what he had done.

"Then came a devastating blow. Through his attorneys, Walter Stockman made a deal with the U.S. attorney, and the very man who had set all this tragedy in motion was allowed to remain free, virtually unpunished."

She lifted her head, allowing the jury to see her emotion, to witness her concern for her nephews, hoping the jurors would think of the twins as human beings, not just defendants in a trial. "We know the pen is mightier than the sword, and how much mightier than the pen is an entire media empire? Through Walter Stockman's wealth and control of a major television network and numerous newspapers, he had killed their father, ruined their mother's health, and permanently besmirched their father's reputation, yet Walter Stockman had received only the equivalent of a slap on the wrist for his crimes. For two young men, raised to revere and trust in truth and justice, Stockman's inappropriate punishment was another crushing blow to their already reeling world."

Karen pursed her lips for a moment. "A human being can only stand so much pain, and these young men had suffered horribly, but there was more to come. As a direct result of the stress of her husband's death and the ensuing public spotlight, their mother suffered a debilitating stroke and underwent life-threatening surgery. Her tenuous physical condition forced these young men, in hopes of relieving the stress on their mother, to abandon their civil suit against Walter Stockman, their one last chance at obtaining justice for what Stockman had inflicted on their family."

Karen shook her head sadly. "In the settlement of the civil suit, Stockman agreed that neither he, nor his attorneys, would discuss the suit, the settlement, or anything about the Jamesons. Stockman held to the letter of that agreement, but he violated its spirit. Using his influence as CEO of United Cable Network, he initiated an unprecedented smear campaign against the late Senator Jameson, digging up and exposing every foible, real or imagined, in the senator's past." She held her hands to her sides, palms up in supplication. "How can two young men, fighting for their mother's life, their own grip on reality tenuous, fight a media giant?

"A human being can stand only so much pain," she repeated, with tears in her eyes. "In the case of extreme physical pain, once the limit has been reached, the sufferer usually sinks into unconsciousness, the body's way of protecting itself. In the case of mental anguish, unconsciousness is not an automatic reflex, so the pain is handled in a different way. With their reason corrupted by the turbulent and scarring events of the past year, Richard and Michael Jameson decided they must confront Stockman and beg him to end the pain, for themselves, yes, but especially for their mother."

She met the gazes of the jurors again. "You've heard the testimony of Dr. Josephs, who explained how, in the Jamesons' face-to-face meeting with Walter Stockman, his threats to destroy their mother served as a trigger, causing Richard's reason, his ability to determine right from wrong, temporarily to snap.

"These two young men are not cold-blooded killers. It wasn't revenge that made them waylay Walter Stockman, nor was it hate that made them pull the trigger. They did not intend to harm him but, naively, hoped to appeal to his human decency. In the recesses of their pain-battered minds, their motive was simple self-preservation, the certain knowledge that unless they did *something*, their mother would die as their father had, and they would never be able to put their fractured lives back together.

"When they begged Walter Stockman to cease and desist the attacks on their family and he stated his intent to continue harassing their mother and their father's memory, Richard Jameson's fragile grip on reality broke, pushing him over the edge. His reason already impaired by tragic events, he reacted in the only way his tortured mind knew to protect their mother's life."

She walked back to the defense table, stood behind her nephews, and placed a hand on each of their shoulders. "There is nothing the law can do to make these young men whole again. Their suffering is beyond comprehension. Their loss is irreplaceable. As the experts have testified, it may take years before Richard and Michael Jameson can experience happiness again as they did before their father's untimely death. Executing them, even sending them to prison, will serve no useful purpose. Their deaths, even their incarceration, will be the certain death of Claire Jameson. In effect, Walter Stockman will have successfully eradicated the entire Jameson family.

"I ask you to return a verdict of not guilty by reason of temporary insanity so that Richard and Michael Jameson—and their mother—can have back the lives Walter Stockman so cruelly stole from them. I ask not for sympathy, but for justice.

"Thank you." She let her hands fall to her sides.

Juror Number Eleven glared at her as she took her seat.

Judge Harding cleared his throat. "Ladies and gentlemen of the jury, let me remind you that this trial is not about character, but about law. The innate good or evil of either the defendants or the victim is irrelevant. The only issue you need concern yourselves with is whether Richard Jameson was sane; that is, whether he knew the difference between right and wrong at the time, with his brother, Michael, as accomplice, he shot Walter Stockman. If you conclude that he was temporarily insane at that moment, you will return a verdict of not guilty. However, if you decide according to the testimony given in court, that he *did* know the consequences of his actions, you must return a verdict of guilty of murder in the first degree."

The jury listened without stirring as Harding described the sentencing options of life imprisonment or death by electrocution, then retired somberly to the jury room to consider their verdict.

Karen leaned back in her chair and closed her eyes. She felt a hand on her shoulder, turned and stared into Carl's eyes. Not a word passed between them. None was needed.

"How long do you think they'll be out?" Richard asked her.

"It's hard to tell. I gave up trying to read juries a long time ago."

She was lying. Judging from the intractable expressions on the faces of the jurors as they filed out of the box, she feared Richard and Michael would be convicted.

The jury stayed out less than three hours. When they returned, spectators and media jammed the courtroom. Karen forced a brave smile for the sake of her nephews.

"Madam Foreman," the judge said, "Have you reached a verdict?"

"We have."

"Bailiff, please pass the verdict to the clerk so that she may publish it."

Karen held her breath.

The clerk, an attractive woman with a swath of gray in her dark hair, stood, avoided looking at the defense table and fumbled with the sheet of paper. Karen stifled a groan and prayed.

"On the count of murder in the first degree, we the jury find the defendants not guilty."

Karen's knees threatened to buckle, and she braced herself on the defense table. Beside her, Michael began to weep.

Chaos erupted in the courtroom with a babble of voices, the flash of cameras, and the hot lights of camcorders, and reporters stampeded toward the doors to file their stories.

The judge banged the gavel and demanded that the room be cleared. But before the jury was led away, Juror Number Eleven caught Karen's eye—and smiled. Karen, sandwiched between her nephews in a giant bear hug, was oblivious to the commotion that filled the room.

She mouthed a heartfelt "thank you" to the juror and allowed herself a broad smile. She had saved Robert's sons from Walter Stockman.

Twenty-four

The following day, Karen rang the bell at the Cobb's Landing house. Mrs. Taylor, Claire's mother, answered the door.

"I'm sorry I've been away so long," Karen said. "I've come to see Claire."

Karen hadn't visited Claire since the week before the trial began. Not only had she been too busy fighting for her nephews' lives, she had feared in her state of complete immersion in the details of the trial, she might let something slip that would alert Claire to her sons' predicament. Her sister-in-law, whose short-term memory had been affected by her latest stroke, believed that her sons were no longer at home because they had returned to school. With her contact with the outside world censored by Ursula and Mrs. Taylor, she had been unaware of Stockman's death, the trial, or its outcome.

"Come in," Mrs. Taylor said. "Ursula's attending Claire's, uh, call of nature, at the moment."

"Are Richard and Michael in?"

"They're upstairs. You can wait in the sun room. Would you like some coffee?"

"No, thanks." Karen followed the elderly woman into the bright, sunlit room and sat in a wicker chair.

Mrs. Taylor settled her plump girth into a chair

opposite her. "I can't thank you enough for what you've done for my grandsons."

Karen nodded in acknowledgment. "I couldn't lose them. It would have been as if Walter Stockman had reached out from the grave to continue cursing this family."

"A horrible man," Mrs. Taylor said with a dismissive wave of her hand. "He deserved to die. But even dead, he would have ruined Richard and Michael's lives if it weren't for you. I owe you an apology."

Karen blinked in surprise. "For what?"

"I had written you off, thinking you were too much like your brother. I even made a point of avoiding you, but you're not like Robert at all."

The bizarre conversation flustered Karen. She hadn't registered Mrs. Taylor's snubs. "What do you mean?"

"I blame all of Claire's unhappiness on Robert."

"You mean Robert's death?"

"No, she was unhappy long before that." Mrs. Taylor took a deep breath and dabbed at her eyes with a lace-trimmed handkerchief. "My poor baby girl. When Robert first started cheating on Claire with his slut of a chief of staff, Claire was actually happy. She used to say the only time she ever got any attention from Robert was when he was having an affair. She actually looked forward to those affairs of his. My poor baby. And Robert couldn't stop himself."

Karen felt icy tentacles reaching for her heart. Inside her chest, she felt a new coldness, a terrible rattle, and in her head, a slight dizziness, the dawning of enlightenment.

"Claire *knew* about Marie Morley?" Her voice was barely above a whisper.

Mrs. Taylor snorted. "Of course, Claire knew. I just told you that. She knew about *all* of them. He used to rub her nose in it, the bastard. He'd tell her about them just to see the look of pain on her face. He was forever shacking up in some hotel instead of coming home for the night. If it wasn't that damned Morley woman, it was someone else."

Karen's mind filled with images, strange disjointed images. Faces swam in and out of her imagination, voices rose and ebbed, entire scenes came and went. She saw the garage and Robert's body. And the blood. And the legs, one askew, one extended. She saw the kitchen and the table, and the strange black marks on the kitchen floor. She saw herself gathering up things to sell or otherwise discard, and she remembered Claire's gardening basket with its trowel—and no gloves.

"When did you and Claire last talk about Robert's infidelity?" Karen asked.

Looking puzzled, Mrs. Taylor thought for a moment. "On the telephone, a few days before Robert's death. Claire was crying over Robert's latest fling."

Karen stared into Mrs. Taylor's eyes. "You're absolutely certain?"

"Why would I lie? You don't believe me, ask Claire. Robert's dead. She has no further need to pretend."

"And you're certain Robert was having an affair then, that week before his death."

"Yes." She drew herself up, offended.

"With whom?"

"With the Morley woman."

Karen closed her eyes. "Then the talk-show gossip wasn't all lies?"

Mrs. Taylor snorted with laughter. "Lies? They didn't begin to scratch the surface of Robert's philandering."

A frightening mass of unconnected thought had been lurking in the dark recesses of Karen's mind, shoved there while she had dealt with more pressing matters ever since Robert's death. Now, the awful heaviness floated unfettered into her consciousness. Small pieces of the once-murky jigsaw puzzle became clear, the pieces still unconnected, but visible at last.

She remembered with sudden, shocking clarity the conversation in her own living room the night of Claire's brush with death. Martha Perry's strident voice echoed in Karen's mind: "As long as we're dilly-dallying over this meaningless suit, we're not searching for the real reason behind Robert's death— the person who pulled the trigger."

Claire had seemed fine until Martha had begun ranting about dropping the civil suit to concentrate on finding Robert's murderer.

Karen jumped to her feet. "I'm sorry, but I have to go."

"Was it something I said? He was your brother, I know, but he treated my daughter like dirt. But you're not like him. Please stay and see Claire. She'll be so disappointed."

Ignoring Mrs. Taylor's ramblings, Karen fled out the front door.

Karen returned home, shut herself in her study with the folder from the investigation of Robert's death and the photographs of Robert's Virginia house she had taken for insurance purposes. When she emerged hours later, she faced Carl in the den.

"I need you to do something for me, no questions asked."

His face reflected her concern. "Sounds serious."

"I want you to fly to Virginia with me. There's something I have to settle. Can you manage?"

"If going to Virginia is the only way to rid you of that panicked look," he said agreeably, "I think I can work it in. Let me make a few calls."

The following day, Karen and Carl drove in their rental car through the gate of Robert's still-unoccupied Virginia house. The realtor had told them that the pall of bad luck that seemed to cover the Jameson family had affected the house's marketability. The property, she assured them, was not likely to sell until either the price was drastically reduced or the public scandal died.

As they stood in the front hallway of the old house, deserted now almost a year, their voices echoing throughout the near-empty rooms, Karen caught sight of herself in the foyer mirror. She looked as awful as she felt. Her face was drawn, her eyes red rimmed, her slumping shoulders an eloquent testament to her inner torment.

"We're here," Carl said with infinite patience. "Can you tell me now?"

Karen nodded and cupped his cheek in her palm. "Thanks for coming with me."

"You've looked like death since you returned from Claire's yesterday. What's happened that's so horrible?"

Karen looked away for a moment. "This is the worst day of my life. I thought it was when Robert died, but I was wrong. This is the worst."

"What is?" he asked gently.

"This . . . horror. I asked you to come with me because you always see to the heart of things, and I'm hoping you'll tell me I'm wrong."

Carl shivered, as if a chill had run down his spine.

Karen motioned him to follow her into the den. She stood in the center of the room, staring at the wall that once held a variety of electronic equipment. now the wall was bare, the outline of the equipment marked by faded wall coverings. The flattened carpet spoke of the great weight that had once stood there, a weight like a feather compared to that which seemed to be crushing her.

"I figure it this way," she said softly. "It started in this room."

She turned, shook her head. "No, that's not right. It really started years ago, when Claire found some kiddie porn in Robert's briefcase. He told her he was on a committee studying pornography legislation, but she didn't believe him. He'd lied to her before, too many times, and the seeds of mistrust were firmly rooted."

She threw a hand in the air. "That's the trouble with lies. They inevitably destroy credibility."

Carl stared at her, not saying a word.

"Eventually," Karen continued, "Robert was able to persuade Claire he was telling the truth, but when she saw that abominable videotape, it triggered something, something snapped inside her. Maybe it was an accumulation of things, I don't know. But the tape was the stimulus."

Carl's dark eyes widened. "You're saying Claire had something to do with Robert's death. Is that what this is about?"

She nodded. "According to Claire's statement, she

went upstairs to the bedroom. I think that's where the idea formed in her mind."

Carl's jaw dropped. "But—"

"Follow me," Karen said firmly.

They went to the kitchen. She pointed to two black marks on the floor. "See those?"

"Yes."

She opened her attaché case, removed a file folder, and placed it on the table, one of the few items of furniture left in the place. "This is Robert's file—the autopsy report, the crime scene pictures, the statements—everything. I read it over and over before I asked you to come here with me. There's no mistake. Claire killed Robert."

Carl's voice was a shocked whisper. "How?"

Karen shook herself out of a fog. "God help me, he was my brother. I can't just let it go. You understand?"

Carl placed his hand on her arm. "I understand. Take it easy."

"It was the black marks that got me thinking," she said. "I can have the lab people check, but I'm sure they're the rubber heel marks from Robert's shoes. And when you look at the pictures, you can see clearly . . ."

"Take it easy," Carl repeated.

She cleared her throat and wiped her eyes with the back of her shaking hand. "Claire came downstairs. She saw Robert sitting at this table, probably with his head in his hands. She was filled with cold fury. Not only, she thought, had he dishonored her with his affairs all these years, he was even worse than unfaithful. He preyed on children to fulfill his sexual appetites.

"She went to the den and grabbed the gun. Then

she came in here. She wanted to kill him right then
and there, but her rage was a controlled rage, a calm,
calculating hatred developed over the years. I've seen
it in clients many times. People you'd consider the
sweetest charmers in the world can perform the most
unspeakable acts. . . .

"Claire stood near the entrance to the kitchen, the
gun in her hand. She heard Ursula upstairs with the
vacuum cleaner. She also heard Toshi working outside with the lawnmower. Lots of noise. It was a
perfect opportunity, don't you see?"

Carl simply nodded.

"So Claire stopped in her tracks, thought about it
for a minute or so, then finalized her plan. Then she
went to the den and wrote the suicide note."

"But you said—"

"I said it was Robert's handwriting, but I was
wrong. Claire often wrote personal letters for him.
Robert hated writing letters. He had a staff at the
office for business letters, but at home, he had Claire
do it. She had become expert at duplicating his handwriting. If a lab compares the note closely with
known samples of Robert's writing, they'll be able to
determine it was actually Claire's handwriting."

Karen fought back a sob. "The evidence was there
all the time, but I was too stunned by my own grief
to see things I should have. And the police—" she
paused and took a deep breath.

"The police," she finally continued, "were local
folks who knew and liked both Robert and Claire
and accepted what they saw and were told as the
truth. They weren't looking for clues, just confirma-
tion. They'd read the suicide note and accepted it at
face value, which predisposed their objectivity and
made them sloppy."

"What about the FBI?" Carl asked.

"They relied on the police in the beginning, and then when the insane publicity with the tape broke, they concentrated their efforts on the people responsible for making the tape, comfortable in the judgment that Robert had indeed killed himself. The blackmail tape presented the perfect motive. They had no reason to question anything, so they didn't. Nor did I, until I started putting it all together."

"Go on," Carl said.

"After writing the note, Claire walked up behind Robert and struck him on the back of the head with the gun. He probably went out like a light. The autopsy never revealed the bruise on the back of his head, because that's where the bullet exited. It was a hollow-point, and they leave a large exit wound.

"Then she took Robert's hands and placed them on the note so his fingerprints would show. An examination of the paper will probably reveal the pattern of fingerprints makes no sense."

Carl shook his head. "This is a lot to take in all at once."

"Then," Karen continued, "Claire grabbed Robert under the arms and started to drag him toward the garage. But she noticed something. The rubber heels on his new loafers were making marks on the floor, the very marks there now. So she stopped"—Karen moved to the end of the marks—"here, and removed his shoes, then finished the job of dragging him into the garage, to the far corner. From her gardening basket, she removed her gloves and put them on. She wiped her prints from the gun. There in the far corner, she positioned him against the garage wall, put the gun in his hand, placed the barrel in his mouth, and started to pull the trigger."

She stopped for another deep breath. "But she remembered the shoes, so she went back for them. Then, with the barrel of the gun in his mouth, she pulled the trigger. That's why the powder-flash pattern on Robert's hands was a little off. The police noticed it, but didn't pursue it. It was impossible to conceive he'd been murdered, especially after I confirmed the suicide note was written by Robert.

"After killing Robert, Claire replaced his shoes and ran to the garage door, which was open. No one had heard the shot. She ran back into the kitchen and into the adjoining laundry room where she tossed her gardening gloves beneath the dirty clothes in the hamper. I remember seeing those gloves—apparently clean gardening gloves—when I sorted the clothes in the hamper before shipping things to Florida."

Carl nodded. "Go on."

"Claire waited until she saw Toshi start for the garage. She waited until he saw Robert's body, then appeared at the door and started screaming."

Karen opened the file folder and removed a photograph. "This is an official photograph of Robert's body. Notice his legs?"

Carl took the picture.

"Notice how one leg is crooked and the other is sticking straight out?" Karen said.

Silence.

"Looks odd, doesn't it?" She was warming to it now, the frustration, anger and hurt clawing at her soul, the sheer weight of the truth pushing at her from all directions. Such a waste! Such a terrible, sickening misreading of another human being.

Claire and Robert had been wrapped in their own worlds, oblivious to the effects of the daily toll, the cumulative damage, like a slow cancer, eating away at rational thought. Claire and Robert were both guilty of selfishness, but Claire's resentment had evolved tragically, mutated into hate, and from there had embraced the unacceptable. Now her sons would have to contend with another truth, this one unassailable.

She wanted to weep, but strangely, her rage made her calm, like Claire's had done.

"There's a reason one leg is akimbo," she said. "When someone dies from a gunshot wound, their muscles twitch. Even an unconscious person's muscles twitch involuntarily. Robert's right leg twitched when the bullet entered his brain. That's the leg that's sticking straight out. But you'll notice the left leg didn't move."

Carl said nothing.

"It couldn't. The left leg couldn't move because Claire was sitting on it, making sure the gun was properly aimed. She had to be sure the exit wound disguised the bruise on the back of the skull. And if you'll look at the picture taken of the garage floor, you'll see there are no heel marks. None at all."

She removed another photo. "Here's the photo taken after the body was removed. Notice? Still no heel marks. If Robert had shot himself while wearing his shoes, his right heel would have made a mark on the floor when his leg twitched. No marks means one thing: he wasn't wearing his shoes when the shot was fired."

"This is incredible," Carl said, stunned. "Claire murdered him."

"Tell me I'm wrong," she said.

Carl looked into her tortured eyes. "I can't. Nor can I say you're right. But you are right about one thing. Only the lab people can determine Claire's guilt for certain, by reexamining the suicide note."

"I can't do that to Richard and Michael. They've been through hell the past year. Reopening the investigation of Robert's death will traumatize them all over again."

"There's one other way to find the truth," Carl said.

"How?"

"Ask Claire."

When Karen returned to Florida, she found Claire sitting at the end of the dock in her wheelchair, wearing a simple one-piece bathing suit, her trim legs uncovered to the warm October sun. Her sister-in-law turned at the sound of footsteps.

"Karen? What brings you here in the middle of a nice day like this?" Her stroke had left her speech slurred and the left side of her face drooping, cocking her formerly pretty smile at a strange angle.

"I need to talk to you."

Claire seemed genuinely pleased to see her. "There's some lemonade in the refrigerator, if you like. Ursula just got back from the market."

"No thanks."

Karen crouched down and sat beside her, staring off in the distance, listening to the gentle slap of waves hitting the pilings. Two seagulls screeched their awful noise in the air above her. A pastoral scene, incongruous in light of what had brought her here.

Claire was still smiling crookedly, but her voice was tentative. "You look tired."

"I was up most of the night."

Claire touched her hand, and Karen had to make an effort not to jerk it away.

"You're still grieving over Robert's death," Claire said.

"I'm afraid so."

Claire stared at the water. "It takes time."

Reluctant to broach the topic that had brought her here, Karen turned her face toward the sun. "Great day. Chamber of Commerce stuff."

"That's what Florida's all about," Claire said. "Water, sun, sand . . . I've always loved it here. How do you know if you really like Florida, Karen? You've never lived anywhere else."

"I've never thought much about it."

Claire laughed. "No, you wouldn't. You're a lot like Robert in that respect. You get so wrapped up in business to the point that nothing else matters."

"Is that how you see me?"

Claire patted her hand again. "I don't mean to be critical. Most successful attorneys are like that. It must be in the genes."

"You're probably right."

"You did a wonderful job, Karen. You performed miracles, in fact, finding us this place, selling the Miami house so quickly, settling the suit with Stockman, and especially encouraging my boys to return to school after the civil suit was settled. I can't express how grateful I am to you for taking the time to look after these things. You should bill me for your time. In fact, I'd feel better if you did."

Karen closed her eyes, then hung her head. She didn't want to see Claire's face when she accused her. She took a deep breath and plunged ahead. "Claire . . . I know what happened to Robert. Mother was right. He was murdered."

"What?"

Karen lifted her head and looked at her sister-in-law, watching the blood drain from the twisted face as Claire met her eyes.

Claire's mouth opened, her throat moved, but no words came out. She stared at Karen, a portrait of shock, her contorted patrician face slack-jawed and wide-eyed, her nostrils flaring as she gulped air. All she managed to utter was a choked, "Murdered? That's not possible! I was there! I saw him with the gun in his hand."

"Give it up, Claire."

Her sister-in-law sighed, then stared into space.

"You killed him, didn't you? I have enough evidence for the police to charge you—the forged suicide note, the marks of Robert's shoes in the kitchen. And you certainly had a motive. You might as well admit it."

Claire remained silent for a moment, as if in shock, and for a few seconds Karen hoped her conclusions had been wrong, that Claire would convince her she'd made a mistake.

"What was I to do?" Claire said with an agony in her voice that made Karen wince. "Throughout our marriage, he'd humiliated me with his stupid affairs. I lived with it because there were other compensations. But his . . . his pedophilia, on top of his renewed affair with Marie, was beyond my ability to accept. It was the end of our relationship, our lives. I'd never be able to look him in the eye, to let him touch me again."

She sobbed, a pitiful sound that, under different circumstances, would have pulled at Karen's heartstrings. "I was consumed with shame. I couldn't bear to be with him another second. But to simply walk away wasn't enough. There'd always be questions, don't you see? I knew that tape was going to become public knowledge someday. Secrets like that always come out. We didn't have the money to pay the blackmail, but even if we had, it wouldn't have worked."

Tears rolled down her perfect skin. "They would have hounded me for the rest of my life. 'How does it feel, Mrs. Jameson?' they would ask. But if I killed him and made it look like suicide . . . there was a chance it would all go away, the tape, the pedophilia, the blackmail. Everything."

She looked into Karen's tortured eyes. "But that terrible tape was a terrible lie. And now I have to live with *that* the rest of my life. I killed my husband for something he didn't do. How will I live with that?"

Karen didn't answer. Heartsick, she rose to her feet, turned her back on her sister-in-law, and walked away.

Twenty-five

"It's my fault." Karen, consumed by an unsettling sense of déjà vu, paced the waiting room near the ICU unit at the hospital.

"You're being too hard on yourself," Carl said gently. "Dr. Dayton warned that another stroke was imminent. It was just a matter of time before Claire had another."

"But just hours after I confronted her with Robert's murder? That's not coincidence."

"If the stroke *is* stress related, it's due to Claire's guilty conscience, not you." He rose, went to her, and gathered her in his arms. "It's you I'm worried about."

In the quiet of the waiting room, empty except for the two of them, Karen leaned against him and took comfort in his strength. "I'll be okay—as soon as I decide what to do about Claire's confession. I can't withhold evidence like that from the police, but . . ."

"But?"

"I'm afraid for Richard and Michael."

"Can't you invoke attorney-client privilege and say nothing?"

"I'm not Claire's attorney."

"You're handling Robert's estate."

"It's not that simple." She broke from his embrace

and began to pace the waiting room again. "How do I tell two young men who've already been through hell that their *mother* killed their father?"

Carl shook his head. "I wish I had an answer."

Karen stopped and faced him with blazing eyes. "When the press gets hold of this, it will validate every ugly rumor Stockman and his paid mouthpieces ever uttered about Robert and his family. God, even though Stockman's dead, he's still ruining people's lives."

"Do you blame him for Robert's death? Even after Claire's confession?"

Karen threw her hands in the air. "I don't know what to think anymore. Would Claire have murdered Robert if that tape hadn't arrived when it did?"

Carl shrugged. "From what Mrs. Taylor told you, Robert's infidelity was a constant factor in their marriage. If Claire had found an opportunity to confront him about his latest indiscretion and vent the rage that drove her to kill him, maybe they would have rocked along as usual, hiding their dirty linen from the public—and their sons."

At the sound of quiet footsteps in the corridor, they both paused. The ICU duty nurse, her face set in grim lines, entered the waiting room. "I'm sorry. Mrs. Jameson is gone."

"Gone?" Karen asked blankly.

"Another stroke," the nurse said. "Her mother was with her when she died."

Karen tucked her arm through Carl's as the minister intoned the burial service from the Book of Common Prayer. On her other side, Richard and Michael sat rigidly, staring at the gleaming casket draped with Claire's favorite pink roses. Beyond them, Mrs.

Taylor wept silently into a black-edged handkerchief, and Martha Perry sat like a statue, emotionlessly.

Lifting her gaze above Claire's casket, Karen stared across the rolling green lawns of Sylvan Abbey Memorial Gardens, dotted with pools of shade from the moss-draped oaks, a bucolic scene at odds with the turmoil of her heart. As she bowed her head for the final prayer, Karen struggled to sort her emotions. The woman being laid to rest had murdered her brother, but in her own way, Claire had been as much a victim of Walter Stockman's thirst for power as her nephews. If Claire had lived and gone to trial, would Karen have fought as fiercely for her sister-in-law as she had for Robert's sons? That was a question for which she'd never know the answer.

After the burial and catered buffet for mourners at the house at Cobb's Landing, Karen, still dressed in her black linen dress from the funeral, drove to her office and met with her law partners in the firm's boardroom.

"I've called this meeting," she said, "to lay before you a situation whose outcome could affect this firm. Because I am personally involved in this matter, I need your objectivity in reaching a decision. Because in asking your advice I must divulge some very sensitive information, I'm invoking lawyer-client privilege."

In her succinct style, Karen related her suspicions about the circumstances of Robert's death and the details of Claire's subsequent confession. When she finished, silence hung in the room like a shroud.

Brander finally spoke. "I can understand your dilemma. As an officer of the court, do you report Claire's confession to the authorities who investigated Robert's death or, as Robert's sister, do you protect your nephews, who have already suffered untold emotional trauma, from the knowledge that their mother was a murderer?"

Karen nodded. She had counted on Brander, as usual, to cut to the heart of the matter.

Darren steepled his fingers on the table before him. "According to the Canon of Professional Ethics, the primary duty of a lawyer is not to convict, but to see that justice is done."

"But what *is* justice in a case like this?" Sharon asked.

"The main purpose of our profession," Brander said, "is to serve the public interest. Perhaps we should approach this matter from that viewpoint."

Len nodded and turned to Karen with an earnest, boyish expression. "It's not as if someone else is serving a sentence for the crime Claire committed, so no injustice would be righted by revealing her guilt."

"And which is more harmful to your brother's memory," Darren asked, "the onus of suicide or the public knowledge that his wife killed him in a rage over his infidelities?"

"Does anyone else know Claire killed Robert?" Brander asked.

Karen shook her head. "Only Carl and I. Not even her mother knows. But there's one other factor in this case that we haven't touched on. The fifteen-million-dollar settlement from Walter Stockman."

Len grimaced. "Stockman was one of the richest men in the world. What's a measly fifteen million among all those billions? It's not as if you're depriving his widow and children."

"From what you've told us," Sharon said, "a very strong case could be made that Stockman's tape was the precipitating factor that pushed Claire over the edge. If Stockman hadn't had that tape created and delivered, Robert might be alive today."

"And Stockman, too," Brander added. "I don't see how the public good would be served by revealing Claire's guilt. The woman's dead, so she can't be prosecuted, not by an earthly court, at any rate."

"The overriding consideration," Len said, "is what harm such a revelation might do. In addition to destroying the already tattered image of Senator Jameson, learning of their mother's guilt could very well maim her sons emotionally for the rest of their lives. They survived their trial, coming out mentally stronger than when they started and, from what Karen tells us, Richard and Michael will be returning to school when the next term begins."

"But," Darren lifted a warning finger, "what if, for some unforeseen reason, the authorities decide to reopen the case of the senator's suicide and discover that he was indeed murdered? If they were to question Karen, she could not lie. If her withholding of evidence should become known, she could be disbarred, and the firm would suffer."

Karen pushed back her chair and stood. "You make a good point, Darren. My actions reflect on this firm. That's why I'd like to hear your opinions on what I should do. I'll wait in my office. You can let me know when you've finished your discussion."

The afternoon hours dragged on as Karen sat at her desk and stared through the wide window, unable to concentrate on work.

At a quarter to four, Liz knocked on her door. "The partners are waiting for you."

Karen hurried up the hallway and slipped into the boardroom, flooded now with late afternoon sunlight.

"Walter Stockman destroyed too many lives with his freewheeling power," Brander said. "If Claire's guilt is revealed, two more lives face ruin. Claire's secret is buried with her, as far as this firm is concerned."

Karen's eyes misted with tears. "Thank you—"

"But," Brander continued, "even though the final decision affects the firm, only you can make it. You are the one who will have to live with it. Whatever you decide, the partners will stand behind you, but the decision is ultimately yours and yours alone."

Karen nodded. "I appreciate your support. I'll let you know my decision."

Two days later, Karen sat in the office of Lieutenant Jack Brace of the Farquier County, Virginia, Sheriff's Department. After relating her conclusions on Robert's death and Claire's subsequent confession, she leaned back in her chair, emotionally wrung out.

"Was Mrs. Jameson's confession a dying declaration?" Brace asked.

"She suffered a stroke several hours after I spoke with her and died a few hours later."

"Then in the eyes of the law—I'm not doubting you, Ms. Perry-Mondori, just stating the facts—her confession to you is merely hearsay and would be treated as such by the courts."

"I understand," Karen said.

Brace shook his head. "I never would have figured Mrs. Jameson for a killer. She was such a lady, and she grew the best roses in the county."

"Will you reopen the case?"

Brace folded his arms on his desk and leaned forward. "What would be the point?"

Karen forced a smile. "The truth? Isn't that a good enough reason?"

"In the best of all worlds." He indicated the stacks of folders on his desk. "But unfortunately, I don't live there. Each of these files represents an unsolved case. I have murderers, child molesters, scam artists, and burglars running loose by the dozens in this county. My department's short on money and manpower. The way I see it, it would be a misappropriation of funds and man hours to reopen the Jameson case. If it's truth you want, I'll place a transcript of what you've told me in the file, but as far as I'm concerned, this case is closed."

"Will you make a statement to the media?"

Brace's kindly face wrinkled in thought. "Senator and Mrs. Jameson did a lot of good for a whole lot of folks while they were alive. The way I see it, if it hadn't been for that son of a bitch Walter Stockman, both those fine people would still be with us today. No point in harming the memory of either one of them any more than Stockman already has. Your statement will go into the archives, where it will probably never see the light of day again."

Karen stood to leave. "Thank you for your time, Lieutenant."

Brace rose behind his desk and extended his hand. "In all the years I've been in law enforcement, Ms. Perry-Mondori, I've always considered defense attorneys about two steps lower than a snake. Since meeting you, I've changed my mind."

The blare of rock music greeted Karen when she entered the foyer of her home. In the past year, her little girl had metamorphosized into an almost-ten-year-old with all the attendant preadolescent trappings—a passion for rock music, teen idols, and the latest fads. The days when Andrea would streak down the stairs into her arms when Karen came home from work were probably gone forever.

"A hard trip?" Rahni asked as she took Karen's coat.

Karen nodded. "Construction work made the drive from the airport even more of a nightmare than usual. Is Dr. Mondori home yet?"

"He's in the family room. Dinner will be ready in an hour."

When she entered the family room, Carl clicked off the television news, rose to his feet, and embraced her. "You look exhausted. Sit, and I'll pour you a glass of wine."

Gratefully, Karen settled into a deep chair, kicked off her shoes, and placed her feet on the matching ottoman. Carl handed her a glass of cold chardonnay, settled on the ottoman, and began massaging her feet.

"You're spoiling me," she protested.

"After all you've been through the past several months, you could use a little spoiling."

"Thank God, it's all over now."

"You talked with Benjamin Rose?"

She nodded. "For three hours. He wants to leave matters as they lie."

Carl raised an eyebrow. "I'm surprised that as executor of Stockman's estate he didn't jump at the chance to recoup fifteen million dollars."

"He said Richard and Michael have been through enough."

"From what you've told me about Rose, I wouldn't credit him with that much compassion."

Karen laughed. "Don't kid yourself. It's to Rose's advantage to let this sleeping dog lie. His reputation is closely tied to Stockman's. Reopening the investigation into Robert's death would also reopen all the allegations against Stockman and his dirty politics."

"And the fifteen million?"

"Rose insists that we could have won the civil case against Stockman, even if Claire had been provoked to murder Robert because of the tape. He says the boys are owed that money, and as far as he's concerned, that's the end of it."

Carl halted his massage and gazed into her eyes. "Will you tell Richard and Michael about Claire?"

She shook her head. "As an officer of the court, I have fulfilled my obligations to the law. As the aunt of those boys, my obligation is to protect them, to protect their memories of their mother and father."

"What if they decide to look into the Virginia records someday and discover the truth for themselves?"

"I would hope by then they'd be wiser and emotionally stronger. They can't take any more emotional upheaval now. I have to allow them to grieve for their mother in a normal fashion. Lt. Brace and Benjamin Rose's refusals to pursue the matter of Claire's guilt let me spare Richard and Michael further heartache."

"So now the boys can get on with their lives."

Karen leaned forward and placed her arms around his neck. "And so can we."

A month later at Thanksgiving, Karen surveyed the group gathered around her table. At the head, opposite her, Carl carved the turkey and passed a filled plate to Bonnie Graham on his left.

"I can't eat that much," the young woman protested with a laugh.

" 'Course you can," Richard teased her. "It's Thanksgiving. The human stomach expands to five times its normal capacity this one day of the year. Isn't that right, Cynthia?"

The young woman seated across from them next to Michael, nodded. "It's a fact we learned the first year of med school."

"I want the wishbone," Andrea told her father.

Carl smiled. "What will you wish for, kiddo?"

Andrea didn't hesitate. "For everybody to be happy."

As the meal progressed, Karen prayed for Andrea's wish to come true. She saw signs of hope. Richard and Bonnie were preoccupied with each other, so much in love it was almost embarrassing to watch them. Michael, in his shy and unassuming way, was showing more than a casual interest in Cynthia Smathers, whom he'd met at the Clearwater Free Clinic. Karen sensed the young men's underlying sadness, the weight of Robert and Claire's absence from the family celebration, but her nephews' depression had lifted, and they were looking to the future now instead of the past.

A tinkling sound drew her from her introspection. Richard was tapping his water goblet with a spoon. "I have an announcement."

Silence descended on the table. Richard stood and pulled Bonnie from her chair to stand next to him. "Bonnie and I want to extend an invitation for next Thanksgiving."

Michael laughed. "Don't tell me you're going to cook, brother. I'll be sure to bring my medical bag."

Richard shook his head, and Bonnie blushed.

"I'm not talking about Thanksgiving dinner," he

said, "but a wedding. Bonnie and I are getting married."

Carl started the applause, and the rest of the table joined in.

"That's wonderful news," Karen said.

Carl nodded. "I have a few bottles of champagne I've been saving for a special occasion. I'll get them now."

His gaze met Karen's down the length of the table, and she nodded at his unspoken reassurance.

In spite of all they'd suffered, her nephews came from strong, resilient stock. Richard and Michael were going to be just fine.